SISTERWIVES

Rachel Connor

ISBN 9780946745586

Crocus

D0433127

Sisterwives

First published in 2011 by Crocus
Crocus books are published by Commonword
6 Mount Street, Manchester M2 5NS

Reprinted March 2012

admin@cultureword.org.uk
www.cultureword.org.uk

Crocus books are distributed by Turnaround Publisher Services Ltd,
Unit 3, Olympia Trading Estate, Coburg Rd, Wood Green, London N22 6TZ

Cover design by Tyme Design www.tymedesign.com
Printed and bound by CPI Group (UK) Ltd., Croydon CR0 4YY

British Library Cataloguing-in-Publication Data: a catalogue
record for this book is available from the British Library

ISBN 978-0-946745-58-6

Dedicated to Elisha and Paul, with love.

Thank you, for very many reasons, to:
Martyn Bedford; the Connor and Cruthers families; Suzannah Dunn; Rebecca Evans; Liz Flanagan; Ilona Jones; Em Strang.

Also to:
Sophie Hannah, James Nash, Tom Palmer and Anna Turner for their feedback on early drafts; the Commonword Novelists' Group; The Literary Consultancy, especially Anna South and Becky Swift; Pete Kalu, Martin De Mello and the team at Commonword and Crocus Books.

I'm grateful to Antonia Honeywell for being such a perceptive reader, and for keeping me afloat in the white water. And to Sara Maitland, the best mentor anyone could wish for.

Final thanks go to Paul and Elisha, for absolutely everything.

So Moses brought Israel from the Red Sea; then they went out into the Wilderness of Shur. And then they went three days in the wilderness and found no water. Now when they came to Marah, they could not drink the waters of Marah, for they were bitter.

Exodus 15: 22-23

It was joy they were both after – the completeness of being. If you evade suffering you also evade the chance of joy. Pleasure you may get, or pleasures, but you will not be fulfilled. You will not know what it is like to come home.

Ursula LeGuin, The Dispossessed

There comes this supreme moment to the glass-blower, when he can either breathe life and form into the growing bubble slowly taking shape before his eyes, or shatter it into a thousand fragments. The decision is the blower's and the judgement too.

Daphne Du Maurier, The Glass-Blowers

I

MARAH

There are two of them reflected in the long bedroom mirror: Amarantha on a ladder-backed chair; Rebecca behind, decorating her hair, fixing the curls with pearls from a purple satin box.

Amarantha sees Rebecca's tongue dart to her lip as she drives home the pin; feels the flush up her neck and a burning sensation across her scalp. When Rebecca grips her chin and angles it to the left she sees everything slantwise then, in the glass: Rebecca's face with its veil of freckles. Thin brows the same red as her hair, with edges that fade to nothing. Witch eyes, the children in school say, because of the green, but there's sometimes a softer light there, too. She listens to the rise and fall of Rebecca's breathing, feels the contact of her abdomen as she leans over, giving off her sweet and peaty smell, like heather.

She wonders what Rebecca is thinking: about tonight, maybe. Tobias's reaction when he takes all her dark hair down again.

Something in her expands at the thought of it. Yesterday, in Tobias's workshop, she felt odd when he folded her into him, with his smell of dust and heat and burnt glass. She's known him all her life but he's never held her like that before. There were patches of sweat, like islands, on his shirt. His smell was sharp as salt; salty like the blue dye when she dipped in her finger and put it to her mouth. He said it was azure. It made her think of the sea, that she has never seen, or a summer sky.

She never expected to want him.

Maybe staying is too high a price to pay, to be with him. It's what her mother would think anyway; it's what she would say if she were here. She's filled with a yearning to hear her voice. A note, at least. She turns to Rebecca.

'There's nothing from Frania?'

'You asked already.'

'She wouldn't want it. All this.'

'Do you?' Rebecca's words are a challenge. The witch eyes fix her in the glass. But she sees that Rebecca is desperate for an answer and seeing her need gives her a rush of pleasure, of power. She hangs onto that silence. Eventually, she says: 'It doesn't matter what I want. Frania left. I've no choice.'

'None of us has a choice, Amarantha. We do what's asked of us.' Rebecca turns away, tidying, laying down the wooden-handled brush and the comb, placing unused pins in the box. There are bright spots of colour on her cheeks.

'But I don't know what they're asking.' Even as Amarantha says it, she knows the answer. They want the same thing for her as they do for Rebecca and the others: the relentless rhythm of Sealings and babies. She was so sure she'd escape it. Frania promised her they would. But Frania's gone and Amarantha is seventeen: still too young to study, too naive, they say, to survive alone in the city.

Rebecca frowns. 'We've been through it before.'

The words jab harder than the pinpricks in her scalp. 'Who should I ask then? Tobias?'

But Rebecca has vacated the rectangular space of the mirror.

Amarantha looks around Rebecca's room, reflected backwards: whitewashed walls, fresh and clean; the voile curtains shifting with the breeze at the window and, through it, the apple tree in full leaf. In the corner, the wide metal bedstead with the patchwork eiderdown tugged across. And on top, laid out so it won't crush, her dress for the Sealing.

When Rebecca comes back into view she's lifting the dress as though it were some exotic flower. She brings it towards Amarantha, instructs her to stand. And then there's nothing but cream and ivory light and the smell of lavender; the rustle of fabric around her ears. Amarantha holds up her arms, feels the tug under them as Rebecca eases down the dress, arranging it. Making it fit.

She's never been dressed by anyone before. The touch of Rebecca's fingers burns her; the contact of skin, then hands skirting her waist. Even through the fabric she feels it.

The anticipation. Tobias's face and his burnt glass smell. Wanting it; not wanting it.

When Rebecca steps away, Amarantha looks at her own reflection. Frania wouldn't know her, with her hair up, her long neck on show. Her skin is transparent, it's so pale. The dress gives her a body other than her own: it pushes up her breasts, tightens her around the waist, expansive as it nears the ground.

Amarantha can't get enough of looking. This strange self, who is nothing like she thought she was.

She closes her eyes, absorbing everything. She hears the Meeting House bell, summoning them. Amarantha imagines them there: Goran and Leah – Tobias's parents – lining up at the front; the rest of his family. The rest of the village, there to witness their joining. Frania's empty seat. Ammie remembers the scrawled note Frania left; beautiful words, but inadequate: *An invisible thread connects us. Think of me and I'll feel a pull on it.*

She can't feel it today, though, that connection. There are women in the house but none of them are her mother. The sound of their voices drifting upstairs makes her absence even more acute. Already, they're swinging into their roles, the women, making *beure manié*, preparing vegetables; chopping herbs that bleed green onto the board, the knife releasing the scent of dill and basil; thyme. As long as she thinks of today, it's the smells she'll remember: the sweetness of roasting vegetables, bitter overtones of rosemary; the lamb brought from the field to slaughter. The scents in this room, too: roses in jars on the bureau, just brought in from the garden. Beeswax where Rebecca polished the floor yesterday, readying the room.

*

The retinue: Amarantha and Rebecca, Sarah and Hannah, Rebecca's three daughters and their cousins. They thread through houses arranged in concentric circles that face in on each other. They're built mostly of wood and straw, rendered with lime, painted in pastels. Each has high windows and roofs with glass panels that generate electricity from the sun.

Past the Olsens' villa, with its atrium that looks like it's suspended in space, then the low bungalow where the O'Gradys live; they come at last to the square of green in the heart of the village: the Piece. In winter after the heavy falls, the children make snow angels here; or they gather in the shade of the trees in the high summer glare. It's here the women meet

4

to bake bread in the communal ovens, reinforcing friendship through habit and familiar routines.

Marah. The word means bitter, brackish. It comes from the river, which weaves like a ribbon through the houses, the gardens and allotments, the workshops and fields. It is a place to fish, a life force, a source of pleasure for the children, who – like children everywhere – swim, make dams, build dens in the vast tree roots that line the river bed. The fields stretch beyond, with their crops of rape, wheat for flour and corn. Some seasons, some years, the fields are more golden than in others. Some years there has been no wheat at all. There are cattle, pigs, sheep and goats, painstakingly reared, then – because they have to be – killed and consumed.

On the perimeter are the kitchen gardens; tidy rows of vegetables: asparagus, tomatoes, peas and beans in the spring and summer; potatoes, squashes and leeks later in the year. Here, in the spring, the glass houses are cleaned. It's a ritual – the start of summer, a cleansing and preparation for the long days and lighter nights to come. By the time they were built, the people here had distanced themselves from the world. The fragile walls retained heat and light; tomatoes thrived. With trial and error, they've come to eat well; failed crops and conflict and broken commitments have given way to pleasure in their own strength and discipline.

From above, this procession of women and children could be a string of bunting flung across baize. Nearing the schoolroom, you might see Rebecca glance sideways. The building is so familiar that it's like home; inside, she nurtures the children of the village, generating a love of stories, injecting their lives with colour and meaning. Here she is now, holding her middle daughter Esther by the hand, ushering along Martha, the youngest, to keep up the pace. They near the Meeting House. She stops to check the hem of Amarantha's dress.

The retinue gathers on the porch. Rebecca bends to adjust the flower garlands in the girls' hair; to remind them about their deportment once inside. She straightens up again. Looks for a moment out to the woods, the distant hills; then, with a deep breath, turns her attention to what is to come.

LOT

From cross-hatched streets and avenues, the city radiates outwards. At night there are lit up billboards, advertising hoardings. The constant thrum of transport: the elevated train; electric cars, mopeds that weave through the streets as though on a chaotic fairground ride. On foot, business people return home, collars upturned, grasping briefcases. The revellers emerge in scanty clothes, faces painted, hair primped out of recognition. The homeless hunch in doorways, faces grey as the blankets they pull around themselves, too thin for any time of year but especially at the year's end.

The smog clears now and then, permits the briefest sight of a couple clinging to each other on a bench, or a man swigging from a bottle and staggering a few steps before continuing his skewed journey.

Lot is constructed in a basin, with hills all around it. They're nothing like the mountains of Marah but if you climb them, you have a bird's eye view of the city: the towering buildings thrusting towards the sky, the vapour that shrouds it in the mornings and at dusk. At night, the uniform rows of lights mark the city's topography. But there are boundaries unseen to the eye, divisions not drawn on a map but, for those who live here, ingrained in the psyche: the Latin quarter; Irish quarter; Little Sweden. The district they call Harlem.

The residents of Lot look not back, but ahead. Looking to the future to transform them. They exist, simply, and wait, losing themselves in pleasure and in dreams about the next day of rest.

The Jewish quarter lies to the west, a hotch-potch of buildings that are taller and more cramped than anywhere else in the city. There are no balconies on the apartments here, washing lines are strung between houses drying linen and rows of white tallits. Decades ago, police swarmed through these narrow streets and dark tenements – looking not for Jews but dissidents of another sort: those who held out against the status quo. Non-conformists, who spurned the Word of God.

This is where, among the Disclaimers, the Elders of Marah once lived. Working hard by day, and trying to stay invisible; single minded, driven by truth. They rejected hypocrisy. If the police arrived, they knew they'd be strong. They had to be.

*

6

The night of the raid, the police moved rapidly, wordlessly up the stairs. The high window at the top let in light from the bar sign across the street; a garish pulse of yellow, orange, green. Enough to illuminate the peeling paint, graffiti daubed on the walls, some in a language they couldn't understand.

There was the unmistakable smell of urine: high, salty and sharp.

The policemen reached the level they needed, a small half-landing. To left and right were shuttered doors that reached from floor to ceiling. They knew without trying they'd be locked and bolted.

There was a hierarchy to their formation: the chief up front; next, his second in command. The new man. Julius, he said his name was – though no one ever referred to him that way. In the mess they had a string of other, more creative names for him.

The chief moved first, hammering on the door, calling for the occupants to come out. There were faint noises inside, shouting, thudding, the cry of a baby. Silence; then the slide of a lock. The door opened a fraction. The chief moved quickly to wedge his foot in the space. A bulky man squared the doorway, the belt of his dressing gown pulled tight across his midriff.

'Are you Micah Kaufman?'

'Who wants to know?'

'We've got a warrant.'

A girl stepped forward from behind the door, a child of about five with an ashen face and red hair pinned in a straight braid. She held fast to the man's leg.

'We've done nothing wrong,' said the man.

As the chief moved close, the girl winced. 'We,' he said. 'Who do you mean – we?'

The man hesitated.

'If you don't co-operate,' said the chief, 'we'll charge you with obstruction.' He paused. 'So tell me.'

A look of panic crossed Micah's face. 'My family – my wife and children, only -'

The chief's senses were engaged now. He felt the knowledge like a current at the back of his neck. There was more to this than he'd

7

realised. 'Are there more of you?'

Micah's eyes slid to the opposite door. It was all the confirmation the chief needed. He gave Julius the command to break in opposite. The remainder stormed past Micah into the hallway. In the Kaufman place there was a wail from the kitchen, the crying of a small baby. The girl with the braids clung to her father's leg.

Through clenched teeth, Micah said: 'What do you want?'

'You know what we want. Where've you hidden it?'

They were levering up the floorboards. Micah's daughter watched as they plunged hands into hollow spaces and produced nothing. She called her father's name, began to cry.

The chief pushed past, moving inside to direct the search. Micah heard the men moving through the rooms, flinging open cupboards and emptying drawers. He turned, wanting to return to Ruth because he couldn't leave her to face this alone. He must attend to his daughter though, first. He picked her up, buried his face in her neck, searching for quiet words of comfort. But her name – Rebecca – got caught in his throat.

MARAH

Rebecca stands on the porch of the Meeting House, waiting for Goran's signal. The community is gathered in the inner room, sitting, not in their customary circle, but in rows with a space cleared in the centre. An aisle. They'll process to the front through this space. To Tobias – who will be waiting, his shoulders squeezed into his good shirt. Goran, his father, will conduct the ceremony.

It's strange, she thinks, to see the back of so many heads, a lifetime of friendships and acquaintances: Carters, Cuthberts and Olsens, all the Christensens; Fitzgeralds and O'Gradys. She takes in the different textures of hair, dresses that have been mended and collars starched for the occasion. At the back, the Miller twins crouch over their spinning tops, ignoring Mariah's pleas for calm. She thinks of her own girls, then, waiting; Naomi standing straight so as not to crease her dress, Esther already on the floor digging about in the gaps between the wooden boards of the porch. And Martha. She lifts Martha to her now, breathing her in as though her girl might shield her from all the day's complexities. Martha's thumb goes to her mouth and she picks at the flowers of her posy.

Rebecca watches Amarantha smooth down her gown. Except that it isn't her gown. It was made by Hephzi with leftover fabric that came with them from Lot. It's been passed from one woman to another – Emilia Olsen was last to wear it – altered, tucked or let out each time. She closes her eyes, briefly, wanting to shut out this image of Amarantha in white. She wants to think of something other than the planning and preparation that have filled her head these past weeks. Rebecca has concentrated on lists and tasks, late into the night because when she lay down to sleep all she could see was Amarantha's face – the smooth skin and full eyebrows with their perfect arch.

All she could think of was Tobias, how he would touch her.

Amarantha will be quick to learn pleasure, of that she's sure.

There's a movement at the front. Rebecca sees Goran step up to the low platform. Despite his stoop, he holds himself with grace. He nods. Rebecca places her hand in the small of Amarantha's back and guides her into the Meeting House.

9

She sees Tobias's profile as they draw level. Watches as he turns – his skin, olive and even; the dark hairs at his neck straying over the collarline. His eyes search for Amarantha, not for her, and she feels a pang of pain. She watches her reaction: the smile on her face that brings her alive, shows her wide mouth, the gap between the teeth at the front, the dimple in the folds of her cheek. Tobias takes Amarantha's hand, thin and elegant, and examines it. The gesture – small but somehow so intimate – makes Rebecca catch her breath.

This connection. Greater than lust. She hasn't seen it before, and now it's too late.

All she can do is bite down on her lip, look ahead of her. She has to bear it. She looks at Tobias's hair curling over his collar; the pearls and pins embedded in Amarantha's. Rebecca is paralysed by her powerlessness. Ahead of her, there's only the relentless onward movement of the ceremony: the vows, the Sealing, the rings.

And afterwards, the lovemaking.

Goran waits for everyone to settle. There's nothing behind him but wall and the intense blue sky through the high windows. She remembers them being built – she was perhaps only six – how she stood on the Piece with the others and watched the men hoist them up into the rectangular frames.

Rebecca forces herself to focus. Goran is speaking.

'Tobias,' he says, 'today you are given Amarantha to seal the Covenant between you and God, and between God and our community.' Goran's gaze scans the Meeting House. 'But there's another person we must call on to join this Sealing.'

Rebecca feels Goran's eyes on hers. They are grey, arresting; she's always been somehow afraid of them, of what he might see. His next words are quieter; reverent even. 'We ask our sister Rebecca to bless this union.'

She has a sensation of falling.

Here, now. She can't distinguish between the raging feelings of anxiety and dread and confusion. Amarantha. Tobias. The two of them together, and what it will mean to her. She closes her eyes, remembering Sarah from Genesis, invoking the determination of those strong women, prophets' wives, who did what was right because it came from outside of them. A good source: the word of God.

When she turns back, the expression on Goran's face is intent, formal. He looks straight at her. 'Tobias is your husband. And today you stand in agreement that he be Sealed to Amarantha.'

Her husband. She thinks about what it means, what it used to mean. Her hands tingle at the memory of her own Sealing to him. What did she feel then? Numb, mostly. Not like this.

'Do you accept that you'll be Sealed to Amarantha also? Do you embrace her as your sisterwife?'

The room lurches. Rebecca can't catch her breath. Can she do this? Take Amarantha into her home, instruct her, support her, work with her.

Share Tobias with her.

The litanies learned in childhood, the tracts the Elders wrote based on the old *Truth's Testimony* mixed in with the scriptures: the ways of God are revealed in the union between men and their wives. You must support each other to ensure the promise of heaven.

But what about earth? Now – tomorrow and the next day, and the next?

Rebecca feels Goran's eyes on her; behind her, the weight of the Meeting's waiting, the silence a taut wire between them, all three of them: her, Tobias, Amarantha.

'Rebecca?' Goran prompts.

She nods swiftly. She mustn't let them see that she might change her mind. She looks straight at Goran. Without glancing at her husband or sisterwife she finds the words.

'It's my duty,' she says. 'I will embrace her.'

Applause bursts out behind her, rushing in her ears. It's the moment they've waited for, the chance to show their pleasure, their congratulations and to share a connection with those at the front. But it's not over yet.

Goran signals for silence and begins the invocation, the speech that calls on the histories: Abraham, Jacob, David, Solomon. He descends the platform, looks around him and calls Rebecca to step forward. He joins all their hands together. Amarantha's fingers are cool on hers; Tobias's grip is strong.

There's a shift, a sudden illumination – the sun moving from behind a cloud. Bleached in the light, their hands become a trinity.

Rebecca sees the pleasure on Tobias's face. As though he's received a gift.

Something in her shrivels. She can't bear to see the reverence in his eyes when he looks at Amarantha like she's a piece he's just crafted, one of his graal vases with the sandblasted layers of colour. She looks away, to suffocate the doubt.

Goran holds their joined hands in the air. The ring Tobias gave – just moments ago, to Amarantha – doesn't fit. A family ring, not even the right size, it rolls loosely down to her knuckle. As it glints in the light, Rebecca remembers the morning and how her sisterwife sat facing the mirror. The way the glass reflected back the two of them, their bodies inhabiting the space; both bounded by the same rectangular frame.

*

The dancing begins at sundown. They've stacked the tables and chairs to clear a space and the musicians cluster in the corner: Gervaise and Ciaras playing fiddle, Seth on bodhrán, his forehead sheeny with sweat. Reeling in concentric circles, dizzy as the colours streak past him, Tobias spins round with Ammie, trying to fix on the garlands round the women's heads and the blur of candles and faces. When the music stops suddenly, she falls against him, laughing.

Ammie.

He picks her up, cradling his hands under her knees. Not caring who sees, he kisses her full on the lips, finding her teeth with his tongue, caressing for a moment the gap there. Aware only of heat; and of the pressure of her breasts against him, her breathlessness, the thudding of his pulse.

When he puts Ammie down again, Kitty takes her hand and pulls her across the hall. She casts one backward look at him, her smile effusive.

'Quite a prize,' says Ciaras, who has found a place next to Tobias, with his violin tucked under his arm.

Tobias is used to his friend's ironic humour. Ciaras knows his unease about the day – his gratitude, guilt, bewilderment, anxiety. In the workshop, in the past few days, they've spoken of little else.

Tobias pulls at the collar of his shirt, starched last night by Rebecca. He wants to be free of these clothes now; longs more than anything for his worn moleskins and old boots. He watches his new wife across the room. She stands in the centre of a group of girls – the Millers, the youngest Cuthbert – and, at a distance, Emilia. Emilia leans in and says something. Tobias watches Ammie flush, her hand go to her throat. He feels a sudden stab of protection.

'It's strange,' he says. 'She's still a child to me.' He remembers her as an eight-year-old, skimming stones on the river, her arm true and straight. He thinks of the pressure of her body next to his just now and it's a strange kind of pleasure, mixed with guilt.

'You know some people envy you?' Tobias catches the look on his friend's face. The tone of his voice might be light, but he is serious.

'Most wouldn't dream of taking on Frania's daughter,' Tobias says.

Ciaras shoots him a questioning look. It makes the fuzz of his eyebrows – dark already, meeting in the middle – more dramatic even than usual.

'The risk.'

A curious expression passes over Ciaras's face, settles into a glower. 'It suits them to call Frania a rebel. Just because she left – it doesn't mean Amarantha should be branded the same way.'

Tobias smiles at Ciaras's defence of Frania. He wonders if Ciaras hoped the Elders might choose Ammie for him.

Tobias looks for her now. The hall has been decked with flowers and ivy leaves, candles placed in the deep sills. They cast a glow that is hopeful, somehow magical. It suits his mood.

His wives are speaking together, looking towards the kitchen, Ammie nodding, Rebecca casting a swift look in his direction. Tobias tries to meet Rebecca's gaze, touched suddenly at the extent of her giving. She's a good woman, a good wife.

Then why does he feel so much guilt?

Because he is betraying the principle. Love all wives equally. Share everything. Surely Rebecca must know it, see it. She must taste the desire for Ammie on his skin.

A discordant noise comes from the corner and when he looks over, Gervaise is brandishing his bow, announcing the start of the music again. People drift back into the centre. He stands, watching, not quite ready to dance again. In the mingling of partners, he loses her. When he catches sight of her again, she's been pulled into the same line as Per and Lucia, Malachy and the Miller children. That the generations blend together is one of the things he loves about this place. He smiles as Ammie ducks under the joined hands of the couple in front.

He senses someone at his side, hears a voice. 'Tobias. I haven't congratulated you.'

Emilia.

He turns to her with an automatic smile. 'It's kind of you to wish us well.'

He sees the slight downturn in her mouth. 'Not at all,' she says brightly. 'I've spoken to Amarantha already. I wanted to be sure to give you my best. You know. Personally.'

The word hangs between them. He notices the flush of exertion on her clear skin, the brightness of the eyes. She has a doll-like beauty but it is empty, somehow. Not for him.

Tobias closes his eyes, and for a moment feels the intensity of the day overwhelm him. He rose early and has been on his feet all day, preparing and organising, issuing instructions, and there's been so little time to reflect. And now, here he is, Sealed to Ammie. He looks around the room but can only see Rebecca at the edge, holding Martha awkwardly on her hip. Then the trace of long thighs through the fabric of her skirt. Laughing, Ammie moves across to her, tugs her hand, insisting that Martha be handed to Ruth or Leah or someone else. It's a game to Ammie, high spirits; but he loves her for it.

Rebecca hands Martha to her mother. He feels his first wife's eyes on his, a question. As though from a distance he observes Ammie's lightness as she takes Rebecca's arm, readying herself for the dance.

Tobias feels a sudden desire to be cool and separate, if only for a minute. To breathe air that he doesn't have to share with the whole community. Right now, his lungs are stale and hot, overused.

The intensity of the rhythm builds. People are laughing, lost in the music, focusing on the dancing or – at the sides – watching, talking to each other. No one will notice if he leaves. He reaches for the handle of the door, and even that is sticky with heat. The door opens quietly and, in a moment, he's outside.

He is drawn, somehow, to the quiet of the Meeting House, finds a seat at the front, side on, so he has a full view of the long window that he loves. Around him, still, are all the signs of ceremony; posies of sweet peas tied to the backs of the chairs. Tobias reaches out to touch them, rubbing the bright petals between his fingers. Already, they're beginning to wilt.

A door opens at the back and Tobias curses, feels a flare of something – anger at the interruption of silence, to his calm. It fizzes through him, the resentment; he wants to ignore it, hope the sounds will subside, and that whoever it is will leave him undisturbed. But then there's a rustling, the noise of a footfall. When he turns, it's Goran.

Goran stands motionless. There's something almost reverential about the dip of the grey head, the stoop of shoulders, and Tobias can't decode it: is it respect for their Meeting House; is it something to do with him? Then instantly Goran straightens, his shoulders pulled back as though to steel himself for a performance. It signals strength. Tobias feels the old rising sensation in his belly, guilt combined with fear. But he remains seated. He'll make Goran come to him.

His father is out of breath, he notices, when he lowers himself into the chair opposite. Even across the aisle the whistling is audible; Goran's expression pained. His face has a grey tint, as though he's fatigued. All the energy and spark of earlier in the day – the ceremony, the lunch – has evaporated.

The question gnaws at Tobias. 'Is something wrong?'

Goran's face is wary, and then a word reverberates in Tobias's head: mistake. They made a mistake in choosing Ammie; now they want to undo everything.

His heart lurches. Why should he think that? Why is it his greatest fear?

He finds his voice, at last; hears the tremor in it. 'Go on.'

'Nothing wrong. No. I wanted … just to … speak to you. On your Sealing day. It seemed the right thing. Today is momentous. A chance to … take stock.'

'Take stock?'

'Of the future. To make plans.'

Goran's fingers move to the bridge of his nose, smooth downwards. It's a gesture that Tobias recognises and yet there's something about it, hesitant and pointed, that makes him nervous. He waits, knowing that Goran will speak before too long, that he has to be patient.

'You know that we're looking for an Elder?' he says at last.

They mean to ask him. He sees it in Goran's face. Tobias feels a rushing sensation in his gut: surprise, pleasure, fear. Anger. 'What does this have to do with me? Now, of all times.'

'It's something …'

'It's my Sealing day. I should be with my wife. Wives.' He stands up, catches the edge of the chair on his thigh and feels the sting of it. Goran reacts as though he's the one who was stung, getting to his feet quickly. Agitation is written on his face, in his movements. He starts to pace backwards and forwards, reaching the furthest chair in the row, then back.

Darkness is gathering outside and when Tobias glances up, the sky through the window is beginning to turn purple. From next door, he hears the whirling melody of violins and thinks of them out there, still dancing – pulling on each other's hands as the pace becomes more frantic – while he's here, trying to divine his father's expectation of him.

He can't take it in. They were expecting it to be Seth. Everyone thought that. And now here, inappropriately, too soon, Goran seems to be asking him. Part of him is exhilarated by the idea of it, flattered. But the request has a weight to it: the constant pressure of setting an example; more meetings, responsibilities. Less time for blowing glass.

What should he say, if Goran asks him?

Rebecca. He thinks of Rebecca and the aspiration she harbours but never speaks about. Ministry, she calls it, the ministry of the church. She'd make a fine Elder's wife.

Tobias blows his breath out hard. Goran stops pacing and looks at him.

'I don't think …' he begins.

'Wait.'

At the sound of Tobias's voice, Goran sits back down. He places the palms of his hands together in front of him, joining fingers with fingers. His listening pose. Then he says: 'Being an Elder means making good decisions. You know that. We need to decide things quickly.' Goran looks at him. 'Sometimes without consulting anyone – friends, wives.'

From outside the Meeting House there's the sound of laughter, drifting across the Piece. People who've left the Hall to catch their breath after the dancing; seeking cool air and respite. Tobias thinks of the lightness he felt earlier when he held Ammie to him and was transported through the dancing.

'But why now?' Tobias can't hide his irritation.

Goran looks at the floor, his posture awkward. 'Because you're Sealed now, to a second wife. An Elder's daughter.'

Then Tobias sees it, like a puzzle falling into place. He feels the anger like a burn, hot and urgent. He stands up. He thought Ammie had been chosen for him because they were meant. He hadn't considered there might be practical reasons. Now they come to him in a rush: a second wife advances his status, makes him eligible for Eldership.

And something else: it solves the problem of a headstrong, motherless girl.

'That's why,' he says, 'why you instructed the Sealing.'

'No!' Goran's protestation echoes around the Meeting House. He can't see his father's face in the growing gloom. But he remembers well his thundering anger, his countenance when he's in the wrong mood. 'You were instructed because … because God willed it.'

'God?'

Tobias feels his father start. Too late. All his doubt is wrapped up in that one word, a question, and now Goran has heard it. He sees him start, hold his breath. What is it, anyway, this God they refer to? This vague, shadowy figure, encompassing everything, yet different for all of them. The elusiveness of it makes him angry and frustrated.

His head is throbbing now. He thinks of the music, the dancing and the lightness. Thinks of the salt he tasted on Ammie's skin when he kissed her neck. He wants only to be back there.

Goran's voice is quiet, comes out of the gloom. 'It isn't your place to question things, Tobias.'

Tobias stands up, overcome with emptiness, suddenly, in this space intended for a gathering. His legs ache, feel unaccountably heavy. 'Then what is my place?'

'To give service.'

There's a long silence. Tobias considers what his father has said. Service. To him, service is making glass. He won't relinquish that.

Goran stands. 'But it seems you're not ready.'

'I need more time.' Tobias is amazed at what comes out of his mouth, at the heartrace feeling he has, facing his father and being asked this. He didn't ask for it. But amidst the shock, even anger, something in him dances at the thought. An opportunity. To breathe life and fire into the way they do things, to shape their customs and rituals; to colour their faith.

'More time,' Goran exhales, considers for a moment. Then nods, slowly. 'I'll tell the others.'

Tobias takes a step towards Goran. He wants to reach for his hand. 'I'm not ...'

But Goran has turned to go. Tobias hears the thud of his father's heels on the wooden floor; the echoing sound, moving away from him.

He stands in the centre of the Meeting House, looking up through the windows. The stars are beginning to make an appearance. He sees clusters of them, cloudy and dense, far away; the puncture of the single ones, piercingly bright. The fullness of the sky never fails to amaze him; the feeling of smallness it creates in him. He closes his eyes, breathing, trying to absorb their light, their expansiveness, their answer.

*

Rebecca has left a lamp burning in the hallway, just enough to light their way upstairs.

In Ammie's new room there's a scent of vanilla; on the nightstand, the glow of a lantern. The bed has been turned down. Tobias imagines Rebecca leaning over it, smoothing sheets; hair swinging forward, red glints firing off it in the candlelight.

From the doorway, Ammie scans the room, mouth caught in an 'O' of surprise. She's still wearing the gown, and he loves what it does to her body; it narrows her shoulders and his eyes are drawn constantly to her neck, bare of hair since it's piled up on her head. He can't stop looking at the bones of her clavicle, her breasts, so often covered but, today, elevated by the cut of the dress. When his eyes move to her face, he sees her tears.

'It's good of her,' Ammie says, then looks at her hands, twisting the fingers together. Tobias reaches out to her, feels the coolness of them, for all the rest of her is so hot. He wants to warm her palms between his but she moves away. She sits stiffly on the edge of the bed, straight backed, eyes fixed to the wall.

Tobias moves to the bed. The coverlet is rose coloured – worn now, he notices – and hemmed with the heads of peonies. He sits behind Ammie, runs his hand along the length of her neck, from the roots of her hair to the nubby bone at the top of her spine. The centre of her, he thinks; the core.

Her body stiffens. He has a sense of trying to grip tightly to something. Hope, perhaps. 'Ammie?'

'I can't believe Goran spoke to you. There's no let up,' she says. He hears the catch in her voice, disappointment. 'Couldn't it wait?'

'I don't think he wanted …'

'What did he want?'

'He wanted … they want ...' He knows he shouldn't say anything. He should talk to them together. Rebecca and he and Ammie, all around the table, working out a way together. But something in him is desperate for Ammie to know. So he can watch her pride in him; that it might set a seal on tonight. He takes a breath. 'They're nominating an Elder.'

'They want you?' Her eyes are wide, mouth open. She covers it with her hand.

He wants to reassure her. But before he can speak there's a noise from the stairs, voices. His brother's booming tones; Rebecca's high laugh. Ammie turns to him and they listen, holding their breath, hearing steps ascending. Tobias watches her face, the dark irises that fill almost the whole of her eyes.

Rebecca's voice is closer now, on the landing on the other side of the door.

'In here, Seth. Thanks. She's too heavy these days for me to lift her. I'll …' The words disappear as they enter the room. Of course. It's late; his daughters will have fallen asleep in some corner of the Hall and slept through the dancing. He imagines his brother's arms cradling one of his girls, and Rebecca ushering him in, covering her, Martha probably, with a blanket.

There's the murmur of voices. Then the sound of a door closing.

He becomes alert, suddenly. The rush of happiness cuts through his irritation at the disturbance and he knows then what he has been waiting for since this morning: for the crowds to fall away, for the day to come to an end. For there to be only this.

No decision to make. Nothing else to think about.

He reaches for her, pulls her to him; he wants to communicate all this to her. Excitement and a feeling of possibility. His fingers brush against the brocade at her waist. He guides her head to his. He explores her hair, looking for the heads of pins, tugs at them and begins to pull them free.

The kiss is new territory for them. Exploratory, flirtatious. There's a new permissiveness about it. He threatens to lose himself in it, because he knows for just these few short hours what he wants more than anything is to forget they're in the house with anyone else.

But even as he holds her, he strains to listen. The footfalls on the landing have gone. Seth will have returned to the party. Rebecca will have closed her door. He imagines her leaning against it, listening, trying to calm her jagged breath. Stuffing her fist into her mouth to stop the crying.

For now, for him, there's only Ammie; only her body.

This desire is foreign to him. It's contrary to everything they believe – that wives should be equal. It gnaws at his soul and at the same time he's overwhelmed by it. He's losing himself in pleasure. He loosens the button on Ammie's dress, kisses the top of her shoulder, closing his eyes against the whiteness of her skin, the contrast of the dark curls that hang, now, around her shoulders.

He won't think of anything else: the interruption, Goran's request. Or Rebecca. He wants to lose himself in the feeling of what he's felt countless times these past weeks. Gratitude. That he has been allowed this gift of another love; unexpected, legitimately given.

And, something else, some other thing. Tobias can't articulate it, not even to Ammie. But he can't let go of it: the regret. An ache of sadness at not being Sealed to her first.

LOT

Goran was dragged from sleep by the sound of crying. Across the hallway, he heard shouting in Micah's apartment. Voices, too, in his own home, coming from the kitchen.

He sat up suddenly. Where was Leah? He expected to see her on the edge of the bed, rousing herself to go to Seth. But when he put his hand out to feel for her, there was only absence, space in the bed.

In the vestibule, the glare dazzled him. Why were the lights on? The doors thrown open? He rubbed his eyes. They were gritty from lack of sleep and from working too hard: too hard in the day at the bookbinders; too hard by night, with the printing.

There were men in the kitchen. Two of them. They had on black uniforms, with microphones pinned to their jackets. Stripes across their shoulders.

Police.

Then the hallway was full of them; in every room they were emptying cupboards, ripping open the linings of curtains.

'Goran Christensen.' The tallest one spoke. Not a question but a statement.

Goran brought his hand to his chest, to feel his heart now, hammering. He couldn't catch his breath for the fear. Now, so help him, he was wishing it was Micah's apartment they'd met in tonight. Goran asked, only at dinner: why should we have to hide at all? He thought now of Micah's response: in times like these there is no such thing as ideological freedom. There is only what the state wants you to believe, and the state is stronger.

Goran had refused to accept it.

'You have no permission,' he said.

'We don't need permission. We've been watching. We know about your secret meetings, your pamphlets. You're breaking the law.'

There was an officer behind him now, jabbing fingers into his back, leading him down the hall. He wondered what the men had inside their padded jackets. Guns, maybe. No, not that. With a rush, he thought of Micah. Goran had seen through the front door the officers in their place

22

too; he thought he had heard Ruth's voice and the cries of little Hannah, their newest child. Younger than his Seth; a baby, still.

As they passed the kitchen, there was the lingering smell of tonight's supper. He thought of them round the table earlier – his family and Micah and Ruth's too. Now, in that room, was the sound of things being destroyed, not created. A ripping. The thudding of drawers being opened; the hollow sound of boots against wood.

They ordered him into the middle of the *familjrum.*

The heart of their home. Goran saw it as they must see it, small and overstuffed with chairs, the cumbersome furniture that had travelled from the old country. There were so many men; men wearing gloves, tapping at the walls, checking for cavities, ripping out phone wires, cables, poking fingers into electrical equipment. Goran closed his eyes, not wanting to think of the care and time that went into choosing the wall coverings, and pasting each strip of paper, matching the tiny flowers on each piece and smoothing out air bubbles. It had made Leah so happy. Leah, who was sitting on the divan, holding the boys to her, shielding their eyes. Nestling against her, Seth had his thumb in his mouth.

Tobias whimpered. Leah reached for his hand and began to trace something – continual circles – on his palm. Goran watched the face of lieutenant, the tall officer with the long, straight nose. He saw the man's eyebrows tighten as though with recognition or at a memory. As if something were being brought to the surface by this action of a woman drawing on her son's skin to comfort him.

Goran looked at Leah, his wife. He saw her as the other men would see her: barefoot, her broad feet firm on the floor, her solid ankles. She'd pulled back her hair quickly into a braid, prominent cheekbones, full breasts that were visible, he saw now, through her nightgown. He wanted to tell her to cover herself.

'Now tell us,' said the lieutenant. 'Where?'

'There is nothing,' Goran said, 'I tell you – you'll find nothing.'

The lieutenant stood for a moment, close enough for Goran to see the pock marks on his face.

'Where are you from?' he said.

Goran could not work out why he was asking the question. 'Why does it matter?'

'You're not from here. Your accent …'

'There are others who speak like this.'

The policeman moved closer still. Goran smelled something on his breath, coffee and old tobacco. He imagined the yellowing insides of this man's fingertips, the fug of smoke as he sat in a car across the street, watching their building. Watching them.

'Your neighbours …' The policeman hesitated.

'What of them?'

'They don't like what you do.'

Goran said nothing. The lieutenant went on. 'The meetings.' He paused. 'The pamphlets. You think we don't know about your so-called faith?' The look on his face was pure malice.

'Faith is … different for different people,' Goran said at last. He would say nothing of their gatherings at night, how alive they made him feel. If that was not faith, then what was? Adding even one person to their number gave Goran a reason to be on this earth.

'You don't believe in anything,' the man jibed.

'We don't believe in your God.'

The words from *Truth's Testimony.* He wanted to say them aloud. *God is inside us, everyone; manifested here on earth. Worship is expressed in simple, daily actions.*

The man's eyes narrowed. 'What then?'

Goran's stomach plummeted. There was no way out. These men knew already. They'd been discovered. All their work, the secrecy of it, subverting what the state wanted them to believe: in one, homogenous faith. What happened to them next was inevitable. It was simply a question of how well Goran could argue.

'We're not like the others, we've committed no crime – no demonstrations or bombs. We believe in peace, only.'

The policeman moved closer still. The breath might be stale but his eyes – his eyes were magnetic.

'Tell me,' said the lieutenant, 'where you've stashed the stuff.'

It was as though Goran had been slapped. His gaze shot to Leah. He saw her face crumple, and he wanted to go to her. But he couldn't

24

move. He didn't have the right words. And they would be watching, these men. Always watching.

All she could do was bury her face in the boys' necks and shoulders, hiding her distress.

Then a splintering noise ripped through the room.

The man in the corner held a hammer and around him, everywhere, was broken glass – large, jagged pieces and tiny studded stones. Goran realised he had cried out in protest; felt a flare of anger at the destruction. It was the pane in the mahogany dresser that was his mother's. It had stood in the hallway of his home as a boy, as a young man.

The state is stronger. Goran had been foolish, so, not to listen to his friend.

Then there was a movement, a flash, a body hurtling towards the dresser, the policeman, the glass. Tobias. For a moment, Goran thought his son was going to attack the officer but Tobias threw himself onto the floor, crying, trying to gather up the fragments.

'Tobias! You'll hurt yourself.' Leah barked the instruction across the room.

His son was kneeling now, holding up a triangular piece of glass between his fingers as though watching the light shine through it. Goran could see the concentration on his face, even in the midst of such carnage, such shame. The policemen had stopped what they were doing to watch the boy.

Goran turned, white faced, to the lieutenant. 'Did you come to search? Or destroy my family, my home? You people – you think you have … authority, power.' He spat out the words. 'Let me tell you something. Power comes only from within. It can't be given by others.'

The lieutenant laughed, a bitter sound.

Leah stood up then, cradling Seth to her. 'Goran, please.'

There was a shout. Goran heard Leah's moan, span around but it was too late: they had prised up the boards with a crowbar, were retrieving something from the recess under the floor. It was a machine, metal, black, something with a crank on the side. The hand press. An old model, brought home from the shop Goran worked in.

Goran rushed forward to retrieve it. Impulsive, but useless because they would see what it was. Would see on it the engraved symbol – their 'D' – embellished in gold.

Goran lunged at it, grabbed the corner and, for all its weight, the two men for a moment played tug of war. They might have been children in the playground.

'You want it?' the policeman mocked.

'You have no right.'

'Is this what you print them on? Your leaflets? 'D'? For dissident.'

'No. Disclaimers.'

'What?'

The mocking tone of the policeman's voice made him flush, shamed but angry. 'We're Disclaimers. We oppose the hypocrisy of the church, its rituals. And hierarchy.'

'You're criminals,' the lieutenant spat out the word. He pointed at the press, then turned to Goran, his face set. 'And this is our evidence.'

An officer stepped forward and took his arms, locked them behind him until he felt a pain shoot up his shoulder. He watched them carry the press to the door. He could not imagine what they might do to it. Or to them.

The lieutenant nodded at the officer who held him. 'Bring him in,' he said. 'The other one, too, opposite. And tell the chief to come and see this.'

The lieutenant dragged him across the room. The gesture was hard, decisive. Goran knew it was impossible to protest. They must face whatever would come next, he and Micah. As they reached the doorway, Goran turned to find Leah. She stared numbly in front of her, not even comforting Tobias, who was crying now. There were tiny spots of their son's blood on her nightgown. Hearing his moans, she stirred, took his finger into her mouth, sucking it gently. Erasing the blood; erasing the pain, too, he thought, and the shame.

Goran's gaze shifted to the lieutenant. He was mesmerised, the look on his face impossible to read – regret, guilt, concern. The policeman nodded once, abruptly, at Leah. She did nothing; said nothing. Stared blankly; kissed the tip of her son's cut finger.

MARAH

Glassblowing, for Tobias, is a kind of miracle. What he loves is imagining a piece and seeing it come into being. Watching it build, layer on layer. He loves the focus required to do it, and the connection it allows him to feel with the thing beyond himself.

He lifts the blowpipe to his lips. The glass expands with his breath, balloons out in the right way. Though he's aware always of Ciaras's presence across the workshop, this part he can only do alone, breathing life into something organic. Sometimes, when he sees tiny bubbles appear under the surface of something he's making, he senses part of himself suspended there forever, his energy and force; everything he is, encapsulated in that moment.

Tobias crosses the workshop. He lowers the glass on the marvering bench for Ciaras to do the shaping. Back at the furnace, he dips the blowpipe, watching for the tip reflected on the surface of molten glass. He turns it quickly as the tail appears, matching the speed of his breath to the rhythm of his hand. The gather forms, neat, round, ready to be shaped.

He steps back, loosening his stance, consciously rolling his weight onto his heels. It grounds him, creates a steady centre he can work from. Across the workshop he becomes aware of a steady tapping, not loud but rhythmic enough to disrupt the meditation of his movements. He misses a count: one, two, and his breath stops, the connection is broken and the glass droops, misshapen, from the pipe.

Tobias inhales sharply. He plunges the pipe into the water bucket. The hiss is sibilant, almost mocking. It suggests something abandoned and unhappy, something that has not yet achieved its shape or form.

'Damn it.' He can't contain his anger. With the glass, with the work; with himself.

Ciaras looks up from the marvering bench.

'Another one?' He plays with the shears, turning them over in his hands. A reminder of his failure. 'You remember,' he says, 'that the craft fair is this month. Not next.'

Tobias is irritated at Ciaras's mockery. But he's trying his best. He's acutely aware of the time slipping away. They need fifty vases by

Friday for the fair in the next district. It's Wednesday already and they have only half that in the annealing oven.

Tobias is aware of the pipe still in the water; the steam still rising from it.

'Should we take a break?' Ciaras's tone is lighter now, more sympathetic.

Tobias glances through the door into the yard, incandescent in the light. Alpha the sheepdog lies asleep in a square patch of sun; in the summer, he comes often from the fields. Tobias feels a wave of fatigue, a sudden need for warmth and space. He looks back at Ciaras, nodding agreement, but his friend has his back to him, already putting the coffee pot onto the stove to heat.

Tobias lifts the cup to his face, inhaling. The bitterness soothes, rather than stimulates: to him, it is a sacred thing, this ritual of coffee.

'So. Will you tell me? What's bothering you?'

Tobias leans back against the whitewashed wall. In the distance, there's a circle of rising smoke from the house chimneys. He feels safe here, amidst the cluster of stone workshops huddled together on the opposite bank to the houses, the school, the Meeting House. He closes his eyes, absorbs the sun and the sounds that are so much part of the fabric of the day that he forgets about them: inside, the constant roar of the furnace; outside, the river, the occasional call of a bird, the noise from Gervaise's smithy.

He likes that Ciaras never rushes him.

'Sometimes I wish I was Seth and only had to worry about farming. It just seems … simpler somehow. I always feel so … caught.'

Ciaras laughs, not altogether sympathetic. 'So many people envy you – that you have that freedom to go outside. But you make it sound like a compromise.'

'Isn't everything about compromise?'

'If so you don't like it,' Ciaras says, 'stop compromising. Leave.'

Ciaras makes it sound so easy. It's true that there is nothing practical to stop him: he has a skill, contacts, regular custom. He could find his way there. Make a life there.

'But think about why you do this. You love glassblowing. And the trading on the outside – it's a kind of service. You need to acknowledge that.' He leans forward on the bench, peers through his spectacles. 'What would we do if you – all the others – Gervaise. If you didn't do this, didn't get out there …' He indicates with his head. 'We wouldn't be able to buy anything. You're our passport, Tobias.'

Tobias is silent for a moment, digging his heel into the ground, makes a mark with it. 'It isn't just that. Bothering me, I mean.'

'What, then?'

'It's just … the juggling everything.' There's the scrape of his heel again. 'Being fair. Like today. What do I do? It's Ammie's birthday. Last year I made a vase for Rebecca. Ammie sees it every day on the dresser. And now I don't have time to do the same for her.'

Ciaras raises his mug, sips his coffee. When he speaks it's slowly, with consideration. 'You've spoken to Goran? He must remember what it's like.'

'I can't go to Goran.'

'Why?'

Tobias looks up, casts his eyes over the hills in the distance, then turns his attention back to his friend. 'If I tell you – can you keep it to yourself?' He takes a breath, braces himself. 'They want to make me an Elder.'

'Ah.' Tobias is aware of Ciaras's eyes behind the glasses, reading him. He takes a slow, careful sip of his coffee. 'What did you say?'

'I'm still thinking about it. It feels like … some sort of bargain.'

'I don't follow.'

'They let me leave to learn my trade. I promise to come back. I'm instructed to be Sealed and then – well, suddenly, they're considering me for Elder. And they assume I won't say no.'

'*Would* you say no?' Ciaras leans forward and places his cup on the ground. He's absorbed, intent on what is being said. Tobias finds himself wishing that his friend would be more direct, sometimes, and say what's on his mind.

'You're always saying ... how much you struggle with it, the way the Elders do things. This is your chance, isn't it? To change all that.'

Tobias hears the cry of a rook. The whisper of breeze beginning to get up, making the leaves shiver, exposing the undersides of leaves so that there is a ripple of light green, grey, green again.

'I don't know, Ciaras.' He turns to face his friend. 'I chose to come back. That's my commitment. I don't know if I've enough energy for all of it. Making glass, two wives, daughters, the community, Meeting. It's not that I don't want to be here. I feel compromised, a lot of the time. But I'm where I want to be ...' Tobias struggles for the word, lays the palm of his hand, deliberately, next to him on the bench. 'In a place I think I believe in. In the end.'

Ciaras's eyes are steady on his. Tobias feels unnerved somehow. He digs again with his heel. It chips at the surface, dust flying upwards.

'But it needs to be less rigid. It seems to me people either yearn to leave, or live here without questioning how it could be better.'

'You think you could change that?' A challenge.

Tobias feels the adrenalin begin to surge through him now, part anger, part frustration, part fear. He takes a breath. 'If I don't change things in some way, I'll feel I've failed.'

There's a sound from behind them. Ammie, standing in the doorway of the workshop. She must have come through the other way. He doesn't know how long she's been there and she looks at him, a guilty smile playing around her lips.

'I was wondering,' she says. She looks at Ciaras, then back at Tobias. 'Since it's my birthday. Will you come for a walk?'

*

Ammie feels a rush of pleasure at the surprise on Tobias's face. He hesitates though, for all that. Ciaras, wiping his hands on a rag, shrugs. They're finished for the morning anyway, he says; he doesn't mind clearing up. Go. Enjoy your birthday, Ammie.

Tobias takes her hand. She thinks about when she used to come after school, asking questions about the glass, talking about her studies and the things Rebecca had taught her that day in the school room. She glances back into the workshop, remembering. The floor is covered with filaments of glass: tiny splinters that have been ground in by the soles of boots. When Ammie looks back, it's dazzling in the midday light, as though someone has cast a million diamonds right across the workshop.

She's forgotten what it is like to walk with Tobias outside. She wants to let it soak right into her, the guilty pleasure of this birthday secret. She absorbs him; his height, the strident movement of his legs, the way his arms swing loosely by his sides as he walks, the action coming from the hips. His skin is olive, the taut hairs around the top of his chest springy and black where his neck is exposed to the sun. She thinks how she'd like to kiss it there, let her tongue linger over the Adam's apple: the place where his voice comes from, the place where her name is formed.

They reach the hollow trunk, one that fell years ago in a storm. It has a space in the centre that is big enough for a child to crawl through, to stay there a while and dream. Under Ammie's fingers, the bark feels crumbly, softened with lichen and moss.

'Tell me what you meant just then. About failing.'

Tobias sits with his back against a tree, legs thrown out in front of him, crossed at the ankle. It's strange to be here with him, in this place that is outside of everything. It's the most peaceful time to be here, with the rest of the women at home, the children at the schoolroom, the younger ones out on the Piece. Most of the men will be in the fields, or occupied some other way: on the plots or doing repairs. Not many – like Tobias – have a trade they work at for themselves. She remembers, when she was young, asking him about his freedom, and his reply: the Elders let him go because otherwise they would lose him. Because they recognised it is the best way for him to serve God.

Ammie watches as Tobias reaches into his knapsack. He brings out an apple and begins to peel it. It comes away in one long strip, curling to the floor like the decoration from a Christmas tree.

His gaze at her is earnest, as serious as she has ever seen him look.

'It's not that I've failed. Just that … it might feel like that. If I were to say yes … to their invitation …'

'Is it an invitation? I didn't think you'd have a choice.'

Tobias continues peeling the apple, his focus intent, as though it might help him decide. Something about his steadiness, his unwillingness to look her in the eye makes her uneasy. And then she realises; the rush of knowledge spills out of her mouth before she can control it.

'You haven't told Rebecca yet?'

He looks up at her quickly, a plea in his eyes. He doesn't want her to talk about it. He wants her to keep the peace until he can get to her, to explain. She shouldn't know this and something shoots through her then, a thrill. She knows something Rebecca doesn't. The knowledge, the pleasure it gives her. It compounds their secret even more.

The silence lasts a good while. She hears him chewing on the apple. The peel lies on the ground now, by the base of the tree trunk. It is red, but now that it has been carved up, no longer shining. He leans forward and offers some to her. The flesh is pale and furry; it's soft and unexpectedly sweet.

'Does Rebecca know you're here?' he says.

Ammie shifts in her seat, unsure how to answer. She doesn't want to admit she's sneaked here; she doesn't want to think what Rebecca would say. Stolen time, secret time; extra to what is apportioned.

She shrugs. 'I can't stay long.'

The thrill of it; that she and Tobias both have a secret they can share with each other. Rebecca on the outside, not knowing.

'She can't argue, surely. It's your birthday.'

'Still a working day. For her.'

'We should go.' He reaches for the water bottle and takes a swig. Then stands suddenly, holds out his hand to help her up. He pulls her to him and there's the feel of the muscles on his back under her fingers, his smell. Even in the open he carries the scent of the workshop with him: a smell like metal and glass dust. 'I want you to tell me,' he says. 'If things get difficult for you.'

'Difficult?' She twists her head round to look at him and laughs. 'Isn't it meant to be difficult? It's what they say. Micah and the others. In Meeting. Plural marriage is a kind of test.'

He shakes his head. 'That's not what I mean. I want you to tell me if you feel at all … restless.'

'What could you do anyway? There's nowhere for me to go.'

'I'm thinking about Frania,' he says quietly. 'That's all.'

'I'm not my mother.'

'You're more like her than you think.'

'I'm not her,' Ammie blurted out. 'I wouldn't just … leave. Not without explaining.' And then, when the anger starts to boil in her: 'I wouldn't leave my child.'

They'd walk to the town, Frania had said, the day she reached eighteen. Uphill all the way to Aroer with its church towers and remains of rampart walls that whisper of a violent past. Then a train to Lot.

And from Lot? Ammie asked.

You can go anywhere from Lot, Frania said. To the coast. To the college towns, with their snaking rivers and bridges and old, old buildings with libraries stocked with books to the ceiling. Such ladders they have, Ammie, reaching to the top.

She puts her hand up to Tobias's chest, feels the breadth of it, his solidity. He looks at her and smiles. When he has that look in his eyes, of delight in her, enchantment almost, she can forget about everything else: the life she once thought she'd have, her mother, Rebecca. Today, she's eighteen. Ammie closes her eyes, feels the pulse of Tobias's heart beneath her hand, feels the sensation of his mouth on hers; feels the energy of desire and life rushing upwards inside her.

They pause, on the way back, in the meadow full of poppies. The bright spots of colour almost take her breath away. She is mesmerised by the movement of the red heads in the breeze. Poppy, he says, such a good word – tall and bright and open. I wanted to call Martha that.

His hand reaches for hers and the unexpected touch is a flare, thrilling, shocking. 'We haven't talked about children. Yours, I mean. How soon.'

Something inside her freezes at that, the thought of things coming up so fast. 'It seems so early to think about it.'

'Not so early,' says Tobias, 'two months.' He pauses. 'Some start right away. Even second time.'

She catches his look. He could probably tell from her eyes, staring away over the horizon, across the surface of the river and over the woods beyond, what she is thinking. That to want it would pin her here, maybe forever. But she knows that the expectation is everything: to produce children, to keep their life here thriving.

'What is it?' Tobias says. He puts his hand on her shoulder. 'What are you afraid of?'

His touch stirs her, that pull that has become familiar now – in her thighs and in the depths of her stomach. When he steps closer, his hand goes up to her face. His chest and groin are right against her; she closes her eyes against the wanting and yet at the same time wants to suck the desire right inside her. The confused feelings she has carried around in these last weeks: to want something so much. To need to hold it away, at arm's length, in case it burns or cuts or harms.

'I'm not afraid Tobias. I just need time. To get used to it all – the house. Rebecca, the children.'

His hand slips inside her blouse, palm flat on her back and she notices how cold it is, even in the heat of the day. How it makes her shiver.

Tobias brings his mouth down on hers. 'A boy,' he says, as they emerge from the kiss. 'A son. I'd love that with you.' The words are swallowed up by another kiss, which is softened by the glimmering light on the water and the sound of the insects amongst the grasses.

When they pull apart again Tobias reaches into his bag. He brings something out. It looks strange to her but something about the way he holds it tells her it's precious to him.

He holds it up for her to see. 'My old Polaroid.'

'What is it?'

He laughs and her ignorance makes her blush, suddenly. 'A camera, for taking pictures of things. If you'll let me … I'd like to take yours. A birthday photograph.'

Ammie nods, shy but at the same time, curious. When he holds it up she is disconcerted. She sees his head, but can't see his eyes. She smiles, tries not to be conscious of how forced her grin must seem to Tobias, focusing on her through the small glass window. He explains how it works. They wait in silence then the camera spews out the square of shiny paper. As they watch, the colours gather, the shapes becoming more defined. It begins to develop, right in front of their eyes, and what she sees

34

looking back is a girl, too young to be married, with wild black hair backlit by the sun. A girl with a gap in her teeth who is far from beautiful, being looked at by Tobias as though for the first time.

*

A kitchen full of dishes is not what Rebecca needs. Not after an afternoon in the schoolroom. It may be Amarantha's birthday, but if Rebecca is preparing the celebration tea, the least her sisterwife could do is clear up.

Rebecca bangs the screen door shut with her hip, arms full of books that she slides onto the kitchen table. She looks quickly away, trying not to think when she'll find time to look through them. Certainly not tonight. There are never enough hours in the day, even with another pair of hands to share the work. This morning she was up at six, weighing the dry ingredients for the saffron buns and the ginger cake before preparing the day's lessons, waking the girls and getting breakfast for them all.

From upstairs, there's the sound of singing. Amarantha's voice. The volume increases as the others join in, Martha first, then the older girls who ran straight up the minute they arrived home. Sometimes she acts more like a sister than another mother.

More like a daughter than a sisterwife.

Rebecca takes down her apron from its hook on the door. Usually she'd have time to play with the girls but there is none of that today. She unbuttons the sleeves on her blouse, rolls them back, runs the hot water. She sets about reclaiming the kitchen, emptying dirty dishes from the porcelain sink, wiping the wooden surfaces, picking up toys from the tiled floor. The movement and routine have a calming effect. On the pine dresser is a row of cakes, each covered with a cloth. She can tell from each one who will have called: carrot cake with orange frosting from Sarah; Lucia's coffee cake; Hannah's lamingtons. If she'd known there'd be so many, she wouldn't have bothered with the ginger, spice and saffron.

Rebecca is trying, really trying, to do the right thing.

Saffron, for example. She was the one who'd remembered to add it to the provisions list. But when the wives went on the trip, they'd run out – as of course they would – she asked Tobias if he would find some in the city. So he came home with it: the majestic bearer of the goods; the giver of the gift.

She pushes away a loose strand of hair. She feels the anger mounting now. After all the effort they've gone to, Amarantha doesn't appreciate it. Rebecca doesn't see why Amarantha can't look after Martha and make sure the kitchen is left tidy. She's managed herself all these years.

Rebecca adds it to the litany of things to discuss with Tobias: Amarantha's work, Amarantha's attitude, Martha's behaviour.

Another child.

That gnawing need of her own. Standing in the middle of the kitchen, running the flat of her hand over her abdomen, she feels the ghost of movement in her womb. There are times when she aches with it, the longing; and she's kept it hidden too long from Tobias. She must speak to him. Tonight. She'll make him see how important it is to her.

They're gathered around the table, all of them. Tobias edges something towards Amarantha, a package wrapped in tissue paper. He explains that the real gift isn't finished, that she will have to wait, but that he thought of her when he saw this small thing.

Rebecca remembers the buns, still baking. She jumps up, crosses to the oven, slides them out on their tray; they sit on the counter, risen and perfectly golden. She turns to see Amarantha pull away the paper, a slim volume bound in maroon leather. A book of poetry. Her sisterwife flushes with delight.

'I thought we could read it tonight.'

Tonight. The word is a slap. No, Rebecca thinks. Tonight is the night for the household accounts; and her night with Tobias.

Amarantha smiles and touches Tobias's hand. 'I'd love that,' she says. And Rebecca watches the flush sweep over his olive skin, as though he were a boy again.

'You remember the accounts?' Rebecca looks quizzically from Amarantha to Tobias.

Tobias nods. 'I meant after,' he says. A pause, he looks away. 'At bedtime.'

Something inside her snaps.

'It's my turn.' Her words ache with a rawness she didn't know could exist in her.

They turn and look. Tobias, Amarantha, the children. Rebecca registers the shock on Naomi's face.

'No, Rebecca. Remember?' Tobias's words are gentle, but she hears the hardness under the surface. 'When Amarantha arrived, we agreed. Birthday nights are extra.'

She can't remember. She can't remember having the conversation, or agreeing to it. She shakes her head as though to clear some blockage. She is, suddenly, so tired.

'Oh yes. Of course.' She forces a smile. Tobias's shoulders relax visibly. Amarantha rises, begins to clear away plates, wipes down Martha's hands.

'But, Tobias ...' Amarantha says. She pauses mid way to the sink and Rebecca sees the puzzlement on her face. 'Surely – don't all three of us need to talk about ...'

Rebecca sees the quick tightening of Tobias's shoulders. The warning look he shoots at Amarantha. His face is thunderous.

Something is wrong; very wrong.

She looks from Tobias to Amarantha, back again. The girls have silently left the table, as though aware of some danger to come. Naomi leads Martha by the hand, towards the door, Esther following.

'What?' Rebecca manages at last. 'Talk about what?'

With each second, the silence in the room grows more taut. The knot in her stomach tightens. The look on her face must be a plea because then Tobias is next to her, holding her. Shamefaced.

'I wanted to tell you,' he says. 'There just hasn't been chance.' He hesitates. She sees the wildness in his eyes, his grasping for the truth. 'They want me to be an Elder.'

The room narrows. She's aware of Amarantha moving to the sink, quietly placing dishes on the surface. That it should come like this, the invitation, the one she has waited for all these years. But to happen like this.

Amarantha knew. She knew, and Rebecca didn't.

The anger surges through her, rocks her. She has to bite down on it to prevent herself from crying out. She was Sealed to Tobias first. But she is last to know.

Air. She needs space to breath. She steps towards the door. Loses her footing and Amarantha is there, suddenly, at her elbow. 'Rebecca'. Her sisterwife is trying to grasp her hand and it is warm in hers, her face flushed. She can't look at her, for fear she'll cry. But she hears guilt in her voice, fear even. A desire to please. 'I want to say thank you. For the saffron buns. All the effort you went to.'

Then Amarantha embraces her. It's a genuine gesture of gratitude. But the pressure of her sisterwife's body is too much. Rebecca feels the tears hot in her eyes and she rushes to the door.

Outside, the air is cool. She feels it light on her skin, soothing after the heat of the inside, the cloying smells of ginger and spices. She walks around the side of the house, leans against the wall, head to the sky, mouth open, breathing. She takes great, deliberate gulps. Eyes searching the hills, the familiarity of the place that has held her for so long.

The screen door slams.

She hears footsteps, braces herself to face whoever it is. Tobias, standing in front of her, reaching out to her. She moves away from him.

'I'm sorry. I'm sorry you had to hear that way.'

She bites down. The ache in her throat from trying not to cry.

'You've no idea.'

Tobias doesn't say anything. He reaches forward, gently strokes her forearm. 'It's just … she was there … it was the night of the Sealing …'

Then she feels a rush of longing, of wanting to know. 'What will you say?'

'I wanted to speak to you first.'

'And what I think matters now, does it?'

She sees him reel at his words, as though slapped.

'I thought it's what you wanted?' Tobias says. 'You always said … you've been brought up to it. Your father … '

'We should be doing it together.' Rebecca is aware that she's

38

shouting. Tobias says nothing but in his eyes she reads regret, perhaps, confusion.

'But I'd decided. For you – I was going to say yes.'

She puts a hand behind her to steady herself. She sees everything, then. Tobias doesn't want to do it. It's something she's always suspected, his distance from it, a lack of respect. Now, it makes sense: he doesn't believe in it.

Rebecca stumbles – she doesn't know how – down the path and away from the house. She crosses the Piece, the backs of the houses, eyes blinded with tears, pain closing her throat. She yearns for the place she knows she'll achieve solace.

Inside, the chairs are still arranged in a circle from last Meeting. She finds the seat opposite her own usual one, sits down in it.

How little there is of silence and stasis in her life.

She closes her eyes, trying to refresh herself with the lack of noise and action around her. She should do this more often, she thinks, be still and do nothing. But her thoughts shift back to Tobias, the confusion that flashed in his eyes, the way he screwed them up, as though to understand. The way the guilt drained him of his colour.

If he has no faith in it, in their system of deciding and doing things, what does it make of her marriage? What of her, and him, and Amarantha?

Rebecca looks through the window, as though the sky might provide answers. Already there is the faintest hint of pink in the sky, in the patch of cloud she sees through the panes of glass. She loves these windows. Tobias has argued over the years to replace them with colour – something that would tinge the light as it falls and bathe them in soft pinks, blues, greens. But Goran disagreed with him: too much like the ornate stained glass of churches and cathedrals. It would be against their principle of simplicity, he said.

Always more than one way.

Two people can be right and wrong at the same time. And life, after all, is nothing more than delicate negotiation.

So why does she feel so wronged?

She shivers, holds her arms around herself. The air is chill in here, despite the warmth of the evening. She moves to the stove. The door is stiff – it hasn't been used since the winter – but she has an urge to light a fire. It might be wasteful, or selfish, but she doesn't care.

Rebecca takes kindling from the willow basket. There is balled-up paper inside the stove already. She lays the kindling on top, begins to lay the logs from the woodpile, focusing on the texture of bark, the way on some of them it flakes away to show the white insides. She notices the different shapes of the wood. However close together she arranges them, she realises, there are spaces in between. They would never fit neatly together. She thinks how the fire needs those spaces – the air in-between – to spark, to catch, to burn.

LOT

Goran Christensen couldn't remember when he was last inside a church. Not even here – in the city that was now home. It wasn't so different from those of his homeland. There was the pulpit with its ascending steps. Wooden benches fixed to the ground. There were lifeless images of people who may or may not have existed. It was alien to be here, surrounded by statues, paintings and candles. Trappings of faith, not faith itself, celebrating a personal God, someone real; distant and external. It was not how they understood God to be.

Their faith required only the presence of a few. There was no special place for it; it had no creed. Goran had loved its transportability, faith that you might wrap in a parcel and take with you anywhere. Community was a thing of the spirit, after all. Not bricks and mortar and hard benches.

Then why did he feel so empty? Why was he longing for some space to call home?

He had been restless since the raid, discontented. To him, it was clear. After the surveillance and arrests, after the way they had been treated, the Disclaimers could not continue as they were. It was too dangerous.

But it was more than that – something internal, something they were grasping for. They were lacking some fundamental precept and since the raid he could see it, see it clearly: it was not enough to criticise and reject what they saw around them: they must seek and find. A home, a resting place, a pattern of their own that grew out of Disclaimer principles but which defined them for themselves.

He knew it was up to him to take the lead.

Except he did not know the answer to the questions he was seeking.

In truth, he was not even sure of the questions.

Goran reached out to the pillar in front of him, wanting to feel something solid under his fingertips. He traced the ribbed pattern of the plaster. The stone was the same flat grey as the cell they put him in. So many hours he had stared at that wall, feeling the throb of his injured hand, his bruises. He could not connect with what he believed, all through the questioning, his confinement in that dark room, the repeated blows of the interrogating officer. Even afterwards, with the sweet relief of the return home. Something had gone, ripped out with the wires and cables. Goran thought it was a numbness that might pass. But he could not shake it.

It was like a riddle he could not work out in his head. He was free; Micah was not. Micah was still, in their eyes, guilty of subversion. Why did they hold onto Micah, when the press had been found in Goran's home, when Goran himself held in his hands the book the police had been looking for?

The book. He needed, suddenly, to look at it, to receive the comfort of its ancient pages. He slid onto the nearest bench, feeling the cold surface of the wood beneath his buttocks and thighs. He rested his feet on a cushion that was embroidered with different coloured threads. When you looked at it from further away, it was impossible to see the individual strands. From a distance, all you saw was a cross.

But the book.

He opened it, realised with a shock how fragile the pages were, how much they had crumbled. They must think about some permanent housing for it, somewhere under glass where it could be preserved: their history, their heritage, these ideas long since passed down. *Truth's Testimony*. They named it so because its full title – formulated so many hundreds of years ago – was clumsy, like a foreign language. He remembered how, when he first came here, he hadn't understood what testimony meant. He hadn't heard of the strange people who held out their faith against government, against the established church. Then he had become one of them.

Only now it wasn't enough.

Goran held the book to his chest, a talisman. *Trohet*. This was what was important. Truth, and faith.

He felt something touch his arm, and looked up. Leah. Her long hair smoothed back, dark circles under her eyes from lack of sleep.

She smiled at him. He saw concern in her eyes, but perhaps, also, fear.

'I was looking for you,' she said.

'I'm sorry. I needed to think, only. Somewhere quiet. Out there

– there's too much noise.'

A frown split her forehead. She looked around her, moved onto the bench beside him. She took his hand, almost as though he were ill. 'But … here?'

'No one can disturb me here.' He paused, wondering how she'd thought to look there. 'How did you know?'

'It was worth a try. Just a feeling. But it feels … wrong.' She lowered her voice to a whisper. 'Like we're making fun of what they believe.'

Goran noticed how restless her eyes were, even though the church was empty. 'You were afraid?' he said.

'We looked everywhere. The boys – I had to leave them with Ruth. I didn't know ...' Her eyes filled with tears. 'Tobias thought – oh!' She turned away. He could not bear it, he thought; what this place did to them, the way it impinged on their lives.

'Please,' she said, 'let's go. It doesn't feel safe. If they find you here … '

A door opened further up the church and footsteps echoed across the space. There was someone coming through a door on the left of the chancel. Goran felt Leah stiffen beside him. A man dressed in black – a priest – peered into the body of the church. He didn't see them and turned back to his tasks, moving around the altar, laying a cloth, lighting a candle.

Leah moved uncomfortably in her seat. 'We need to do something, Goran.' He could hear the panic in her voice. 'Ruth is distraught. The children …'

'It's what I've been doing here. Thinking.' He turned to look at her, noted the gentle shape of her round face, the premature grey beginning to show at the temples. He loved her. He loved the history they shared. Working together, he knew it was possible for them to change things.

'We must find another way,' Goran said. 'A way of our own. As long as we live here, they'll come after us. They'll never understand.'

'Leave?'

Her jaw slackened. The word hung between them. A tantalising glimpse of a possible future. She took a breath. Turned to face him. 'But why? Surely we don't need …'

'If we stay, we'll have no freedom.'

'They didn't find anything.' He sees her face begin to drain of its colour. The extent of her fear. If we lie low, don't put out any more pamphlets for a while. They can't prove anything. They didn't find this.' She touched the *Truth's Testimony.* 'To them, we're just ...'

'Non-believers?' He laughed bitterly. 'But we do believe. Not their beliefs – in sin and heaven. They feel threatened. And so ...' He feels his bile rising, sees the disgusted face of that policeman the night of the raids. 'So they try to make us afraid. Rip apart our homes. They arrest us, make our children fearful. And you know ...' He turns now to face her, to look at her white, terrified face. 'You know it will always be like that.'

Through his outburst Leah had been silent, playing with her rings. So many rings, Goran thought. Did she need so many? So many and yet the finger that counted – the one that should have borne her wedding band – was bare. He was struck, suddenly, with anger at everything they owned, the accoutrements they had dragged with them through their life together. Part of him wished they'd given away everything they owned, in boxes, that night in the apartment.

Leah turned to him, reached out, stroked his cheek with the tip of her finger. 'Goran. You've just been released. It's understandable you're angry.' She looked at her hands, playing with the ring on her middle finger. 'But ... ' She hesitated. 'They're not so malicious as you think.'

'How can you say that? After everything?'

She hesitated. 'One of them – the policemen. He came back.' She took a breath. 'The other day,' she said quickly, 'when you were out.'

A hot column of anger surged through his body.

'Did he threaten you? Touch you?' Why would the policeman come back? He could sense Leah's breathing, rapid and light, right next to him. He could not bear for her to be so afraid. 'Why didn't you tell me?'

'I wanted to,' Leah said. 'I just thought it would ... worry you ...'

'What did he want?'

'To apologise. For the mess. He offered to pay whatever ...'

'Apologise?' He laughed aloud and the sound of it had an echoing ring. 'It is too late – the children saw it all. Can we undo what has already been done?'

'He was …' Leah hesitated, 'kind.' There was something in the way she lifted her chin, so. A defiance, almost. 'Understanding.'

She said the word without looking at him.

And he saw it. The truth. The lieutenant. Why he'd come back. Goran remembered Leah that night, how she looked with her hair mussed from sleep and the outline of her breasts visible under her nightgown.

Abruptly, he stood. He needed to escape this place.

'Goran.' She tried to catch his hand but he pulled it away. He saw anxiety now in her face, real fear locked into her body, in the frown between her brows. 'Please,' she said, 'let's go home.'

He pushed past her. He caught his shin on the bench, hard against the bone. His steps down the central aisle of the church. Ringing, rapid. Panicky. Leah's voice behind him, calling his name. He was dizzy. It was like seeing the world through a haze of black dots. This was wrong, wrong. Everything was wrong.

Goran reached the heavy wooden door. It was still propped open. The heat and light poured in from outside. He grabbed the rusting ring of the handle, pulled it hard, slammed it shut.

After the gloom in the church, the sun was intense. Goran winced. He squinted hard against the blinding heat of the day, descending the stone steps to the square.

*

They'd waited too long already, crammed into a circle in Goran and Leah's apartment. The mismatching furniture meant they were at different heights: Goran on the low footstool; Leah, cross legged on the floor, with Gervaise and Niamh beside her; Eliza and Per and Lucia Olsen on kitchen chairs. Ruth sat upright on the battered divan, Jude lounged next to her, denim-clad legs flung out in front.

Two seats were vacant still: those belonging to Simeon and Matilda.

Goran glanced at the mahogany grandfather clock. 'We should start,' he said.

In front of them, the teak table was littered with empty bottles

45

– wine mostly, beer and mineral water – as well as bowls holding potato chips and the dusty residue of peanuts. The noise of the city permeated the room: a hoot from a car horn, drunken shouting, the occasional whine of a siren. And the rain, spattering against the window.

'Shouldn't we give them more time?' Ruth voiced everyone's concern. There was a pause as they looked at the empty seats and tried to decide what to do.

'They're half an hour late.' Jude said. 'I say we proceed.'

'No,' Eliza snapped, 'we should wait.' She raised her hand swiftly. She sometimes had a habit of flicking her wrist, as though to free it from something, and it was always accompanied by a sound like the clink of a spoon on a wine glass. It was the charm on her bracelet, a tiny bell. 'Everyone must be here,' Eliza said, 'when we make decisions. You know that's how we do it.'

Again, the sound of the tiny bell was audible in the room.

Jude frowned, irritated. 'They haven't been seen for two days. Their van is gone. Their phone disconnected. Do we need any more evidence?' He was a tall man, slender and long limbed – in this sense, very like Goran. His dark skin and slick ponytail gave him the look of a Native American. His voice gave him an air of authority. When he spoke, people listened.

'I think Jude's right.' Ruth was speaking now. 'They've gone.' Her voice dropped in volume. 'While it's still safe.' The implication was clear to them all: she wished she and Micah had done the same. Now, though, it was too late.

'Should we start anyway?' Goran said. Most nodded their assent; only Eliza remained silent, lips clamped shut, a thunderous look on her face. She kept working her lip, chewing at the top one – from agitation, rather than nervousness. It was what she did to hold herself back from speaking.

'As you know, we need to decide what to do,' Goran said. 'Now they've found us, we're exposed. There's always that risk, that they'll come back.'

Gervaise leaned forward. 'Will he cave in, do you think? Micah?'

At once Ruth stood up, visibly shaking. 'Are you saying Micah is weak?'

Goran intervened, nodded to Ruth to sit down. 'No one's saying anything. But until he gives them what they want, they'll hurt him.' The words hung in the air. Like they hurt me.

'He won't give in.'

'That may be so. But there's still a risk.'

'It's simple.' A voice from the corner. Jude. 'We comply. On the surface I mean. So we attend church. We send our children to their schools. But in secret we carry on as before.'

There was a silence as they considered this. Per raised his hand to speak. 'It could work – I think.' He pushed his spectacles high up his nose. 'But it'll be dangerous.'

'Subterfuge *is* dangerous.' Jude's voice cut across the room. Ruth jumped with shock at the sudden volume.

Goran leaned forward, joining his palms together. He brought his hands up to his face. 'To me, it's clear,' he said. He looked around at them all. 'Since the raids I've been troubled. I have doubts about whether … if what we're doing is even right.'

'You want out?' Eliza's tone was snarling.

'No. No. Not at all. I'm saying we need to change.'

'Change?' Leah said. 'What do you mean?'

'Haven't you had enough of living in fear? Wondering always if our homes will be raided, our children persecuted?' Goran looked from one face to the next, gauging their expressions. He turned to Ruth. 'You've paid the highest price of all, Ruth.'

'But he'll be freed – they'll let him go.' Leah's words snapped out of nowhere. Her eyes met her husband's, challenging him. 'And then we can continue as before.'

Per sighed. 'I think, if we listen to Goran's concern – what he's saying is that it can't remain as it was.'

The sound of another siren punctuated the silence – whether it was ambulance or the police they couldn't tell. These days the emergency services blended together.

Leah kept her eyes fixed on the carpet. Then, suddenly, she gathered her flared skirt and got to her feet. She darted a look at Goran, and began to clear away the empty bottles. Hands full, she moved to the doorway of the kitchen. Her husband didn't even raise his eyes to look.

'But – that danger,' Eliza was saying, 'isn't it the price we pay for our belief? What's the alternative?' An angry edge crept into her voice. 'Do what Jude says and fall in with them?' She laughed. 'Profess a belief in God.'

Jude protested. 'I said *appear* to believe. We don't have to …'

'Then that would be hypocrisy. Which is also wrong.'

'Friends, we must listen to each other.' This was Per. The strident note in his voice made them stop. An obedient silence settled in the room. 'What we believe,' he continued, 'is now rooted in something very old – centuries old. For those first Disclaimers – it was very different. We must think how to adapt.'

Goran nodded. 'We've suffered enough.' He glanced at Ruth, who was twisting her hands in her lap, trying to contain her emotions. There was a hush in the circle. No one could deny that they'd suffered. Goran injured, Micah detained – and depressed, Ruth reported, frighteningly insular.

Goran reiterated his point. 'We were lucky this time. If they'd found *Truth's Testimony* …'

Ruth was crying now. She balled a handkerchief in her fist and held it to her face. Strange, strangulated sounds came from her throat; attempting to hold back tears that were forced out anyway.

'What exactly are you proposing, Goran?' The voice was Jude's.

Goran steepled his hands together, and looked at them all. 'I'm proposing we move.'

'Move? Move where?'

'To somewhere we can be entirely – independent,' Goran said.

'What do you mean – independent?' Jude said the word slowly, deliberately.

'Somewhere remote. We would live more simply, so we will need less. Then we focus on practising what we believe – not being in fear, or having to fight.'

Ruth raised her head sharply, exhaled. 'So we'd cut ourselves off? Entirely?'

'Not entirely. That would be out of the question. We could grow our own food but there'll be things we can't produce ourselves. But in the main – we would be as self-sufficient as it is possible to be.'

There was a stunned silence.

'It would be such hard work, Goran,' said Lucia Olsen. 'Have you any idea? We don't have the skills.'

'Then we'll learn.'

For the next ten minutes, for each question fired at him, Goran had a response. It was clear he'd thought through every detail. After a time, they fell silent, sipping their drinks, looking sideways at Goran, trying to absorb his plan. Eliza was thinking how ridiculous it was; Ruth was wishing Micah could be involved in the decision. Per performed checks and balances in his head.

'What about the children?' said Niamh at last. 'Their education?'

'We teach them ourselves. We are capable, intelligent. We could nominate teachers, or do it in turn – by rota.'

'Hold on. We're teachers now as well as farmers, and gardeners?' To the others, Eliza's tone was patronising and bitter. Her negativity made them uncomfortable.

'It formalises only what we do now,' Goran said. 'Don't we spend time at the dinner table already, talking to them about our beliefs? What difference if we add some geometry or grammar?'

'How would we communicate? I mean … with the world. Outside.' This was Leah, standing in the doorway to the kitchen, arms folded across her chest. She looked directly at her husband. The aggression was palpable, seemed to stretch across the room, a taut wire of anger.

'We wouldn't need to,' Goran said. His gaze locked with Leah's and she bristled. 'Would we?'

Two spots of colour appeared in Leah's cheeks. Her body reflected an anger that the others put down to an earlier disagreement, a conflict of opinion between man and wife. Leah didn't want to leave the city she was raised in. Goran was a migrant; it was different for him. But his question remained unanswered.

'It's too big,' Jude said. 'We just don't have the resources.'

'I agree,' Eliza said. 'We stay. Try to find a solution right here.'

Goran sprang quickly from the footstool. 'Let me show you something.' He crossed to the corner of the room, reached behind the dresser for a tube of paper: a map, which he unrolled on the floor in the middle of the room. 'Look. This is the area I was thinking of – sixty kilometres north of Lot. In the Aroer valley. It's mostly forest and there would be some clearance work. But in this area ...' he pointed a finger to a ribbon of land, 'either side of the river, so, there are pockets of land we could farm.'

Niamh crawled forward to look more closely. 'There'd be no shortage of wood for fuel.' She moved her hand across the map. 'And open space for building on.' She smiled at Goran, her young face alive and smiling. 'Sure, it'll be like home.'

'Here's another map, more detailed.' This one was flat; Goran unfolded it, tracing the orange lines and spaces that corresponded to the stretch of land by the river. 'Fields here for cattle and crops. And we can make kitchen gardens. Productive plots on the edges, and a fruit labyrinth. There.'

His words came out in a rush: plans for a community space, a schoolroom. More freedom for the children. Families eating together on long benches; men with the other men, groups of wives, all of them working alongside, supporting each other as they rear each other's children. A resourceful community, aspiring to live peaceably, industriously.

'It's all very ... idyllic,' said Gervaise. 'A land of promise. I see what you're driving at. But what does it have to do with faith?'

'We'll have ...' He corrected himself. 'What I propose is that we build something here, where we meet to observe – matters of the spirit.' Goran's finger rested on a spot in the fold of the page. 'The Meeting House,' he said. 'A kind of home.'

He looked at Leah, who had her hands thrust in the pockets of her jeans. She stood above the others, who were leaning over the map on the floor. Goran's words were directed at her: 'It would bind us together. I know it.'

She bit her lip, looked away.

Goran looked at the others, crouched over the map. 'It will bring us together.'

Jude sat back on his haunches. He started to laugh.

'There are so many things wrong with this plan,' Jude said. 'There's the legal ownership, the amount of work. The size of the group. I mean – how sustainable can it be, to live out there? And what about children? It would be … incestuous.'

A curious look passed over Goran's face – anger and raw hurt. 'We're small now, that is so. But we can let in others,' Goran said quickly, 'we check first, of course, who they are. We need people with skills as well as faith.'

'What kind of faith?'

'Like ours, only …' Goran began refolding the map. Slowly the others returned to their seats.

'What?' Eliza said, 'Like ours only … what?'

'I think we need more structure. Some guidance to follow. Something … written down.'

'We have *Truth's Testimony.*' Eliza said

'That's philosophy, not a guide book.'

'What do you suggest? That we write one?'

Goran shook his head, looked at the others. His eyes rested on Leah. 'I mean … we take examples – extracts, I should say – from the Testament.'

There was a rush of voices, exclamations.

'Goran. Are you mad? If we read their book, use it, we become like them.'

'It's a metaphor, only. It could give us a framework, something to direct us. It doesn't mean we agree to their creed.'

In the silence he looked around the room. He continued: 'If we had prayer meetings – discussion groups, it would pull us together. Don't you see? This new way. It's an extension, only, of what we believe now. That we are equal. And all of us sacred.' He glanced at Leah, and she flushed. 'That sin …'

'We don't believe in sin.' Leah's retort was bitter. 'Freedom of the spirit. And the body. That's what we believe in. Remember?'

For a moment, Leah and Goran looked at each other. There was a hardening of something between them.

'And it won't change,' Goran said. His voice was gentler now. 'In that valley,' he indicated north with his head, 'the world won't pose any dangers for us. We'll be founding something new. Based on what we have always believed, but more – what's the word? Authentic. Because how we live and organise ourselves, it will be … more equal – everything will be shared.'

There was a long silence.

Ruth spoke first, her voice tremulous. She turned to Goran, touched his arm. 'I don't like the idea of a move. It's too radical.' Then she looked at the others. 'But if we can find a place to be safe, I'm in favour.' Tears shone in her eyes. 'And if … if he were here, I know Micah would agree.' Her voice broke and she covered her face with her hands again. Leah crossed to sit next to her – in the seat that was Simeon's – to comfort her.

'Of course we'll wait to move – until Micah is back with us.'

Jude got to his feet. 'I'm not with you on this.' He reached over the back of his chair for his jacket. 'I've felt connected here. With all of you – until now. But … I'm just not into isolation. And the faith thing – if I wanted the God of the Testament, there are other places I could go.'

Goran stood up, so he was on the same level as Jude. The men faced each other. Goran's hands curled into fists, then uncurled. 'You've misunderstood,' said Goran. 'I'm not proposing we change our belief, just … refine it. It's time to move on, Jude. A new start.'

Jude didn't respond.

Goran continued. 'If you're opposed, then you should go. We need people only if they're committed. Only if they are …'

Jude's laugh was one of disbelief. 'Crazy?'

Around the circle there was a hush, expectant. Niamh clamped her hand to her mouth. But Goran didn't flinch. He levelled his chin and returned Jude's gaze.

'*Trofast.*' It came out quickly, the word from his first language, as though it had been on the tip of his tongue all the time.

'What?'

'True.' Goran's voice dropped nearly to a whisper. 'Faithful. Those are the ones we need.'

Jude laughed. 'See, Goran, you are driven by … something personal. I don't know why, or what it is, but it's dangerous. I don't want to be there to witness it.' He crossed to the door, pushing through the circle of chairs. He looked around the group and, finally, at Leah. 'I wish you well. All of you.'

He closed the door behind him, and was gone.

For a moment no one spoke. Ruth, still gathered in Leah's embrace, began to sob. Eliza's face was stricken. Per looked to the ceiling, Gervaise from one face to another.

Goran said: 'We owe it to Micah to try. We owe it to ourselves.' He turned round to find his seat again, sat down, and waited.

It was Per who galvanised them. He reached for Lucia's hand, looked steadily at her face, speaking a question without words. She smiled at him, and nodded.

Per said: 'Friends, do we agree with Goran? Are we willing to join him?'

Leah stood up. She made to say something, looked at Ruth, looked at Goran. Then she clamped her mouth shut, sat down again. The others turned to each other, their expressions revealing fear, doubt, excitement. But Goran was smiling, a smile that encompassed them all. It was beatific. It shone bright into the future.

II

MARAH

Ammie kneads the bread like Rebecca showed her, turning the bowl with one hand, thumping the pale plump dough with the other, stopping now and then to add more flour. It is only three Sundays since Rebecca taught her how to do this but now, with Rebecca in the school-room and Leah out in the gardens, Ammie is left with Martha, baking bread.

Martha kneels on a kitchen chair, leaning over the drawing on the table, with the pile of crayons spread out beside her like a rainbow. Watching her provokes a rush of feeling – safety and security; the heat of the kitchen protecting them from the cold autumn outside.

Ammie senses a movement at the window and looks up. Whoever it is has her hood up. She braces herself for the knock and with the teacloth removes as much as she can of the dough from her hands. When she opens the door there's a chill blast and a swirl of leaves and there's Emilia Olsen standing on the porch.

Emilia's smile, the one she had ready for Leah, seems to fade. A gust of wind gets up and sweeps a lock of blonde hair across Emilia's face and she pulls it away with a blue mittened hand.

'Well? Are you going to invite me in, Amarantha?'

Ammie stands aside and Emilia sweeps to the table where she puts down the basket and pushes off her hood.

'Mama sent this over for Leah. Where *is* Leah?' As Emilia speaks, her eyes range around the room, stop at Martha, move back to Ammie. 'It's a pie. It isn't cooked.' She pauses. 'So mind you put it in at the right temperature.'

Ammie watches as Emilia speaks in exaggerated tones to Martha, patting her on the head and exclaiming over the drawings scattered across the table. Ammie thinks how the voice is too loud, too overpowering.

When the tea is brewed they sit at the table and Ammie offers the cookies Rebecca baked yesterday.

'And so,' Emilia says, 'how are things? You're busy, no doubt? With the celebrations and all?'

Emilia has a way of answering people's questions, as though she's not at all interested in the answer but only in her own voice doing the asking.

'Thank you,' she says, 'things are … pretty well.'

There's an awkward silence.

'So,' says Emilia, 'how long now since the Sealing?'

'Three weeks.'

Emilia smiles, rolls her eyes to the ceiling, dips the tip of her cookie into the tea. 'I suppose by now you feel settled here?' Then a pause. 'It must be like being Rebecca's daughter,' she says.

'No.' Ammie knows her tone sounds defensive. 'She's a sister, a sisterwife.' Ammie fights the image of her own mother. The leaving, that day, and the weight of Frania's hand on hers that morning; the scent of her coming in from the cold – already smelling of the outside, of clean air and open spaces.

Ammie watches Emilia's concentration as she balances a second cookie above her cup, holding it carefully so it won't collapse.

Emilia opens her mouth wide, pushes the cookie into it and darts her gaze back at Ammie.

'And Tobias?' Emilia says.

Ammie waits for the question that must surely follow: is he well? Where is he today? But then she realises Emilia is pretending to ask those things when in fact she means something else. She feels a sudden, sharp wanting; the memory of Tobias's body close to hers in the darkness. 'Tobias?'

Their gazes lock. It's like being in the schoolroom again, both waiting for the other to blink or to break the hold by looking away first.

'Well.' Emilia shoots a cautionary look at Martha, and leans across the table. 'You know. How is he?' She lowers her voice. 'As a husband.'

Ammie blinks, looking into the other girl's face, at the broad cheekbones and the florid skin and wonders whether Tobias has ever wanted to kiss Emilia.

Ammie motions to the counter, to the dough covered with a cloth and the waiting loaf tins. 'If you'll excuse me, Emilia, I have bread to be going on with.'

Emilia's face broadens to a smile. 'It's so strange to see you in the kitchen. Instead of out with a book somewhere. Tobias must be worth it, that's all I can say.'

Clearly Emilia won't be leaving. Ammie tries to concentrate on the bread. She can't remember how long to leave the loaves in. But it will be written down somewhere, in amongst Leah's recipes. She inches over to the bureau, willing for Emilia not to see her.

'Looking for something?'

Ammie whirls round. Emilia has Martha on her lap and a crayon in her hand with the drawing beside her, and she is smiling.

Ammie fumbles with the handle. 'A recipe. For the ... timing. The bread.'

'Oh. You need a recipe?'

Ammie feels the heat flush up her neck and cheeks and curses the moment that Lucia Olsen sent Emilia off with a basket full of pie. Emilia isn't even Rebecca's friend but a girl her own age sent on an errand by her mother to spy on Ammie's skills as a sisterwife.

Emilia shoos Martha down and gets to her feet. 'Let me help.' And before Ammie can protest, Emilia is right beside her, unwanted and way too close.

The cupboard is a chaotic jumble of things – lengths of string, jam labels, broken toys, and stacks of paper that might tumble at any moment if they're not sorted. She wrestles with a stack of papers, intending to bring them to the table and wishing now she'd waited until Emilia left.

'Here, let me.' Emilia steps forward to take the papers. Ammie pulls sharply away, then there's a sliding sound, the sensation of papers falling and the soft shuffle as they land on the floor.

Emilia smiles sweetly. 'I'm so sorry, Amarantha. Shall I ... ?'

It's that moment Martha chooses to cry, holding two halves of a crayon in her hand. Emilia looks pointedly at the wall clock. 'Oh! Is that the time? I've been enjoying myself so much eating cookies that I lost track of time. I must run. I'm so sorry.'

Ammie feels a rush, a sensation of panic, of too many things happening all at once; a crying child, the proving bread, Leah's chaotic kitchen and a crowing Emilia Olsen who is buttoning up her cloak and running through the ritual of goodbyes.

'Be sure to thank your mother,' Ammie says, clenching her teeth, 'for the pies.'

And Ammie hears the slam of the screen door behind her. Standing in the middle of the kitchen surrounded by a stack of spilled papers Ammie feels the need to cry herself.

Once Emilia has gone and Ammie has put Martha down, she starts on the mess of papers that litter the floor. It might be all Leah's life laid out before her. The heel of Ammie's boot leaves an imprint on a five-year-old list of Meeting House maintenance tasks. There are notes all around her, in Leah's untidy handwriting; notes for committee meetings and notes on herbs and their properties that must stretch back years. Each piece is yellowing and has something else on the back – printed, not written by hand – rows of numbers and letters. There is something about the formality and permanence that makes her think it must have come with them, a residue of their long ago life in the city.

Ammie crouches, gathers up the papers into rough bundles and puts them back in the cupboard that smells faintly of mace and the herbs Leah stores in there sometimes, the ones that look like dried grass. Something tucked amidst the sheets of paper catches her eye, an envelope. She picks it up, feels a sharp sensation and lifts the finger quickly to her lips. She licks it and looks at it. There's no blood, just a burning cut, small but deep.

The envelope has an address on the front. They learned in school how in the city they used to communicate by putting a sticky coloured square on a corner and placing it into a box. They printed the details of where they lived, each piece of information on a separate line. Ammie looks at the envelope. On the top line is a name: Leah Christensen. There is a stamped circle, black with blurred numbers and letters, but she can see clearly that the word in the centre is Lot. Why would Leah have a letter from the city?

The tightness in Ammie's stomach that tells her that she shouldn't be here, in Leah's house, reading her papers. But she is driven with curiosity now; she has to know. Maybe the letter was sent when they still lived there, and she has brought it with her and it has found its way amongst all the things that make up their life here.

When Ammie opens the letter, she sees a page filled with writing that is tight, with hardly any gaps, sloping to the left. Her eyes scan to the bottom and she tries to decipher the single letter written there: 'I' or perhaps 'L' – she cannot tell. Her eyes return to the top of the page.

Dear Leah,
I don't know if you will even get this letter but I want to write it anyway. I wanted to tell you that since you sent me the herbs the eczema is so much better. Thank you for that.

Ammie frowns. She didn't know that Leah worked outside Marah. She thought she only healed people here, in her tiny consulting room at the top of her house. Why would Leah have gone outside? On one of the trips for provisions, perhaps, with the wives; she might have met someone in need when she was there. But how would she have sent herbs from here? Ammie gets to her feet, stands in the middle of the kitchen, reading and rereading the letter. She shakes her head; it feels muffled, as though she has water in her ears and can't hear properly.

Even if this doesn't reach you, I have to trust you'll know, somehow, that I'm thinking about you. I can't imagine where you live, except that it's remote and hundreds of miles from here. I always hope when walking down the street that I might spot you but you might look different now. The picture is so old.

A curious thing to write: you might look different now. Different from what? And why would this person have a picture of Leah? Ammie's head begins to throb. Exhausted already after Emilia's visit, she now feels completely drained. She doesn't have the energy to try now to work out the puzzle of who wrote the letter and why. Sometimes there are things about this place and its history that are beyond her. Ammie begins to fold the letter, taking one last look at the cramped handwriting, to put it back into its envelope.

Then her eye snags on a word: University. She can't help but scan the rest of the letter, heart hammering as she soaks up the words. Her stomach flutters at the thought of that other life, to have the freedom to roam around the libraries with high ladders.

... enjoy what I study and made friends quickly. I moved into an apartment with one of them. The bedroom is cramped. There isn't even a desk so I have to use a wooden board balanced between the chair and the bed that I take down again when I'm finished! My address is on this letter and if you were ever nearby I would love to see you.

Ammie thinks about a cramped bedroom in an apartment in the city. She wouldn't care about not having a desk. She would be outside, anyway; walking through the streets and looking at the faces, listening to the sound and smell. It's the smell, Tobias always says, that makes it different. Meat cooking on stalls in the open air; the grey smoke that comes in clouds out of the back of the cars they use for transport in and out of the city. If Ammie ever visits she wants only to stand somewhere and watch. And then she would go home. Home to a tiny bedroom with a wooden board for a desk, and draw it, the city, straight from memory.

The screen door slams.

Leah. Leah is back. Quickly, Ammie crouches to the floor again. She balls the letter in her hand and pushes it into her pinafore pocket. But the envelope, the envelope. She sweeps it up with the sheaf of papers so when Leah enters the kitchen, there is no trace of the envelope, or of Ammie having seen the letter.

'Amarantha?' Leah is unwinding her scarf and at the same time frowning at Ammie crouched on the floor. Ammie is conscious of the paper in her pocket, dreads having to move in case it rustles and gives her away. Leah mustn't know what she's been reading; she mustn't know that Ammie knows about this place in the city, the home of a University student, someone Leah has met before. *My address is on this letter.*

'I'm so sorry, Leah. I just – Emilia was here and we were looking for something.'

'Oh?' Does Ammie see Leah's face tighten?

'A recipe. For bread.'

'Heavens, girl, you shouldn't need a recipe! Where are the loaves?'

Leah busies herself at the counter, checking the dough and checking the oven and looking around for the padded gloves. Ammie stands on and watches. But she doesn't feel helpless. It is as though her thigh burns with what she is hiding: the address, a glimpse into another life. A secret. Ammie clears up the rest of the papers, drawing them all together in a stack. She places them back in the cupboard and stands, looking at them, touching her hand to her pocket with silent resolution.

*

They commemorate the anniversary in the way they know best: a ceremony in the Meeting House. It is thirty years since they left the city and founded Marah; since they built their homes, their schoolroom and their workshops. Thirty years since they put the roof on this structure, this church – of a fashion – in which they sit, as they do on Sabbath days, in a circle. The inner ring is occupied by the Elders: Lucia, Eliza, Goran, Micah. It is their role to listen to the silence, and judge when it is time to speak or lead the prayers.

They are dressed for a celebration – the women in bonnets and in long best skirts, the men in button collared shirts and jackets. Some, like Per, sit with their eyes closed, reflecting on the significance of the day, the number of years they have been here; and also, in some cases, the journey they have been on since they arrived. There are others who are intent on absorbing the atmosphere in the room, which is decorated with swathes of ivy. Stems of autumn leaves and berries have been placed around the room on simple wooden tables. In the corner of the room there is a cluster of music stands, when the young people will come together – when it is time - to provide the music and sing hymns and songs that reflect the day.

Mariah struggles to quieten her baby, stuffing rusks into his mouth. Her other two are occupied with a picture book. But she looks around her constantly, waiting for the moment they become restless so she can lead them to the outer room. All the children are impatient for the party afterwards. They've seen their mothers prepare sweet treats; they themselves have made the decorations in school. For once, they remain in the main room with the adults and although the ceremony is short, they are fidgeting already, impatient for their role – the part where they will place symbols on the Jacob's Ladder to recall the events that have happened to them: the founding of Marah, the poor harvests, the many births, the few deaths and, with each year, the steady trickle of new joiners.

At last Micah stands. There is a rustle in the room, a heightened sense of attention. People sit upright, alert, waiting to hear what he has to say. He sighs, looks up, begins to speak then closes his mouth as though he has changed his mind. He looks around the circle. Eliza nods encouragingly. When he speaks, his voice betrays his emotion. He tells of the day he and Goran discovered the place that became Marah, both of them translating the contours of the land from a map. The map is a symbol, he says, of the idea, the theory of what they do here: that they are all connected, through each other, share everything, and this finds its expression in the land. He speaks of the joy of finding the place. Like Moses – leading the Israelites out of Egypt and discovering milk and honey – they had known that they were home. Micah goes into the centre of the circle, where there is a table with a model of a ladder. He tells the story of the boy who dreamed, with his head on a rock, of a place he couldn't see and a ladder leading up to it. In a moment, he says, he will invite the children up to place something on it they made together at school. But he will place the first object on it. It is a tiny paper scroll, a map; a symbol of seeking, and of journeying to places unfamiliar and unknown.

*

In the Congregational Hall Rebecca is agitated. Tobias is late. Earlier, he had given her a cursory kiss outside the Meeting House, said he must work and that he'd be back later to rejoin the party. Now the villagers are beginning to spill into the Hall and she is sitting with a sleeping Martha on her lap. She leans back, sighing and looks up at the exposed roof beams. Every time she sees them she marvels, still, at how they managed to build it all themselves.

Most of the wives are in the kitchen. Rebecca watches through the doorway with a mixture of guilt and exhaustion. She should be there, ensuring Sarah and Hannah have everything as it should be. Instead, she watches the young people in the corner, faces flushed and excited, giggling over the notes and chords they missed during the ceremony but, now that it is over, not really caring. Even Emilia is there, having prised herself away from Gideon, standing with Kitty Miller and Silas Cuthbert. She throws back her head and laughs but it is forced, Rebecca thinks, not a natural exuberance like Amarantha's, or even Kitty's. Rebecca can't say she welcomes Emilia's Sealing to her brother. Gideon somehow doesn't see past all that blonde prettiness. Really, she's a child, still, wanting to be at the centre of everything.

Amarantha hovers at the edges, trying to include herself in the conversation. For a brief moment, Rebecca feels a rush of protectiveness; as though Amarantha were Naomi in the schoolyard, being ignored by her friends. It shocks her, this feeling. She buries her head in Martha's curls, inhaling the smell of rosemary.

Still no Tobias. How long? Rebecca thinks.

She is sure that Martha is fully asleep now, which means she can move, at least. She might put her down on the bundle of coats and jackets at the furthest end of the hall, away from the door and the draught. When Rebecca has settled her, her arms feel empty. It echoes the emptiness she feels often, these days, a physical ache that fills her stomach – her longing for another child. She squares her shoulders to face the room. She mustn't think of it now.

Rebecca joins Leah and Eliza and Niamh in the centre of the room, pulling up one of the wooden chairs in the centre of the space. On the table in front of them are the albums, so many of them – large, embossed and some embellished in gold with a large letter 'D'. Niamh has one on her lap, turning the pages: so many images and memories from the old days. She closes her eyes, thinking of those terrifying moments from her childhood, what she remembers of their life in Lot: shouts and footfalls, and her father being away for a long time.

'Where's Tobias?' Leah looks around the room, trying to locate her son.

'Working.'

'Not today, surely?' She frowns and Rebecca sees, as though for the first time, how much her mother in law is ageing.

'There's a fair coming up. You know how anxious he gets beforehand.' She tries to muster a smile. 'He'll be along soon.'

Niamh continues to turn the page of the album. 'Oh look,' she says. She points at a group shot of the community in front of the Meeting House. 'Was it really so long ago? Thirty years. I can't believe it!'

Rebecca leans in so she can see the pictures. They have a white border around them, the ones on this page black and white. Someone – Lucia, probably – has scrupulously marked each page with the date and the name of each person. The photograph of the men is deliberately posed, an optimistic group shot in which they hold up their hammers, their bright and hopeful faces looking thinner and so much younger than they do now. She nearly misses Micah, not recognising him without his beard. The shots of the women and children are closer up; she sees herself, Sarah, Mariah and Hannah, children all holding hands. In herself, in all of them, it's possible to see the faces as they will emerge into adulthood. There are Tobias and Seth, a little apart from the other children. The wives: Ruth, Niamh, Lucia, Eliza.

Rebecca runs her finger across the surface of the cellophane page. It has air bubbles in it, creating ridges that obscure some of the photographs. 'I can't see you in this one, Leah.'

The other women look at the picture. Rebecca looks up suddenly and catches something on Leah's face that no one is meant to see, a tight look of anxiety. It passes so quickly that Rebecca thinks she was mistaken.

She swallows. 'Perhaps I was taking the picture?'

'No,' Niamh says, 'it's always Malachy takes the photos.'

'Then what was the date?' Leah pulls her spectacles closer to her eyes. 'Ah. That would be … yes. I must have been away. For my training.'

'I didn't know you'd been away, Leah.' Rebecca is surprised by the sudden stab of jealousy that shoots through her: that Goran's wife has had experiences she hasn't, that Leah was able to leave behind the responsibilities of motherhood so easily. 'But the boys must have been so young.' She looks back at the photograph. It's grainy, black and white and the image isn't clear. Tobias looks about six or seven, Seth about four. 'How long were you away?'

Now there is a rigidity in Leah's shoulders. She feels guilty, Rebecca thinks, guilty for leaving the boys behind. She doesn't want to talk about it.

'If I'm truthful, I try to … block it out … that time. Everyone was very good. Tobias and Seth are the same age as Jacob, after all. So Lucia took them on, in a way. Made sure they had a motherly influence. Not,' she says quickly, 'that Goran neglected them at all.'

'Did you train in Lot?

'Oh no,' Leah says quickly. 'No, no. On the coast. Quite a distance. It meant I couldn't come back. For visits.'

It's strange that she hasn't spoken of it before: months on the coast when her boys were young; training on the outside and bringing the experience back with her. It must have coloured her view of things here.

Niamh nods. 'I remember …' She screws up her eyes, as though to recapture the memory. 'You were gone some months, I think. The boys struggled. Tobias used to ...' Her words trail off as she catches sight of Leah's face.

There's an awkward pause.

Niamh and Eliza exchange glances. Niamh is agitated, places down the album and shuts it quickly, picking up the next.

Leah is looking at her hands. Rebecca notices that she runs her tongue over her lips as though her mouth is dry. She hesitates, and Rebecca imagines that she might be about to absent herself. But she remains in her seat, resolute, and her eyes follow the turn of the page. The years move on. These photographs are in colour. The group shots are bigger than the last ones, almost double.

'This one,' Eliza taps the page. 'It must have been taken that year we had the influx – all those new people. There's Frania, look.' Rebecca peers at a woman with shorter hair than the others. Even then Frania had a detached, faraway look, as though she was regretting having come at all.

'Would you look at Amarantha!' Niamh says, 'All that hair, even then. What a beauty. How old would she be there, would you say?'

There's a shout from the children; they are rampaging around the hall, sliding along the wooden floor. Rebecca feels the anger rise in her; at the women discussing Amarantha's merits, at the children – her children – conducting themselves in that way, even if it is a party. But before she can get up, her mother is already there, picking up Esther who has fallen over, dusting off her pinafore, and speaking firmly to the boys who lead the mischief.

Someone calls from the kitchen. Food is ready, and for a moment Rebecca is disorientated as a mass of people stand suddenly to make their way through to the side room where the lunch is laid. She hesitates, unsure whether to find her girls, not sure if she should go to the workshop to fetch back Tobias. Feeling angry and resentful, she realises, because he is missing. Just then, she is aware of another absence.

Amarantha. Where is she?

Rebecca's eyes scan the room, darting back to the place where she saw her sisterwife last. But Kitty and Seth and Emilia are linking arms and are heading, with the rest of them, towards the food.

Rebecca is filled with a sudden panic. Something is wrong, something missing. She turns to make for the door, but before she can reach it, it opens. She holds her breath, waiting for Tobias to come through it, but it is Amarantha who stands there, a high colour in her cheeks. Rebecca is thrown. The expression on Amarantha's face is haughty, victorious but – Rebecca thinks – with perhaps just a hint of guilt. And then she watches Amarantha rejoin her friends, touch Silas's shoulder and smile.

Rebecca crosses to the door. She isn't sure why she does this, only that it might give her some sense of where Amarantha has been. There was no reason for her to leave the party, no reason to absent herself. She reaches the door, frowns, opens it silently; then closes it again. As she looks down, she sees traces of mud on the floor. They are like jigsaw puzzle pieces, shaped like the ridges of the soles of boots. They could belong to anyone, she thinks, it's an autumn day after all. But she knows that if she went close to Amarantha, examined the bottom of her boots, that she would see the mud there: mud from the dirt track that might lead to the workshop, for example; where, even now, Tobias is working.

*

The foundations of the Meeting House had been laid the week they arrived, an act more symbolic than practical. But then their attention had to turn to their homes, the tents and temporary shelters made from interlaced branches of willow and ash, reinforced and the roof rainproofed with canvas.

Today, before the weather turned and the colder weather set in, they were raising the Meeting House. Its wooden structure stood in the centre of the Piece, and in the light of dawn when the men began to stir, it might be the ghostly hull of a ship.

Goran and Per stood to catch their breath, swigged from a bottle of water they passed between them. Per pointed at Micah, struggling with the weight of the cross beam and laughed that he looked like Atlas. But Goran said that he must surely mean Samson, because it was more fitting for the building of a temple, and they laughed. But Micah's bulk and strength was a blessing to them. Carrying the weight of the roof cross beam was no easy matter. Swinging it up into place should have taken the strength of more men than they had here, but they had done it, they had achieved it. The cross beam was in place and as the sun climbed in the sky, there was only the matter of securing it and they began the methodical task of driving the nails into the beams, attaching and reinforcing. Across the Aroer valley, the hammering rang out, startling the birds, stilling whatever small mammals were seeking out ground to rest in, hide in, overwinter.

As the morning wore on, the rest of the village joined them. Some of the women – the ones without small children or who were not pregnant – could join in the physical work, forming a chain from the wood store to the site of the building, heaving the smaller of the planks and readying them for the men. The younger girls – Rebecca, Hannah, Sarah – sat in a circle sorting nails, grouping them into piles of ten as they had been asked. And the boys fetched tools, passed hammers and ferried nails, nuts and bolts, unable to contain their energy and excitement at the collective enterprise; for all their youth, they were proud to have a hand in the construction of their Meeting House.

By the afternoon, the sun was high, warming the skin of the men as they worked. One or other occasionally stopped and looked up, taking in the sky like a hopeful blue banner above them and the colours of leaves as they were beginning to turn. The contrast – deep blue, offset by crimsons, reds and rusts – brought a spirit of lightness to their work. And there was the scent in the air of smoke from the fires, the smell they associated now with the end of the year: the start of the leaf mould, the smell of afternoon mists.

When they were not being given a task, the boys raced around the base of the building. Tobias was in charge of the game, shouting instructions in a voice that – from the food tent where the women were gathering, beginning preparations for the meal – bordered on the hysterical. One or two, hearing the harshness in his tone, turned to look. Ruth called Tobias over, telling him how unlike him it was, that he was to take care of Seth in Leah's absence, not order the poor boy around.

Tobias returned to his game. He picked up his hoop moodily and began to send it round and round the foundations of the building. Goran, looking down on his son from a height, knew it was time to speak to him. The wooden frame became a ladder for him to scale down; the boy looked up, saw his father, bit his lip.

Goran led him to the edge of the Piece and invited him to sit under a broad oak tree. His son. So tightly wound up, like the curls on his head. His long limbs, the shoulder blades narrow and sharp. Somehow, Goran thought, as though he was waiting to take flight.

'Tell me what is troubling you,' Goran said.

Tobias looked at his father, his expression defiant.

'Nothing is troubling me.'

'You are sure?' Goran's hand automatically reached out for the top of his son's head. It hovered there a moment, then he placed it down. 'Because Leah … because your mother. You know that there was no choice? She had to go …' Goran looked up then, his eyes lifted to the line of the mountains in the distance. 'Where she is going she will learn a great many things. To help us all. Do you understand?'

The boy's eyes fixed on his father's face for an instant. Then he turned away. He pointed to the rectangular frames high up in the structure.

'Micah says these will be windows.'

Goran nodded. 'What of it?'

'Where will we get the glass, Papa?'

Goran watched and listened to all that was going on around them. Everywhere you could hear the rhythmic swinging of hammers, the ringing out as the head hit the heart of the nail. 'The glass will come … from the city.'

'From Lot?'

'Yes. From Lot.'

'But you said – you always say – nothing good comes of there, that we no longer need what they have. I don't understand, Papa. Can we not make our own glass here?'

Goran sighed and crouched down. When he reached the boy's level, he reached forward and caressed his son's face. 'Some things we cannot do without. We need glass to see through. To make our Meeting House light and beautiful. We can't make our own because – we don't have the right equipment ...'

The son was beginning to lose patience. His hand twitched on the hoop, his gaze moving in the direction of the other children.

'Go now,' Goran said. 'Go and play.'

In one leap, all his energy gathered into the gesture, Tobias sprang from his father. Only when he was a few steps away, did he turn and look back. The expression on his face was somewhere between a smile and a grimace.

'One day,' Tobias said, 'we'll make glass here ourselves, Papa.'

Then he was off, back with the others, rolling the hoop and laughing.

When Goran rejoined the men, he felt a presence next to him, a light touch on his arm. He turned, and there was Deborah. She had joined them only weeks ago, arriving on foot with all her possessions in one pack on her back. Standing beside him now, Goran felt her glance in Tobias's direction and then turn her attention back to him. Her face radiated empathy and charm. The smile was so subtle that he almost might not have noticed. He looked at her, as though for the first time, the earnestness of her eyes, the shapely hips, her broad, open face. He was overcome by what she provoked in him – confusion and curiosity - and turned away quickly.

Deborah watched him turn and walk back, exchange a word with

Per, bend to retrieve his hammer. She watched as he shinned the structure, back to the top where they were working now on the roof. She watched as he precariously straddled two roof struts, bending to work, concentrating all the time on his balance. She threw her long plait over her shoulder, revelling in the fact that – just for a moment – she had enjoyed a moment of connection.

October brought the potato harvest and for a whole week the community concentrated their effort on digging. The year, their second there, was moving to a close and they had worked hard to establish the crops. In the summer they had grown hay and managed to raise wheat. They had watched their herbs thrive and tomatoes grow rounder and redder on the vine under cover – in the glass house built from old window frames scavenged from the city.

The day began with a mist and the fumes of breath on the air. Tobias and his friends stamped their feet and blew on their hands to warm them, excited by the prospect of a day with the men, a day away from school. The men divided the field into areas, each taking a few rows, men at the fore doing the digging, the children following behind with trowels and buckets, ready to retrieve the earthy vegetables. Micah and Goran worked alongside each other, with Malachy and Padraic and Per spreading further out towards the wall.

Goran worked without words, feeling the rhythm of the spade striking the ground and taking pleasure in it. When he looked up, his friend had stopped what he was doing. Rebecca, behind him, held out a potato in her hand and he was frowning at it. He took it off her, turned it over in his hand. Goran stopped. Tobias – working with him – stopped too and watched as Micah placed it carefully on the ground, then struck the tuber with the edge of his spade.

His face contorted into a grimace. 'I knew it,' Micah said. 'Blight.'

He picked up the split potato and examined it. Goran came close enough to see the spoiled core, brown like a rotten apple. Micah screwed up his face and threw it. It spiralled into the air, landing in a patch of weeds close to the glasshouse.

'It will affect the whole crop?'

'Undoubtedly.'

'But … it was going to be …' Goran bit his lip with disappointment. 'We were relying on it. Our main crop. How could it have happened?'

Micah sighed. 'Sometimes the elements are against us. We've had so many damp months – the climate hasn't been ideal. The peas failed, too, remember?

'So what do we do now?'

'Well, once we've dug up all the diseased ones and burnt them, we dig over the soil, let it lie fallow. In time, it might be fine to use for potatoes again.'

Goran stared directly ahead of him. His mind was turning over the implications. 'When do we tell the others?'

Micah saw the fear on his friend's face and guessed the reason for his question. This would compound the resentment that some were already feeling: that the life was harder than they had realised, than they had been led to believe, at least.

'We need to call a meeting. I know it's disappointing, my friend. But it's what we've taken on here. Next year, we may have more luck.'

'But … we can't afford to wait. How will we feed ourselves?'

'We get busy. All that wheat – we can grind some for flour. At least we have the bread ovens.' Micah drives his spade hard into the ground, frowning. 'It's the only thing of substance we're likely to be eating this winter.'

It was the largest gathering in the Congregational Hall since they built it. With the number of bodies crammed into it, it was stuffy and hot, despite the chill in the air outside. It was men, mostly, a few of the older boys; the smaller ones were at the front with their fathers. Of the women, there were few: Eliza and Deborah, Niamh with her baby held close in a sling. The men were still in outdoor work clothes and boots, fatigued from a day of digging and clearing. Some of them had the smell of smoke clinging to them from the bonfire. The smoke had spiralled above the village; a pyre, driving the stink of rotten potatoes into each house in the village.

Micah was explaining the course of action they had decided on.

Padraic stood first. His face was red and angry, the freckles standing out even more than usual. He tugged at his ear, irritated, not used to speaking out in such a way. 'Why weren't we told about this?'

Goran glanced at Micah and stood as though to defend his friend. Micah shook his head: he should be the one to answer to this. 'Because we needed to act fast,' he said. 'We made a decision based on …'

'We? Who is we?'

'The men who were there at the time.'

The silence became more acute; there was an awkward shuffling at the back. Somewhere there was an intake of breath.

'Isn't this the problem?' Padraic looked directly across the room at Micah and Goran. 'The whole point of this community is that we make decisions together. We share. We come to a consensus.'

'The crop was diseased,' Micah said.

Padraic's voice rose in volume. 'It's not just about disease, or crops. It's everything. The Elders have all the power.'

Eliza Cuthbert sighed, put her head in her hands. Her bracelet rattled with the movement, the faint tinkle that accompanied the silence in the room. Lucia Olsen looked briefly, sideways, at her husband. The atmosphere was fraught. Padraic was struggling, lips trembling. But he held his ground.

Goran coughed to clear his throat. 'But there has to be an overall vision. There has to be some person, or persons leading. Think of Moses, who brought the chosen ones out of Egypt …'

'But that's my point!' Some of them jumped at the increase in the volume of Padraic's voice, his unfamiliar anger. 'We never believed in God! We left the city because we wouldn't conform to that! We believed in human greatness, in what can be done now, here, on earth. And spirit. But now here you are – quoting *scripture*.'

Goran faltered, rocking back and forth on his heels. He swallowed, and his face was hard with anger. Micah placed a hand on his friend's elbow, a warning, a gesture of conciliation or of support. But Goran shook his head, took a breath, stepped forward.

'You're right, Padraic. We never wanted to believe in their God.

72

But we need a template.'

'We have our template within ourselves,' Padraic said. 'Remember *Truth's Testimony*? "Be patterns, be examples"...'

'But that's all scripture is – don't you see?' Goran looked around the room. He took in Per's watchful eyes and Ruth's encouraging ones; he took in the children gathered at the front, seated on the floor. He missed Leah's calm presence to reassure him. But his eyes fell on Deborah, and she nodded. An encouragement. He went on. 'What they did – those prophets. It is just a guide, an example. We don't have to believe it was real.'

'So you're saying you read the scriptures – their scriptures. But you don't believe in their God?'

The room was silent.

Deborah stood up. 'I think what Goran is saying is that we have to forge our way, find our own way. As a group and also ...' She turned back to look at him, standing there, facing the hostility. 'For ourselves as individuals.'

'I still believe that sharing everything – that is the way. Like the prophets, the focus of that vision ...'

Padraic's response cuts through the room. 'So let's say God – your God. Do you expect him to be able to save the potatoes?'

'I expect that we have enough resources and faith amongst ourselves to manage.'

Micah nodded, and there was a sudden shift of the energy in the room, with others nodding, breathing out. Some turned and frowned at Padraic, who sat back in his seat, face glowering, but some looked nonplussed in Goran's direction.

Goran caught Deborah's gaze. He held it for a long time, taking comfort from the expression in her eyes, her respect, of her confidence to speak out and hold the floor. A thought was forming in his mind. He whispered to himself under his breath, words that might give him inspiration. A prayer that he might draw strength from the prophets: patterns, examples.

*

Friday evenings are Tobias's best time. There is the joy of a solid, pleasurable week's work done: there is the security of the community gathering for prayers. The waiting in silence for the Meeting House to fill up; time to prepare, to turn inside himself and examine what he finds there. They are precious moments in a life often crammed with too much. They are rare moments too; his work is important, the pieces he forms as though from nothing, from misshapen hunks of heated glass. It weds the hand to the heart, the spirit to the craft, and he often finds that his mind takes flight as he works. In a life so caught up in doing – working, fathering, husbanding, worshipping – this Friday ritual, with its simplicity of silence followed by the quiet power of words, calms and uplifts him.

Tonight, though, Tobias is fatigued from working all day without pause. The latest commission is finished but his arms ache and his head echoes still with the rush and roar of the furnace. What he wants is a hot soak. He wants to be able to close the door – just for an hour or so – and let the noise and activity of his life float over him and sink right down until his shoulders are submerged, his chin breaking the surface of the water.

But he isn't free to bathe, or to escape. Tonight he has to muster up the energy to lead prayer. Duty, the memory of it, causes his chest to tighten, the ritual he must lead this week because the community depend on it, on the sharing of tasks, the taking of turns.

His first as an Elder.

Imperative to find, even more than usual, a surety of words, the right pitch. He thought the anxiety of all that would have dissipated by now, the question of whether he is good enough, whether he will be perceived to act and speak in the right way as an Elder's son. The truth is that he has always found it hard to submerge the questions about whether their way is the right one. With Seth, ever since childhood, it was clear he was so much more faithful. Tobias thinks of the two of them as boys in Meeting, Seth's composed expression, his willingness to sit for so long, while Tobias's eyes strayed to the window where he could see the sky and the tops of the trees moving with the breeze.

The problem for Tobias is that, unlike his brother, he still remembers the time before; a time when worship was not the isolation of silence, or sober words printed on a page, but experiential: something else entirely, involving dancing and singing, and people's laughter.

Tobias leans back, head resting on the hard bench behind him. His fatigue, he knows, comes partly from the fights with Rebecca, her silent moods and their hissed, tight-lipped conversations. Ammie is young and strong; malleable. And beautiful. Rebecca will see that; it must make her heart shrivel. And he could never say it to Rebecca, but he feels himself blessed.

Blessed, and exhausted.

Tobias crosses to the table in the centre of the circle and picks up the bible. He can't help himself, running his fingers over the embossed gold patterns on the surface of the binding. It is compulsive, as much of a ritual as the prayers themselves and he can't remember a time when he hasn't done it. It calms him. It helps him focus on what he needs to do. He finds the ribbon that marks the page. Exodus 3, Moses at the Burning Bush. He sighs. How will he make sense of this passage, especially to the children? Their view of the world is so literal. How can he find the words to illuminate the story so that it speaks to them, so that they do not walk around with the constant fear of shrubs and foliage around them bursting into flame? But then at the same time, how can he produce something rich, something thought-provoking that they might all learn from?

There are times when he is struck by the irony of it all. That he should be charged with instructing, informing and guiding. Of all of them, he is the one most in need of guidance; some advice that would bury the doubt about their rigidity and isolation firmly at the back of his mind.

His thoughts are interrupted by his children crossing the Meeting room. Esther climbs onto his lap, pleading a hug. She is only beginning to understand the significance of Friday prayer. Most weeks, she attempts to curl herself into Rebecca's body, a gesture Rebecca discourages because it is never too early, she says, for her children to learn to sit upright as they should, as she taught Naomi to do. The fact that Esther is a different child seems to count for little. Naomi sits at his feet, legs crossed in front of her, back perfectly straight and upright. For a second, Tobias feels a flash of remorse – even of anger – towards Rebecca, towards the way the community dictates things. That even just for this quiet half hour on a Friday evening, the childhood has been sucked out of his six-year-old girl.

Esther wriggles against him, thumb in her mouth. He bends to kiss the top of her head, taking in for a moment the creaminess of her skin, the length of her lashes. He will store up that pleasure for later, when he will stand at the door of their room in the darkness and watch them while they sleep. There is nothing so pure, he thinks, as the sight of a sleeping child; his own sleeping children, safe and protected and loved.

The Meeting House door opens, and when he looks up it is Rebecca. Even from the threshold she seeks out her daughters, checking that they are where they should be. She crosses to Tobias. Just for a moment as she bends to coax Esther from his lap, her eyes meet his. It is a reproof. He sees the firmness around her mouth as she whispers to their daughter. He senses Rebecca's frustration as her eyes meet his again; she is tired, he thinks, he sees the way the skin is saggy and smudged underneath the eyes, the green of the irises less bright than usual. He releases his hold on his daughter and catches Rebecca's hand. It is an attempt at reconciliation. He wants her to know that he respects her child-rearing choices.

What will happen when Ammie's children come along? Instinctively, he knows, she will make different choices, that unlike Rebecca she won't be guided by what the community dictates. Ammie's children will be free to run around, Rebecca's tight lipped and straight backed.

Rebecca's hand is warm in his. She meets his gaze and smiles. For a second there is only that connection between them. An understanding. Their girl. Their way.

When it is time, the others enter: the Cuthbert family, the Olsens, Eliza. Micah and his three wives. Filing in like this, in a group, formally dressed, sombre, he is struck, as he always is, by how different they are to the outsiders. The dark clothes – long pinafores for the women, jackets and tight buttoned shirts for the men – have become so much a part of their way of life here. He can't imagine how they would have dressed before they came here: casual, tight-fitting garments, in lighter fabrics, and in colours. In his forays to the city, he's dazzled by the variety, and by the colour.

Goran and Leah take their usual seats. Goran lowers his head and

Tobias knows that he will be remembering Deborah. Tobias thinks about her now too, though he doesn't very often. He has long suspected that she was his favourite wife, although Goran would never admit it. But since Deborah died, his father has never taken another wife and it's something that puzzles Tobias.

The door opens noisily. Ammie enters, flustered, wiping her hands on her skirt, clearly just having finished some errand. For all that he catches his breath at the sight of her. The sweep of her white neck, the voluminous curls. His luck creeps up on him in these most ordinary moments ever since she came to them, when she enters a room, when she turns to look at him in the middle of a chore. More even than the sight of her lying naked: the length of her, the smooth pale skin of hips and torso and breasts; and how it flushes under the touch of his fingers.

Ammie slides into the chair opposite him, the colour high in her cheeks. She places her hands on her knees and bows her head swiftly, indicating her readiness. Tobias watches as Rebecca turns to look. He can't see the expression on his first wife's face but from the set of her shoulders he senses her agitation. Later, there will be a hushed conversation in the corridor, perhaps a strained attempt to contain their raised voices.

It is time to begin.

Across the room, the young people pick up their instruments. The notes from the flute begin to ascend, beautiful haunting notes that are calming and uplifting. Kitty Miller, playing as though she is translating the music from somewhere sacred. When Patience begins to sing, it brings tears to his eyes, the purity of it. It is worth it, Tobias thinks, all of it – the work, the endurance – for moments like this of clarity, a glimpse of something beyond their being here on earth. It is worth it for the beauty and the simplicity of what they do.

But the muscles in his upper arms still ache. He is too acutely aware of Esther fidgeting. He is aware of Rebecca's irritation. He picks up the force of Ammie's still flustered presence and of the weight of expectation from his father. Tobias closes his eyes and tries to focus on the work in hand, on how Moses must have felt when he witnessed the angel and the bush before him bursting into flame. Astonishment, he should think, privilege, amazement. Like his own life, and luck.

When his eyes flicker open, the first thing he sees are her eyes on his. Expectation on her face in the arched eyebrows and the smile that plays at the edges of her lips. He wonders if she has been watching him the whole time. Ammie nods, a gesture that is almost imperceptible but at the same time daringly overt. He looks at Eliza and Micah. He looks at Rebecca, Goran and Leah but they are all elsewhere, caught up in their thoughts or prayers.

He feels a surge of energy then, in the intention that he sees in Ammie's eyes, that giving of energy, her belief in him. It galvanises him.

Tobias opens the bible and begins to read.

'I don't agree with you,' Seth says. He is breaking hunks off a loaf of bread, tearing at the crust until he reaches the soft white middle. 'The bush on fire is a sign of power. God's power, and his will being done unto mankind.'

Across the table, Ciaras shakes his head. His face is charged with energy. 'That's too absolute. It is about power. But not the power of something done *to* us. It's about what we can change from within ourselves. I think Tobias is right. It's about transformation, power from within.'

Usually, Tobias loves these mealtimes. It is one of the pleasures of the way they live. He loves the formality of the men's dining hall, the oak-panelled walls and the clean lines of the long benches. These Friday dinners give them time away from the women and children, to eat undisturbed; an opportunity to speak with Ciaras as well as observe his fraternal duty of eating with Seth. He enjoys the reflection and the debate on the meaning of the week's passage. But on the evenings of his own testimony, he is too anxious about the ways he has interpreted the text, what Goran, especially, will make of it.

Ciaras is looking at him. 'Tobias?'

Someone has asked him a question.

'Do we need to repeat it?' Seth is impatient. 'The purpose of the fire. In the text?'

Tobias has his fork in the air. He pauses a moment, lowers his fork again. 'I thought I'd said – in Meeting ...' He looks questioningly at his brother. He tries to keep the irritation from his voice, takes a breath. 'For me – it is about communication, listening. To the Spirit, I mean. The fire isn't just about power – though clearly fire is powerful.'

'Spoken like a glassblower,' Seth says.

Ciaras rounds on him. 'Let him finish.'

Tobias pushes the stew around on his plate. 'I see it as ... as the fire being the symbol of Moses' task of leading. Fire is transforming, and Moses transforms history and the lives of the Israelites. But it's an outward ... manifestation ... of his knowledge. That he has the ability, that he can choose to do that.'

'How could he already know something that God ordered him to do?'

Tobias looks at his brother, sees something hooded in his dark eyes. There is something behind the question, Tobias knows, but he cannot get at it.

'I think the fire *is* self-knowledge, it's the spark of realisation. The inner spirit, and its voice. The risk of speaking out, and doing it anyway. *They will heed your voice; and you shall come.* Do you see?' Tobias looks around him, biting his lip. He is no longer sure that is what he thinks, whether his interpretation is tenuous, has too much licence in it.

Padraic looks up from where he is sitting. He has been turning an empty glass round and round in front of him. 'Well,' he says, 'for what it's worth – I was moved by that. Really moved. The idea of the spirit in us all – it's ...' He glances at Goran. 'It felt to me like the old days, like the things we used to talk about and believe in all those years ago.'

There's the murmur of agreement from someone else – one of the younger ones, Francis perhaps.

Goran leans over and scoops more stew from the pot in the centre of the table. 'I think we should not be speaking of inner spirit. It is what Moses did next that matters. Leading his people through the countryside – looking for the right place to settle. That is the real story. Not burning bushes.'

Silence falls around the table. Tobias places his fork, with his food uneaten, quietly down on the plate. Goran looks around him. 'Brothers. If we have finished eating, let us go and join again the women and children.'

Goran slides his chair back and stands, throws his napkin down onto the table. Tobias looks at it, sees it is pure white, but crumpled; spattered with the juice of the stew.

*

When it's time for bed, Tobias is there already. He lies on his back, unmoving, with his hands behind his head, as Rebecca goes through her ritual: splashing her face with water, unbraiding and combing her hair then rebraiding it; hanging her robe on the back of the door. She sits on the edge of the bed and opens the drawer of the nightstand. Takes out her bible, blue leather with faded gilt lettering. She won't read from it tonight. Just to touch it, to feel the familiar warmth of the leather, is enough. If she were alone, she would bring it to her lips and kiss it but she is too aware of Tobias next to her, his expectancy. The uncertainty of what will pass between them before they fall asleep; replaying the earlier tension at the children's bedtime. He had come home after the men's dinner with a brooding anger she could not reach. It was not like him.

Rebecca switches out the lamp. In the darkness Tobias pulls her closer into him and his chest becomes a pillow, with her face up against the brushed cotton of his shirt. She listens, as she always does, for the steady pulse of his heart. When he speaks finally, she hears the vibrations of the words in his body and his words come out muffled.

'I'm sorry. About earlier, it shouldn't have come out like that.'

'It's Naomi you should speak to.'

Rebecca turns over and shifts across the bed, thinking of Naomi's stricken face, reacting to Tobias's harsh tone. On her back, she tries to extend her body by stretching through her feet. She waits for her eyes to adjust to the darkness, calculating the location of the spidery cracks in the ceiling, the patch of damp directly above their bed.

'You acted without thinking. You should know better, Tobias. Really.'

The silence tells Rebecca exactly what she wanted to know. That Tobias is suffering. But she feels loss too, in a different way. An ache in her belly that she carries around with her each day and, more than that, Tobias's ambivalence to that deep need.

When Amarantha arrived, she thought she would feel it less. But her sisterwife's presence has exercerbated the need, if anything. Something from her body, something of her very own, that Amarantha can't own. It is with her always – at school, even, as she battles through mathematics or, perched on a blue plastic chair, working on letter formation with the little ones. Little 'a'; big 'A'. Rebecca's mouth speaking the words. Her pencil moving correspondingly across the page. Keeping up the chant, pointing to the row of pictures forming a bright border round the top of the walls in the classroom. A is for apple, for aadvark.

For Amarantha.

Rebecca feels Tobias move next to her, a brushing sensation against her thigh. He takes her hand and the warmth of it causes a surge of something in her: affection, guilt. He loves her, after all. She knows that.

Tobias says simply. 'I know.'

'Well, then.'

Tobias sighs. 'But you can't let everything … get in the way. You carry it all around with you, this need. It's … suffocating.'

Rebecca feels a hot, rising anger. She has to breathe, consciously, to make her voice come out calm. 'So now I'm suffocating you?'

Tobias makes an irritated noise, a sharp breath, the click of his tongue and a stiffening of his body. There's another silence. But Rebecca feels him yielding, softening.

'I'll speak to Naomi,' he says, 'tomorrow. I'll explain that things are difficult since Ammie arrived. That …'

Rebecca stiffens. 'Surely that's the wrong thing to say? They need reassurance, not to be told of adult concerns they don't understand.'

'Don't they need to learn …'

'Not yet.' Rebecca's words snap out suddenly, into the darkness. 'They're so young. Let them find out in their own time, not be thrown headlong into our troubles.'

Tobias turns towards her, lying on his side, propped up on his elbow. Rebecca's eyes have grown used to the dark now and even without the lamp she can see the confusion on his face, the uncertainty in his posture.

'Our troubles? What happened to teaching them early about our ways? You always say you wished it was like that for you. As a child.'

Rebecca feels a growing panic at saying something she might regret. What she wants at this minute is to find a small space somewhere, bury herself inside it. Lock the doors so that nothing can hurt her family or disturb them.

She swallows, trying to ease the knot that clamps her throat. 'I think ...' The words are so hard to say. 'Lately, I think differently, perhaps. About such things.' She knows she is not being clear. She can't express to Tobias what she wants to say. That, since Amarantha, everything is different. That she has so many questions about the rightness of this, of what they are doing. And she wants to guard her girls from this same difficulty. The pain, even. There, she has acknowledged it: the pain of sharing her marriage.

Amarantha is always there. She has entered the marriage, Rebecca's home, her bedroom.

Tears force themselves into her eyes. Rebecca can't bear even for Tobias to see her like this. But in the night, in the darkness, still feeling the rawness of everything – the harsh words spoken to Naomi earlier, Amarantha's distractedness, her own desire for a child and Tobias's uncertainty – she is unable to help herself.

Then Tobias is there, his arm under her back, his body heavy on hers, and he is holding her. Rebecca lets go, into the security of his embrace, forcing herself not to think about anything but this connection: the man she has married comforting her, empathising with her. She blinks away the image of Amarantha – in the kitchen, playing with the children in the garden. She blinks away the images of her girls' faces and their excitement and their joy.

She feels Tobias's mouth on her temples, the light kisses as he works along the edge of her hairline, the weight of his hand underneath her head. She closes her eyes and leaves the traces of tears unchecked as they roll down her cheek. She dare not shift position because the wrong turn of a head or the movement of an arm might undo this moment, the detachment of it all. Just the two of them: two bodies, two people, finding comfort in each other. When his mouth moves down to hers, only then does she feel free to shift her arm above him, around him, placing her hand round the back of his head, feeling the texture of his hair and how profuse it is, how hard the skull beneath it. And we are all bones, she thinks, bones and bits of flesh that will wither, at last, and decay.

But the thought is gone. Tobias is lifting up her nightdress. They struggle together to get it over her head and then she feels the smooth coolness of the sheets against her skin and the roughness of Tobias's, the scratching, the traces of stubble where his mouth looks for the crook of her neck, then her shoulders, then breasts, then nipples.

'A' is for Amarantha, thinks Rebecca, as the twinge courses through her, breasts through to abdomen, through to womb. She remembers how her breasts swelled up over the months, the veins blushing blue over transparent skin. How, with each one of her children, they filled with milk, weeping into the warm bath water for weeks before the birth.

Tobias's mouth begins searching for her breastbone, and for the skin of her belly. The shock of flesh and moisture. The relief that she can let go. Of tension, of anger, and fear.

A. Annunciation. In her mind, Rebecca sees Mary's face as she meets her cousin: her high smooth forehead, her eyes black as olives. Elizabeth's face is etched deep with lines, lighter in the creases where the sun has been unable to penetrate. She feels Mary's dread at telling Elizabeth the news. She has been sent by God. But her cousin – old, barren Elizabeth – is smiling and Mary calls out *my soul magnifies the Lord*. Elizabeth is nodding; slowly, she moves her hand across the mound of her own ample belly.

The day Goran Christensen took his second wife, the community gathered at the top of the hillside. They stood in the place where, a few years earlier, he had imagined Marah where Marah now stood. The whole village had made the climb and they stood in two loose circles, the children on the inside holding onto the hands of their parents and the more recent members of the group in the outer ring. Rebecca – who at nine was tall and willowy already, with fair skin and eyes that fixed you in an earnest stare – was in charge of keeping the little ones in check: her brother Gideon, the Cuthbert toddlers, young Mariah.

It was a warm day, the day of the summer solstice. They had chosen it deliberately so that there were more hours of daylight and because this Sealing was partly a celebration of all they had achieved – of what they had done, built a village, started a community, begun a way of life. When they got back to the village there would be feasting well into the night. There were no absences. Those who did not believe in the day, in what Goran was doing, had left altogether: whole families, and Tess, a single woman with her two children – who refused to embrace what Goran was purporting to do.

Micah held up his hands, to indicate they should start. Deborah smiled at him, excited, glanced around the circle, then finally at Goran. She had prepared for this ceremony all morning. In fact, she had prepared for months – from the time she set out to make him love her. He had schooled her in their beliefs and their ways, had sat side by side at Leah's kitchen table, reading scripture and tracing the lives of the prophets who went before them, whose names she reeled off to herself in bed at night like an incantation – Abraham, Sarah and Hagar; Jacob, Rachel and Leah – and on and on. Those people whose example they would follow.

'But why,' she said one night, frowning, with her finger still on the page. 'Why – when you all spent so long rejecting these writings – why do you turn to them now?'

Goran smiled a slow smile, and leaned forward to move a strand of hair from her face. He held it between his fingers briefly, looking at it.

'It is not,' he said, 'the bald words that matter, but how we interpret them. It is a framework, that is all. And for a community which is bound together, which shares everything – what more can tie us together than husbands and wives? It means our lives weave around each other.'

Deborah brought her hand to her chin, leaning on it, smiling. A rush of happiness bubbled through her – she had been chosen, after all, for this. To be the second wife of an Elder. To lead the way in a new belief, a new way of life. 'Weave around each other. I like that.'

And they wove their words around each other that day, binding themselves to each other. They had written their vows themselves. Goran spoke of Deborah's openness and bright nature. Deborah spoke of Goran's strength and wisdom and of how much she loved him, how grateful she was for it.

On the hillside, with Micah standing in the centre of the circle, the children encircled Goran and his soon to be new wife with ribbons. They wove in and out of each other until they were enclosed in bright bands of crimson and yellow, blue and mauve. Everyone cheered. Goran clasped Deborah around the waist and pulled him towards her. He kissed her and for a moment she closed her eyes, murmuring something – though whether it was to him or herself, or to the sky, no one could tell. When they parted, the two of them stood in the centre of the circle, hands joined, looking at each other.

Leah looked on, detached, awkward. She looked into the distance, towards the village, clamping her lips together.

Micah's eyes shot towards her and when he saw the expression on her face, a look of pain passed over his.

'Leah,' he said gently, 'sister. Will you join your husband in the circle?'

Leah looked confused, looked wildly around her, her hands for a moment fluttering agitatedly. Her sons stood beside her, resolute and unmoving. Since her return she had noticed their distance. They loved to come into her new consulting room and arrange the jars on the shelves, even label and catalogue the herbs. In such moments she thought she knew them, saw that same spark. But something vital had been lost forever, some part of their emotional being closed to her, she thought, perhaps forever.

As though to steady herself, Leah placed her hand on Tobias's head. 'In the centre?' she whispered, looking back at Micah. He nodded encouragingly.

Deborah's eyes were on Goran's face, trying to assess his reaction. Her eyes darted from his face, back to Leah. She did not want the other woman in the circle because then she could pretend that it was she and she alone being united with Goran before God. Goran hesitated. This was not in the script, this was not what they planned. But there was something so right about it – that it was a union not just of Goran and Deborah, but of both his wives to each other too. He looked at Deborah, lifted his hand and stroked her face, the wide cheekbones, the fine skin. Then he stretched out his hand towards Leah, inviting her to join them in a gesture that was generous and expansive. For all they had been through, this was a new beginning; and Leah knew that. It was an invitation to a new way.

Leah took a breath, raised her eyes to the sky. She looked down at her boys – at Tobias's sulky expression and Seth's shy smile and saw how scarred they had been by her absence. She breathed out, a commitment to something – a determination.

She took a step forward into the circle, touching first Goran then Deborah lightly on the arm, as though encircling them with her acceptance.

It is only when Rebecca reaches the porch, and she and the girls are knocking snow off their boots, that she notices the house is empty. There's no light in the kitchen. Rebecca pauses with her laces half undone. She opens the door and it hits her, an unfamiliar cold. The stove must have gone out. On the table there are the remains of a meal, a plate with breadcrumbs on it and a knife smeared with something – jam perhaps – that has also stained the tablecloth.

No Amarantha, no Martha.

Rebecca slams the kettle under the faucet. As she fills it with water, she looks out onto the garden; in the darkening afternoon, the branches are bare against the sky, the layer of white throws the landscape into relief.

'May we go to Leah's?' Naomi asks. Rebecca nods, asks her to take her sister and she is left in the abandoned kitchen, sighing as she piles the wood in the stove to relight it. After the day she's had, she shouldn't be doing this.

The flames have just started to take when the door bursts open. Amarantha is on the threshold, cheeks flushed. It's more than just the cold though, Rebecca thinks; she's breathless. Somewhere inside Rebecca's head there is the beginning of a high-pitched hum, faint but relentless. She brings her focus back to the room. She doesn't need to say anything: the look on Amarantha's face speaks her guilt clearly enough.

'Oh – I'd hoped to be – I'm sorry, Rebecca. Did the stove go out?'

'Where have you been?' She finds it difficult to keep the irritation from her voice.

'Caught up. You know, with work to do.'

Rebecca finds she is clenching her eyebrows; she wonders if the noise, becoming painful now, might be the onset of a migraine.

'And Martha?'

'Leah said she didn't mind.'

Rebecca catches her breath. She can't believe this flagrant admission, the careless abandonment of her duties. 'She didn't mind?' She tries to keep her voice steady, to phrase it as an open question.

'Only for a short time. I had … something I needed to do.' Amarantha's tone is belligerent. Rebecca is reminded of the girl in the schoolroom from years ago, standing on one leg with her ankle hooked around the other and chewing the ends of her hair. There's a drift of voices from outside, the muted sound of the girls' laughter from Leah's garden. They're chanting some song or playing a game. Rebecca thinks of all she has to carry: responsibility for the girls, the family as well as the education of all the community's children.

'I came home to a dark house,' Rebecca says. 'After the day I've had – it's thoughtless, Amarantha.'

'There are other ways of being thoughtless.'

The air between them is suddenly charged. Rebecca is alert, aware of Amarantha's body, poised for argument. She's aware of her own taut shoulders.

Rebecca's voice is so tight she can barely speak. 'You're saying I'm thoughtless?'

Amarantha moves further into the room. She's still wearing her cape, her black woollen mittens. 'I'm saying that ...' she hesitates for a moment then lifts her chin, speaking clearly and carefully into the room '... there's thoughtlessness in how you treat me.'

Rebecca feels the shock crackle through her. That Amarantha should be so ungrateful when she and Tobias have taken her in, fed her, provided for her, given her a home. She has so few real responsibilities, save cooking and looking after Martha, and even then she abandons her to Leah's care. Rebecca wonders how many times it has happened before.

She turns abruptly, takes off her coat and places it on the back of the chair to dry out. Then she sets to on cleaning up, removing the dirty plate, whips off the table cover, finds a cloth to wipe down the table. She pulls so hard that it catches on the grain, leaving particles of blue fluff clinging to the wood.

'Let me do that.'

Amarantha has taken off her cape, is removing the cloth from Rebecca's hand.

'No!' Rebecca tries to snatch it back. They each pull at it; Amarantha steps closer to get a better hold, Rebecca veers away to the side, knocking into her. Something falls from Amarantha's cloak, something from the pocket, and floats to the ground. They stand for a moment, the two of them, looking at it: a sheet of blue paper, so thin as to be almost transparent.

Amarantha scoops it up, balls it up instantly in her hand.

'What is it?'

'It's nothing,' she says, 'nothing.'

'Let me see.'

'It's private.'

Rebecca laughs. Even to her ears it is sharp and hysterical but she can't help herself. 'Private?' She looks at her. Amarantha colours, a flush tingeing her cheekbones. 'We're sisterwives, Amarantha. Nothing can ever be private.'

Amarantha clutches the paper to her chest. She can't meet Rebecca's gaze. She is defeated, Rebecca thinks; and she holds her hand open in a gesture that orders Amarantha to place it there. She is secure in her authority – at least, here, for now – and her greater age and status as first wife.

Amarantha places the screwed up paper in Rebecca's hand. Rebecca uncurls it, straightens it out and holds it in front of her. She is aware of exaggerating everything: slowing down the moment, of playing up the importance of her own gestures. But she doesn't care; all she wants, in this instant, is to make Amarantha suffer.

Rebecca begins to read it. The writing is looping and spacious and the words have a breathless tone about them: *so delighted to hear from you* and *please come, you'll be welcome to stay as long as you like.* Then the words become a blur and Rebecca finds herself struggling to read and her throat is tight and hot.

'I didn't want you to find it.' Amarantha's voice is quiet.

'How did you get it?'

'I can't say.' Amarantha's gaze is fixed to the floor. With her toe, she draws a line in front of her. The gesture is indignant, a refusal to speak.

'You mean you won't say?' Rebecca takes a sharp breath in, trying to absorb, trying to consider and wondering what on earth she will say to Tobias. Tobias. The next sensation comes in a rush, the tumbling knowledge of being outside of things.

'Tobias?' Rebecca can hardly say her husband's name. 'Did he help you? Has he been – have you been there with him?'

'No. Don't blame Tobias, it isn't him. It's …'

'Who?' The word echoes in her head, the sound bouncing back to her, reverberating. She nods at the letter. 'Who is this person?'

'Someone Leah knows.'

Rebecca steps back, hip bumping against the table. She feels the edge of it dig into her. Tomorrow she'll have a bruise there, flowering over her whole outer thigh.

Amarantha's words come out in a rush. 'It's – when I'm out walking I see the …'

'You go *walking*?'

'I take Martha with me. I see the mailman and he helps me, sometimes – well one day I asked him if he could take something – a letter for me and … '

Rebecca shakes her head suddenly, trying to release the image of her sisterwife in boots and long skirts with Martha in the papoose on her back, laughing up at the mailman. And the backdrop for all this: the streets, the stores, a post office.

'You've walked to Aroer?' Rebecca can hardly believe it. Not simply that Amarantha can do that, physically do that, walk there and back in a day, but that she has been doing it in secret all this time. And that she knows someone, something about Leah that none of the rest of them know.

Rebecca feels a thrusting momentum. She moves forward and now she's close, close enough to see the texture of Amarantha's dark lashes, the flecks of amber in her eyes; the creaminess of skin around her neck, her collarbones. And it is pure gut instinct that makes her raise her hand and strike. The next moment Amarantha is clutching her cheek. The air still rings from the slap. Rebecca feels the sharp sting of Amarantha's flesh. Rebecca gasps, holds her hand to her mouth. So help her, she has lost control.

Amarantha is sobbing. She lifts her face slowly to Rebecca's and it is dead white, with the beginnings of a red mark where Rebecca's fingers have been. 'What was I supposed to do?' she says. 'You're all out there – doing things – busy with your own work. No one thinks to ask

90

about me. It's like being in ... in prison.' The spittle flies from her mouth as she shouts. Her shoulders heave.

The anger has passed and Rebecca is flooded with exhaustion. She gropes for the chair, sits down on it. She looks at Amarantha's hand, clamped to her cheek and sees the length of the slender fingers. No wonder, she thinks. No wonder men are enchanted by her. How could Rebecca ever compare?

And now she has struck her and she feels hollow. Sullied.

One more time, Amarantha bends to scoop up the letter. She straightens again and looks straight at Rebecca, her mouth curling into a knowingness that Rebecca can't read. Amarantha smiles. She waves the letter in front of her, like a prize.

III

MARAH

The stranger blew in with the winter drifts. She arrived at the start of the year, during the first Sunday gathering, opening the door with hardly a sound and standing for a while at the back of the Meeting House. She saw what she had expected to see: a group of men, women and children of differing ages, simply dressed, drawn together in prayer. Really, she thought, they could be from another time, the women in long pinafores they clearly stitched themselves, the men with their trousers and jackets cut in an old-fashioned way. There was something about them, a kind of directness. Their integrity was palpable, hugely present in the room. Just how she had been told it would be.

When Micah looked up he saw the olive-skinned woman – not much more than a girl he thought, at first – with dark straight hair in two braids. She held a shawl around her, but still it couldn't conceal the clothes of the outside: a tight-fitting jacket with decorative buttons. And trousers: denim ones that betrayed the curve of her thighs. The shawl she held around her was plain, a neutral colour: a kind of disguise, as though she were trying to hide her badge of outsideness.

Why was she here?

The woman hadn't stamped her boots before she came in; the water had begun to pool around her feet. The heat from the woodstove brought colour to her face, a flush that could also have been anxiety or excitement. On her face was a look that might have been detached amusement, like she had caught them in the middle of some forbidden act.

Goran opened his eyes, and saw her. He stopped chanting the prayer. It brought instant silence to the room. When the other villagers looked up, looked around them, they sensed something was wrong. The woman took a step backwards, brought the shawl tighter around her. Goran glanced at Micah, who lifted his eyebrows in a question. What were they to do? Nothing like this had happened in twelve years. Away from the rest of the world, they had never been visited in the middle of worship.

It was Goran who signalled at her to sit down. Nothing would interrupt Meeting: they would finish first and speak to her later, find out where she had come from and what she wanted. Whoever she was, they must extend a civil welcome.

Goran nodded at the seats vacated by Tobias and Gervaise who had been gone for months now to begin their guild in the city. Even now, the debate still rumbled as to whether or not they should have been given permission to leave. But Goran knew his own son. If he hadn't agreed, Tobias would have left anyway, perhaps never to return.

The woman hovered close to the chairs, looking for affirmation from Goran. He nodded again then she smiled gratefully and sat down. The seat she chose was Tobias's.

Even though the raids were a distant memory, newcomers were regarded with suspicion. Goran was sure there was nothing sinister about this new person, this young woman. She was a seeker, it was clear. There was something solid about her presence, an absolute groundedness. She was young and fit, that she had an openness which would serve their Meeting well. She did not know the words to their prayers, but when the time came for silence she sat unmoving, as though thirsty for it.

During the rest of worship, each person tried to assess this woman, this newcomer in their midst. She is like a squaw, Leah Christensen thought, with the woods in her hair. Goran thought how she reminded him of Leah, a similar steady smile and a calmness about her. Some held her at a distance; others tried to connect their silence with hers, to forge those bonds of spirit that go beyond words.

And the woman herself? She was not used to prayer, or even to silence. To her, now though, the silence was a kind of prayer. The quiet was a balm; there was something nourishing about it she had not encountered before. She tried to sink deeper into herself, to feel the boundaries of her physical self, her muscles and sinews, and what lay beneath. She brought her hand to her abdomen, and drew a single long breath.

Leah watched the woman's gesture, noticing for the first time that, under the coat she had taken off, there was a swell to her belly. She was pregnant; no doubt seeking sanctuary. The Elders would have to decide what to do with her. But for the most part, there was something about this woman with her smile and her lustrous hair that made Leah uneasy. It might be envy. But it was more than that, Leah thought. Something about the way she brought in the outside; something about her connection with the city.

If the woman stayed with them, Leah would deliver the child. And, if the woman stayed long enough, Leah might watch this child grow up.

When the silence ended and they shook hands, the Elders signalled to each other and left the room without a word. The woman looked around her, disorientated, not sure what to do next. It was Rebecca, sitting next to her, who touched her hand lightly on the woman's forearm and told her they would want to speak with her.

When she had left the room, the others looked around at each other, uncertain of whether to wait or to proceed – as they always did – to the Congregational Hall for refreshments. They fell back into a silence but it had a different feel to it; a prickling curious energy circled the room, more alive and less grounded than the one they experienced during worship.

They were gone a long time. When the children began to agitate, Sarah rose and led them all off, to the hall no doubt, for games. The silence returned, and they waited.

When the door opened, Goran came first into the room, his face tight and ashen. His eyes met Leah's, briefly, for a second, flicked away again, back to the circle. One by one, the Elders returned to their seats. The woman went back to where she was sitting. She was flushed but triumphant, relieved.

Micah remained on his feet. 'Brothers and sisters. Our visitor today comes with a request to join us.'

Malachy stood up. His words came out in a rush. 'This is too sudden,' he said. 'Surely we must all decide – not just the Elders?'

Goran's voice rose above the others. 'We are satisfied that it is the right thing. Circumstances …' He paused, looked around him, 'mean that it is best discussed amongst the Elders.'

'But …'

Malachy's protest was silenced by Micah. He raised his hand and looked directly into the eyes of the challenger. 'Malachy. The decision is made. Our visitor will join us for a trial period.' He nodded towards her.

'She is trained in teaching, and as we have need for help in the schoolroom, she will be useful there.' Micah smiled, across the room, at Rebecca. 'I'm sure Rebecca would welcome it.'

Rebecca nodded her affirmation, blushed, looked at her hands. Then she sought out the woman, wanting to see her reaction. Their gazes met; they smiled. Rebecca was sure she would like her – so exotic in so many ways and yet, although from a different place, she was, like her, just a woman.

Eliza asked the question that they had all been thinking. 'Might we know the visitor's name?'

The woman got to her feet. She had taken off her jacket but the shawl was still around her. It fell loosely away from her shoulders as she stood, and her pregnant belly was obvious for everyone, now, to see.

'My name,' she said, 'is Frania. And I want to thank you all for giving me the chance to join you.'

There were murmurings around the circle, some of approval, some of dissent. Frania sat down in her seat, hand behind her to guide her. The test was over. She had won them round. Her hand moved across onto her belly, smoothing circles there, as though to soothe herself, as though to relax the child who had woken inside her and now was kicking: active, restless, eager to get out.

Frania loved the schoolroom. It was like a secure and bright cocoon: the alphabet frieze with its gaudy homemade pictures running round the top of the wall; the shelves and cupboards lovingly made by various men in the village. So much care for such a tiny school – only thirteen pupils of all different ages. Yet the industry and ingenuity of the people in this village touched and amazed her.

She paused at the desk, where Rebecca sorted pencils in a box, setting aside those which needed sharpening. The baby inside her gave a swift kick, a reminder of the life inside her. In the weeks since Frania had come here, she felt the baby turn and grow, move in the confined space as though fed by the security of being here. They had given her a small caravan on the edge of the village, overlooking the garden. And although it was winter and the ground still covered in snow, Frania looked forward to spring, to the day she could see rows of planted vegetables, perhaps even help put them in the ground herself.

Rebecca looked up from her task. 'I thought they would be bored by now, of the snow. But listen.'

Voices from the Piece, as she had learned to call the green area where all the houses clustered. Shrieks of laughter and cries that carried in the clear air. Through the window, Frania watched their childish figures, bundled up in layers and hats and gloves. The winter sunshine caught the sheet of snow, a surface like glitter. Surely, she thought, this place is almost perfect.

She turned back to Rebecca. 'Doesn't it bring out the playfulness in everyone?'

'Is that how it was in the city?' There was a hunger in Rebecca's eyes – for information, for a glimpse of a different world view – which surprised Frania. She had thought the Elder's daughter to be content here. But here she was, desperate for details of the outside.

'Children are children. Things weren't much different. Yours are more patient, more able to sit still. But when it comes to play – and snow – well ... even the adults reverted sometimes.' Frania laughed at the memory of herself in her first year as a teacher, out rolling snow balls and making igloos with her class.

'Which do you prefer?'

Frania noticed the emotion wrapped up in the younger woman's voice, an edginess that was stronger than wistfulness; it was almost angry, even. Perhaps she was angry. Angry that she had never had the chance to go there? Or angry with Frania that she had the privilege of seeking refuge here?

'You mean, do I prefer living here or there?'

'I suppose that's what I meant, yes.'

Frania sighed. How could she begin to relate the complexity of how she felt? That she admired everything they did here but constantly felt like an outsider? That she waited daily for the man she loved to arrive, as he had promised he would, and that until then she could not help but feel lonely. She could never explain how when she woke in the inky blackness with the pressure on her bladder, she could think only of the waiting: for her baby, for her lover, the child's father. Then her life here could begin.

'There's something I love about this place. The simplicity. It's like – all my life I felt there was something lacking – the way I was living, the damage and self destruction that people do to each other. But ...'

'You're not happy?' Rebecca's voice was gentle. Frania could see empathy in her face.

'I feel sometimes ... on the edge of things.'

'I think that's the way here. At first, for those who join – it takes time.'

Frania looked steadily at Rebecca, at her neat straight red hair, her straight posture. At eighteen she had been so grown by this place she belonged more than the moss that lined the river bed, or the trees that grew on the Piece. Rebecca could never know what it was not to belong.

'It's more than that. It's your faith.'

'Our faith? You mean – you don't believe?' She had shocked her, this young woman who was so devout.

'I'm open to it. But it's not the same.'

The children's voices floated in again from the outside. Rebecca turned, slowly, and looked out of the window. Frania followed her glance. Outside, the children had formed a circle around the snowmen they had built. They were holding hands and laughing, so much part of a group.

'That. That's what I missed. I've never had it – that kind of belonging.'

'Tell me,' Rebecca said, 'what it was like.'

As Frania spoke, Rebecca sharpened pencils. One by one she turned them against the blade, keeping the pressure against the blade until the shaving came out in a satisfying continual loop. Frania spoke of her childhood, her years at university, her friends, her hopes and ambitions. Her loves. In all the years Rebecca had grown up here, she had not had so much detail or information from her friends, her mother, her brothers. The intimacy – all these personal details – almost a shameful thing, she thought; as though Frania were desperate for contact, desperate to make some emotional connection. Rebecca wondered, really, if she were the right person to be listening.

'And so – after all that … wandering – it's good to know that I can belong here. And when Julius comes, he …'

The breath almost stopped in Rebecca's chest. 'Julius?'

'He's the reason I'm here. How I knew about you all. Not that I knew you as you all. But you know what I mean. He told me about this community he knew. He admired their values and that he'd always hoped to come, he said. I think he might know Goran, maybe – and your father?'

Rebecca could hardly breathe. Julius. She had heard the story of the raids so many times. Remembered now, if she closed her eyes a voice, the name being called, echoing down the hallway of the tiny apartment they had in the city. Julius. The name of the man who took away her father. There must be many men with that name. It couldn't be the same one.

'He's coming here?' Rebecca said. Did anyone know this? Her father, Goran? Did they know of this link with the past, with the violence that had made them flee the city?

Frania hugged the papers she was holding close to her. Her face was lit up with hope. 'We're going to build a house! I've found the spot, right in the woods. And when this little one arrives, he or she can have a garden to play in. In the city – we wouldn't have had space.'

Rebecca felt the tension creep through her body. She lined up the pencils, now all with sharp points, on the desk. She looked at Frania, unsure what to say, what to do. But Frania had picked up the hand-bell they used to call the children back. She was standing at the open door and there was a cold rush of air; the bell clanging, clanging and the children rushing back to the school room. Rebecca did not hear their chatter as they entered, the thump of boots against the wooden steps as they were instructed to knock off the snow. She couldn't focus as Frania led them to their desks and explained the lesson they would be doing next.

All Rebecca could see was the face of a man from her childhood. Coming here. Living here. She stood up, feeling dizzy and disorientated, propping herself up on the desk. She moved to the board at the front of the schoolroom and smiled, weakly, at the children. She must concentrate on what to do next. It was time for the lesson to start.

LOT

Ammie loves this place, the noise and hubbub of the café and the continual stream of traffic outside on the street. If you sit for long enough you see all of humanity on this corner. You can watch the passing shoppers and commuters with their heads bent, watch the customers who come in, setting the bell jangling when they enter and shouting their order over the counter at Frank. During the week, when Libby is at work, Ammie comes here to sit at the table in the window. She's fascinated by these city people, by the clothes they wear especially. One girl's stockings are pink like the heart of a fuschia, and full of holes she doesn't seem to notice. There's a man in a dark overcoat which skims the floor because it is so long; he has boots with metal chains and they clank as he walks. She envies these people their courage; the way they invent themselves and the ease with which they flow through life. Their fluidity is the thing she most wants to possess.

She feels fluid herself though, today, a Saturday; she is warm everywhere, especially on the inside. In here the three of them – she, Libby, Finn – are spending the afternoon, insulated from the November cold. Their wet coats and jackets steam on the back of chairs as they dry. Ammie finds comfort in the strange smells at Frank's: oil, frying eggs, the bitterness of charred toast.

Today they have a table in the corner. They're playing cards, and Libby is frowning, trying to work out her next move. When she has a realisation, she smiles; she could be a child again, younger than her thirty-something years. Though she has the faintest lines around her eyes, the smile makes her seem innocent, open. Even now, Ammie is amazed how readily Libby accepted her, opening her home to a stranger who came bearing a letter from a mutual friend. It's as though the name – Leah – was enough, a key to a new home, a new life. No questions. Ammie has been grateful for that.

In this light, Libby's hair encompasses so many colours – pure copper, chestnut brown, black – even, Ammie noticed yesterday, wisps of grey. She is older than Ammie, but somehow beside her it is Ammie who feels old.

Libby picks up a card from the pile, places it, face up, on the table. Ten of Hearts. Finn shuffles in his seat. His turn. He deliberates, looks around and for a moment Ammie catches his gaze. His eyes speak of his capacity for laughter and pleasure, a life of lightness. He grins at her and she looks quickly away, back at her own cards. She needs only the King of Hearts. Her heart begins that queer skipping rhythm, excitement at the knowledge of the game coming to a close. She knows now why they never play cards back home. Too addictive. Too much pleasure.

As Finn picks up Libby's card, a look of elation passes over his face and he places his run down on the table for the others to see: Ten, Jack, Queen, King. A run of Hearts.

To celebrate, Finn buys them hot chocolate. Frank makes them with extra milk, whipped up, and sprinkles grated chocolate on top. Finn lifts his cup in a toast.

'To Ammie,' he says. 'To your first month here.'

Libby clinks her cup against Finn's. Ammie isn't sure what to do, but raises hers too, looks up to see an expression of fondness and amusement on Finn's face as he looks at her. Those eyes. She has spent weeks trying to work out the emotions they evoke in her. Sweetness, she has decided. Her response to him is different from the desire for Tobias that cuts right into her. With Finn, there's a gentle affection she wraps around herself. He makes her feel safe.

She watches Libby take a sip of chocolate. Her hands, she notices, are raw again around the knuckle, and dry. Ammie catches it in hers, stroking the fingers against Libby's skin. Libby recoils at the sudden gesture. She doesn't take her hand away but Ammie feels the arm tighten. Something in her withdraws and Ammie's stomach plummets with the fear of having done the wrong thing.

'Sorry Libby – I didn't want ... it looks sore, that's all.'

'It's fine. It's healing.'

Ammie senses Finn's eyes dart from her face to Libby's.

'Leah's herbs. Are they working?'

Libby's eyes widen; more with guilt than surprise, Ammie thinks. Why is that? It's not as though Libby doesn't know where Ammie comes from. When she arrived she told Libby how Leah's letter was the beginning of the trail that led her from Marah, across the countryside until she reached the city and to Libby's apartment two flights up a tenement building. Libby had been open, and welcome. She pressed Ammie for details but never reciprocated. Libby helped Ammie shed her old life, offered clothes and talked her into swapping the shapeless pinafore for second-hand jeans that clung close to her legs and made her feel strange. But the one-sidedness strikes her now, with force. Ammie does not know Libby; does not know how she knows Leah. And because the information hasn't been offered freely, she's not even sure she should ask.

Libby's eyelids flicker. Her gaze shifts, avoiding contact with Ammie's face.

'The herbs, yes. They've helped.' Her words sound distant. Then her head swivels round to the window. 'The rain's stopped,' she says suddenly. 'What shall we do?'

Ammie thinks of the busy streets, the crowds, the allure of lights and the rich colours of the winter season that decorate each shop. For days, when she first arrived, she wandered, fascinated by the amount of things being sold, wanting to touch; one day, when she has found a job and a place of her own to live, she will own things. But today she wants more than anything to be away from crowds, away from all things that are unfamiliar. She wants to breathe, spin round with her arms outstretched, and to be able to see the sky. Since she arrived here, she has been less aware of the sky.

Ammie glances at the café window. It is running with condensation; and outside people are moving shapes, a blur of greys and dark blues on the high street. Soon, it will start to grow dark.

'Let's go somewhere quiet,' she says.

In the park the paths are lined with leaves, sodden and clinging together. They're lumped in a great mass, slimy brown with the odd shot of gold or red. Finn is ahead of them and Ammie watches as he balances on a low wall, one that borders the flower beds. Libby hooks her arm through Ammie's and they walk without speaking, watching and looking around them.

'You could do worse,' Libby says at last.

'Worse?'

Libby stops walking, nods towards Finn. 'Than him.'

Ammie's stomach turns. It is the queerest sensation; a rush of feeling that is at once anger, embarrassment and pleasure. Because she's pleased that Libby has noticed something. It makes it a possibility, something more tangible than a hope or a thought. She looks back at Finn, how he holds his arms wide in the air, starfish like. Behind him, the backdrop is of trees with branches stripped bare, a steel sky. For all the world, he looks as though he might be about to freefall through it.

He jumps suddenly off the wall and calls out to them, challenging them to a race. Ammie doesn't stop to think. She takes flight, leaving Libby behind her, crying out with laughing protest. Ammie picks up speed; her heart thuds, her hair blows out behind her. When she reaches Finn there's a pain in her chest so acute that she bends double, hands hipped, gasping air into her lungs. And in the next instant the three of them are laughing together, dancing, jumping in the leaves heaped up next to the path. Ammie remembers a moment from childhood: in the yard, bright confetti leaves floating towards her against the bluest sky.

Ammie stoops to the leaves around her now. They're soggy and cling to her but she ignores the wet sensation of them on her skin and scoops them up, gathering a bigger and bigger pile. Then she throws them into the air, mould and spores raining down on her, probably. But she doesn't care because they land on Libby and Finn, and the three of them are covered with sodden leaves, laughing.

At weekends they become three, together almost continually: Ammie, Libby, Finn.

Tonight they're in the sitting room, listening to music. Libby takes up the space on the sofa, so she and Finn lie on the floor, her head resting on his belly. When he speaks, she feels each word vibrate in the back of her skull. He's talking about jazz, about famous people with sonorous voices, long dead. It's new to her, still, this music. She finds herself moved and perplexed in equal measure by the clarity of its sound. The high notes come from a saxophone, she learns, and she tells him she'd love to find one, somewhere cheap, and learn to play it. He'll help her, he says; he'll learn alongside her. He'd love to.

Libby gets up from her prone position. The wine bottle is on the side table and she lifts it high to pour a refill. Her movements are so deliberate. When Libby raises her glass to toast the weekend, Ammie feels a stab of something she's missed: a lifetime of routines like this, weeks measured out by the units of days, the Mondays to Fridays; journeys to work; journeys home. The freedom of Friday and Saturday nights. In Marah, even when the tasks are so varied, the days all meld into one.

'Sure you won't have some, Ammie?' She feels the pull in her stomach at the directness of Libby's gaze, the grey of her eyes; a pull at the thought of the decision. Accept or refuse? She's afraid to drink it, of what it might do; but she wants Libby to like her, to approve.

Finn raises himself up onto elbows so that her head rolls away. 'Just a sip. Go on. It's Cava.'

Libby lumbers into the kitchen for a spare tumbler. The liquid has bubbles in. It's pale and inviting and celebratory. She raises it to her mouth, feels the effervescence on her lips; the newness of it, tastes the danger.

'It's bitter.' She pulls a face, and they laugh. She doesn't feel ridiculed, though. She's found that she likes it, her difference; she likes that they find it a novelty, that it makes them affectionate towards her.

'I can't believe you haven't tried it before.'

Ammie pauses. 'We just don't.' She bites her lip to prevent her from saying what she was going to say next: 'where I come from.' She's used the phrase too much lately, to explain, to justify. She senses Libby's weariness whenever she says it. Less and less, she wants to talk about Marah. It stings; the thought of everything she's left there. Her childhood. Tobias.

There's a pause. The three of them look at each other. 'What about you?' Finn directs his question at Libby. 'Did you drink? When you were young?'

'Oh, he always let me try. It was a way to get me out of his hair.'

'He?' Ammie is still piecing together this woman, this friend of hers, the one who's shown her the way here; who's given her, when she thinks about it, a new life.

'My dad.'

'Didn't your mother … ?'

Libby's response is too quick, the hurt too obvious. 'There wasn't one.'

Ammie is aware of the music shifting key. A woman's voice sings about dreaming a dream and in the background, there is the climbing scale of a trumpet. She'd like to talk to Libby about her best memories of Frania: the two of them working in the garden in Marah, the sun warming their skin and the sight of the hills through the open gateway beyond. What she wants to transmit to Libby is this: the preciousness of it, the being connected to a mother.

Libby waves her hand, dismissive. 'It's alright. I've got used to it. By my age, you have to.'

'Don't you … didn't you … miss it? Having a mother.'

Libby says nothing. From across the room Ammie takes in her downward glance, the motion of Libby bringing her glass to her mouth in a gesture of consolation. The slug she takes is deep and needy.

Finn stands up and moves across the room. The track has changed; it's a different singer now and Finn turns off the deep chocolate bass of his voice, searching for something else to play. For a minute all they hear is a clicking as he flips through the discs in the storage racks. Ammie watches his frown of concentration. What she admires is his sensitivity to the mood in a room, that instinctively he knows what to do. When he puts on the next tune, it takes a few bars for Libby to react. Another trumpet; the chime of something metallic in the background. Then a grin spreads across Libby's face. 'Night in Tunisia,' she says, euphoric with recognition. She starts to sway her hips. She crosses to Finn, grabs his hand and he responds, smiling.

Ammie feels the music resonate in her belly. She's felt this sensation before, the beat of the bodhrán on her Sealing day. Tobias's face as he whirled her round until her breath nearly gave out and she went spinning into the knot of women in the circle. The music that day: the reedy, Celtic pipes, the strings; a frantic beat. She remembers Tobias's breath against her neck, the smell of him.

Libby and Finn. They're in the centre of the room; eyes closed, together but not touching, bodies translating sound and rhythm into their own version of movement. They thread around each other in their dance, smiling lazy smiles and making eye contact. They're in the room with her; and yet their imaginations are elsewhere, somewhere exotic and colourful, amongst a swinging crowd. All Ammie can do is watch, envy their freedom, their lack of inhibition. It frightens her, what she's come to, who she'll become if she stays long enough in this city. A girl caught in a bubble, continually watching others. Unable to join them. Unable even to tap on the glass to call for help from outside.

Every day Libby leaves money on the kitchen table. Ammie plans a meal, shops and cooks. It's become a ritual, a daily challenge.

She still isn't easy being dependent on Libby. Libby dismisses her protests, saying how grateful she is to have someone keep the place clean, and good food to come home to. When Libby leaves in the mornings, Ammie feels a mixture of things: panic; loneliness, awareness of the long hours to fill before she returns. But there's pleasure, too, at simply occupying the space. Often, she walks through each room, breathing it in.

Today Finn is home first, and they eat alone. She watches how he takes in his food – quickly, with his head lowered, not even raising his eyes from the table. She still isn't accustomed to the speed at which people eat here, how rapidly mealtimes are over. He wears a necklace that swings forward as he eats, not a piece of jewellery as such but a leather lace strung through soapstone with a hole in the centre. His hair is fair, wiry and coarse; the softest wisps of it feather his cheeks, so blonde as to be imperceptible. There is something so fascinating about being loved by someone other than Tobias. She loves the unfamiliarity of Finn's gestures, how when he kisses her his hand curls round the back of her head and his fingers find the flesh on the back of her neck and stroke it. Her excitement exceeds her guilt. It allows her to push away all thoughts of Tobias, and home.

Finn pushes his plate away, and smiles. 'That was great, thanks.

You'll have to teach me how to cook it.'

'The mustard seeds are the important part.'

'Yeah?' He plays with the fork on his empty plate, turning it over and over. 'I thought they were a band.'

'What?'

'Joke.' He grins. 'It doesn't matter.' Ammie watches his eyes slide sideways to the clock, noting the time. He picks up the fork, turning and turning it again. He drops it in the end and it clatters against the plate. She winces and he apologises.

'When's Libby back?' he says.

Ammie stands, stacks the plates on top of the other, beginning to scrape the leftover scraps from her plate onto Finn's clean one. 'Late, I think. She's …'

'Let me do that.' He springs to his feet and she feels his hip brush against the top of her leg. The sudden contact is a shock; she freezes.

Finn puts down the plates. 'Ammie?'

Her words come from nowhere, not words she'd intended but prompted by the touch of his body and her own fear. 'I'm not sure any more, about this.'

The space between Finn's brows creases.

'Hey.' He comes closer. His hand goes to the space between her shoulder blades, fingers finding the flesh there, kneading it. She feels something release.

'I don't want to upset Libby.'

'Why would Libby be upset?'

'I don't know. She approves, I think … of, you know. Us. It's just that it all seems so … close.'

'I'm her lodger, not her lover.'

'It's not what I meant.'

'Then what?'

She's at a loss as to what to say: that though she wants to be with Finn, part of her isn't her own to give. That she's tired of living and loving someone under the gaze of other people. She wants privacy; she wants space.

Finn reaches for his jacket. For one wild moment Ammie thinks he is preparing to leave. She doesn't want him to. She wants to be here with him in Libby's apartment, even with the rusty stain on the ceiling above her bed, and the specks of mould in the bathroom.

He takes something from his pocket, holding it out to her, a small parcel wrapped in white tissue paper and tied with a gold bow. The paper is delicate; if she digs her fingernails into it, it will rip. It rustles as she fingers it.

'What is it?'

'Open it,' he says, nodding. His face has coloured and she can almost hear him holding his breath, waiting for her to open it, waiting to see how she will react. It's too much, suddenly, the thought of what he expects of her. She sits with it on her lap, stroking the paper still. 'It was my grandmother's. I think she'd be happy that I gave it to you.'

Ammie breathes in, a sharp intake.

'Oh.' The life goes out of Finn's face as it tightens. 'You don't want it?'

'I don't know what it is … '

'Please,' he whispers, 'open it.'

When the paper falls away she catches sight of something shiny, something that glints in the light of the bulb that hangs over the table. When she holds it up, she sees it is a butterfly, its wings studded with small white stones, so shiny, so bright.

'It's beautiful,' she breathes the word out. Finn smiles and takes it from her, putting his hand inside the neck of her shirt and pulling the fabric away from her skin so he can attach it to her. Ammie's neck is hot, she lifts the hair away from the nape of her neck, and there she is, pinned, decorated, with her scalp tingling at a memory: Rebecca's fingers moving around her head; the butterfly pins she pushed into her hair on their Sealing day.

Finn's eyes fill with tears. Ammie holds out her hand, puts it in his. When his arms fasten around her, she wonders how it might feel to stay. To build a life here, a future, without turn-taking or village ceremonies and looking after children that aren't her own. Maybe here – in this damp flat, with doors that stick and are grimy with age, with the windowless bathroom and the yellowing tiles – she has found a place where no one else is needed. There is only herself. And she wonders how it would feel to belong only to one person, to someone like Finn.

Ammie burrows into him, smelling the scent of him, so clean, so different from Tobias. He lifts her chin, kisses her and when his hand cups the back of her head, her insides explode in a rush of wanting. The tenderness is still there, but there is a stirring of something deeper, more base. Ammie pulls away suddenly. She needs to see him. He looks at her, open mouthed. He lets out a quiet groan and his eyes are wild, a mixture of confusion and desire. It makes her heady, seeing how much Finn wants her.

She smiles, a smile of permission. He gives a grateful sigh, and as his hands slide under her shirt and his fingers begin to seek out her breast – the nipple – she blocks out thoughts of Tobias, of Rebecca, of Marah so far away. There is only here, now: Libby's sitting room, Finn's tongue on her skin, the heat of her own human flesh.

*

Tobias has never been in City Square in the dark before. The tower with its thousands of tiny squares of light seems to stretch to the sky. Tobias's eyes follow it upwards. He thinks of the energy needed to power it; how their tiny hydro in Marah would creak under the strain.

The lighting of an empty building at night: it is just one of the things he finds it difficult to comprehend, such excess, the waste. His distaste – his separateness from it all – makes him feel like he is looking at a cold world as though through a pane of glass. Usually it doesn't matter; he is only a transient passenger on a journey, travelling through it. Now, if he is to find Ammie, he has to engage with it, become accustomed to it.

When he finds her, then what? Tobias doesn't know. He only hopes it will become clear, what he should do. What is best in the shifting circumstances he finds himself? He has two wives in two different places, young children, a responsibility to his community. But a deep desire, on some level, to be free.

The noise is incessant. It hit him as soon as he left the platform, walking through the lofty concourse of Central Station, caught up already in a throng of people; flanked by them, hemmed in on all sides. Down steps that smelt dank – of old urine and the sweat of bodies. The different coloured faces. One man's face was so black it seemed almost purple. And he's aware of them looking at him, too, curious perhaps at how he is dressed, his old-fashioned moleskin trousers, his waistcoat, his triple-cornered hat. This is not his first time in the city but whenever he returns, he might be discovering it all over again. He's forgotten the pulse of movement here, the pace of the place. And the smells. As he passes a food stand at the side of the street, his nostrils detect fried onions and fat, and charred animal flesh. He sees a hunk of meat turning on a spindle, the vendor slicing into it as it revolves. His stomach contracts, despite himself. He hasn't eaten since the morning.

From the square, he follows the crowd towards a sign that reads 'Subway', ducks under a concrete lintel and descends some steps. It is lit with long thin bulbs that are encased in plastic and spattered with flies. He steps onto a moving staircase, looks up, amazed at the height of it. Catches the faces of those travelling downwards; their blank stares. It makes him wonder about their lives – where they come from, what their homes are like. Everywhere, his eyes are assaulted. Coloured posters blazoned across walls; the garish clothes they wear, the things they carry. Plastic – everywhere. Shiny plastic in colours that cheer them, perhaps, see them through the winter.

Tobias reaches the top. There are gates here, barriers, and signs with the names of places he doesn't know – blue routes and green routes with diagrams and an endlessly moving list of times. He digs in his pocket for the address he'd copied out, his only clue as to where Ammie might be. People brush against him, irritated, jostling his elbow. He feels each contact like a shock. But he can't hold his ground, and he is pulled along in their flow. For a moment he looks around wildly as he is funnelled towards the yellow line, not knowing if this is the right place. Then he finds a pocket of empty space as the corridor opens out and he is deposited at the edge of the crowd, at the opening to a tunnel that branches off right. Tobias looks at the ground, littered with old tickets, empty packets. There is a heap of blankets, red with a border of gold and purple, seemingly abandoned but stark against the grey of the floor.

Stepping closer, Tobias is about to pick it up. Something under it moves and he jumps back. What emerges is a grey face, grubby, bearded, and ingrained with dirt.

'You want – what? To take?' The man's face voice comes out broken, cracked.

'No, no, I ... I was just ...'

'Don't touch my stuff.'

'Sorry.' Tobias backs away. He's acutely aware of not knowing the spatial codes of this place, what's permissible and what isn't. He forgets, each time he arrives here. People's proximity to each other, the distance you have to keep. It's as though each person is surrounded by a force field, which no one is permitted to penetrate.

He wants to get away now, is about to head into the right-hand corridor when he hears the voice behind him. 'Wait!' Tobias turns and the man is standing with the blankets pulled around him, his hands clutching them up near his chest. 'You are a stranger here?'

Something like relief floods through him – at a brief moment of empathy from this man, who is dishevelled and homeless and has no conception of what life is like for him.

Tobias returns to the man. Close up, he has remarkable eyes, astonishingly blue and yet covered with a fine film of white, a milky substance. Tobias has never seen anything like them before.

'A stranger?' Tobias says. 'Yes. And no.'

'Tell me.'

It strikes Tobias that what is being offered is a tacit exchange: the man is offering kindness in return for a story. What could Tobias say? He thinks of Goran's hardened features when Tobias told him that, since they had no word from Ammie, he had no choice. To follow her, Goran said, would be the will of man usurping the will of God. He spoke of the dangers of Lot that Tobias would no doubt encounter if he went to the heart of the city with only a few details from a letter that might lead nowhere.

But Tobias doesn't see danger. All he sees in this vagrant is a desire to connect. He is not like the traders Tobias meets at craft fairs. He has nothing to take, and nothing to give.

The man senses Tobias's hesitation. 'You afraid?'

Tobias looks around him, at the fast-moving throng. There is nowhere else to go. He could move on, pretend he had never met this man. Or he could trust him.

'It's just that it's different. From where I come from.'

The man almost doubles with laughter. Tobias wonders for a moment whether he is drunk. He hadn't picked up that sour smell on his breath but he is unhinged in that way Tobias has seen before with others, after the fairs.

'Yes. For me too – when I came. Difference everywhere. Confusing. Come …' He indicates Tobias to come closer. When he steps up to him he sees the deep lines cutting into his forehead, the untidy hair of the beard that covers most of his face.

'So why you here?'

Why, he thinks? Why am I here? Chasing a dream, or a memory. A desire. But he has to find her; he can't settle until he has, until he knows her intentions.

'I'm looking for someone.'

The man leers at him. 'A girl?'

'Yes,' he says, then swallows. 'My wife.'

Tobias remembers the Polaroid, pushed deep into his pannier. The man is patient while he digs around and finds it. Somehow it is important. He may have seen her; may be able to help. Tobias holds out the picture. He watches the man's grimy finger trace the shape of Ammie's face. Tobias feels not irritated, or even proprietorial, but oddly moved.

The man's face takes on a serious expression. 'Losing a wife in the city – it is not good. Anything could happen.'

Again that fear assaults him, the crowding in of images: Ammie's fair skin ruptured with a knife; her body mangled as she is hit by a speeding car. He can't stop them. They undo him.

'My friend. Do not be a slave to your imagination.' The man touches his arm. The blanket moves; underneath Tobias sees the frayed sleeve of a jacket and, to his amazement, something gold that holds together the sleeves of the shirt. 'You are by foot?'

'I only have …' Tobias thinks of the rumpled note in his pocket.

112

'There's a – the name of a street.'

'Let me see.' The man brings the paper up to his nostrils, almost as though he is trying to smell out the details written on it. Tobias watches his eyes roll in their sockets as he tries to read. There's a pause and Tobias thinks that he can't see. But then the man turns to face him.

'I know where this is, which quarter. I take you to the train?'

Tobias takes a breath, looks around him. He sees a wall of tiles with dirt ingrained in the grouting. He breathes the hot smutty smell of the subway passageways, diesel fuel, bodies. It is stale, here, with the air of too much breath breathed in, nothing like home, its clarity after the rain.

Tobias looks at the man with the milky eyes, and nods.

The man's name is Thebes and while they wait together, he points out the route on the wall on the platform, making sure Tobias knows where to get off. The train comes to its rushing stop, Tobias gets on and at the last minute – just before the automatic door pulls closed – Tobias feels the rasping touch of Thebes' skin and something being thrust into his hand. Tobias stands with astonishment, watching Thebes on the platform, grinning and then making, from forehead, across his shoulders to his heart, the ancient sign of the cross.

When he has found a seat, Tobias looks at the gift he has been given. When he uncurls his palm there's a coin, of much greater value, he is sure, than Thebes can afford. Tears spring to his eyes. Through the blur, he tries to make out the miniature version of the map, above the door. Three stops. Tobias looks again at the paper and tries to memorise what Thebes told him. Right out of the station, straight ahead, right again. Right, straight, right: Tobias murmurs it like an incantation.

He leans back in his seat and feels something hard against his thigh. There's a book wedged into the space between the seat and the window. Tobias holds it in his hands, unsure what to do with it. If it has been left by a traveller they might never see it again. Was there someone at a station to hand it to? But he's afraid to stop to talk with the people in uniforms he's seen at the barriers. He's sure they won't listen to him, or else think him suspicious.

Tobias looks at the cover. It shows a red sunrise or sunset, a black silhouette of a man, and words written in bold white letters across the top: *The Dispossessed*.

Something tugs at his insides, a yearning.

Possessions. Those Tobias has, here in the city, are numbered: a ragged piece of paper with an address written on it; a grainy photograph, cracking from so much folding. Should he add to it the book – something that someone somewhere has written for pleasure, and with the intention of giving pleasure?

He knows he has to keep it.

His stomach churning, he looks around the carriage to see if anyone is watching. His hands tingle with excitement, and with the sense of something illicit; he has never read anything like it before. He turns the pages quickly, and words stand out in bold at the top of the page: Anarres, Urras. His eyes run down the page, looking for things that might be familiar. There are marks in margins and places where the page has been folded over. He has a sudden desire to devour the whole story.

The train lurches to a stop. Tobias looks up quickly, trying to ascertain the name of the station. It's the one he needs, the one that is only a street away from Ammie's house. Quickly, he stuffs the book into his pannier. He slings the bag over his shoulder and makes for the door of the train. Negotiating the gap between carriage and platform, Tobias is thrust again into the heat and noise of the subway, and follows the signs to the exit.

When he reaches the Northern Quarter, Tobias checks the address. He knows this is the right apartment block, yet there's still a wrenching in his guts. In front of him is a row of illuminated buzzers, eight in all. Each bears a name: Montefiore, Jacobs, Audel. At the last one, he feels a pulse, a shiver of familiarity at the combination of vowels and consonants. He knows this name.

He's aware of the insistence of his finger pressing the button. For a moment there's no response. There can't be anyone home. Then there's a crackling sound, a click. And a voice. One word: 'Yes?' It's a hard voice, urban, slightly breathless. He thinks of someone well groomed and always in a hurry. He wonders how Ammie has come to know this person, surely so different from anyone they know in Marah.

Tobias explains what he wants. He's aware of the street noise behind, of competing with the traffic as he speaks. He's embarrassed by the public nature of it all. And he's irritated by this barrier, this device which conveys sound but not meaning. It's disembodied. He can't see the woman's face.

There's a pause at the other end. A low buzz. He wonders if she's cut him off. But it continues and he realises that the door in front of him has loosened. It's the sound of it opening.

Inside, the lobby is dark. It takes a moment for his eyes to adjust, then he realises there are blue lamps on the sides of the walls, lighting the way up. He finds the stair-rail. Whenever he's pictured this moment, his belly has always knotted up, yet now he feels light, insubstantial, as though there's no connection between body and emotion. Amarantha, here, after all this time. He fumbles forward, losing his way momentarily in the dark, trips on an object, something – a stray shoe – left on the bottom step. He picks it up, runs his fingers over canvas fabric, a white rubberised toe. The laces are frayed. He doesn't even know if it belongs to a man or a woman. He wonders how Ammie would look wearing it and finds that he can't imagine it. What did she wear in Marah: clogs, like the children? Heeled boots like the women? Tobias places the shoe back on its step.

He begins his ascent. He's aware of a sound above him, right at the top. In the next moment there's a shift in the light and his way is illuminated more clearly. He sees the detail of the banister work, the cheap wood carved into spindles. He sees shadows of patterns on the tiles, passes the doors to other apartments with their umbrella stands outside, their tangle of shoes and toys on doormats. He hears a voice that is clear, distinct. Deeper than Ammie's.

'Hello? Are you there?'

He doesn't know how to answer, doesn't know where he has reached in relation to her. From the sound of her voice, she is right at the top.

'I'm here,' he says.

Tobias continues upwards. The hand-rail guides him as he walks, as he feels his way to the top like a blind man. Then it becomes brighter. There's a square of stained glass at the top, a roof light guiding him upwards. But when he looks again, he realises it has been decorated with a sheet of stick-on plastic, which is beginning to peel. He swallows hard, sick at the thought of its cheapness, the artifice.

He rounds a corner, nearly at the top.

The girl leans against the doorframe. She is dressed in black, except for a vibrant scarf knotted around her shoulders. Her hair is dark and loose, her arms folded.

'You're Tobias.'

'How do you know?' He's in front of her now, not sure whether to shake her hand, in the way that strangers do here. In the end, he stands with his arms stiff by his sides.

'I just know.'

'Is she here?'

'Ammie?'

He feels a rush of irritation at the way she mirrors his questions, as though she's playing with him, as if she might be deliberately delaying things. All this way he's come, the journey, the seeking; all he wants now is to see her, hold her. His eyes skim past the girl, into the apartment behind, but he can't make anything out, just the gloom of an unlit hallway.

'What if I said she wasn't here? Would you go back?'

It's a test, he thinks. The mocking smile on her face. He feels the beginnings of a twitching in the nerve below his eye. Please, he thinks, please. Let me see her.

'Is she here? She must be.' The paper is still in his pocket, the address like a compass. He touches it now.

'Of course she's here.' The girl starts to laugh. 'Where else would she be?'

She uncrosses her arms and takes a step forward, holds out her hand. Tobias takes it; the fingers are cool and he's aware of her eyes sliding over him. He's aware suddenly, acutely, of how he's dressed. But then he focuses on her. Close up, she's not a girl at all. There are the beginnings of lines around her eyes, hints of grey in the dark brown of her hair. It's her figure and demeanour that are girlish. She could pass for five, even ten years younger.

'I'm Libby.'

'Can I see her?'

'Are you going to take her away?'

'I just want to see her.'

A noise in the background, the opening of a door. Tobias looks up and hears a movement in the hall, sees the shadow of a presence there.

'Ammie?'

In that moment he hates Libby. He wants her somewhere else, away from this hallway so that it can be just him and Ammie, alone in this corridor and the strange half light.

Ammie moves into the doorway.

The first emotion he's aware of is shock. She's wearing trousers – the uniform of so many of the girls on the streets here – and a close-fitting shirt that shows the shape of her breasts. Her hair is also loose. She has lost weight. He feels his throat constrict; the echo of a sob at the back of it. Relief, anxiety.

Ammie turns to Libby. Something passes between them, something like regret or understanding. Libby looks at him then, shrugs, smiles; it's a kind of welcome, an acceptance. All he wants is to touch Ammie, absorb her. But he can't. Not with Libby looking on like this; not when he doesn't know if Ammie wants that too. She ran away. What if she won't have him now? Now that he's here, now he can see her, his arms are heavy with the loss of her, with the anticipation of her presence, her solid bodily self.

Ammie steps towards him. 'Tobias …'

Her words are lost as they cling together. He holds her, as though to inhale her, to fold her into him completely. As though to make up for the days without her, and replace her body in the gaps of his memory. Tears course down his cheeks but he doesn't care. He doesn't care that this moment of reunion didn't happen how he wanted, that it has taken place on a strange stairwell in the city, witnessed by a stranger. He's here, with her. For now, this – her body, her self – is his home.

Ammie and Tobias have managed, finally, to wrest themselves from bed. They've left behind the confines of the apartment, the Northern Quarter and its occupants, to which they've confined themselves the last two days. It's a steady climb up the embankment but from the top it is possible to see the pulsing heart of Lot's central districts and the suburbs flung beyond. The landscape is bare but not desolate; in the foreground, thin skeletons of trees cling to the hillside. The buildings rise from the valley basin, the slanting afternoon light making them oddly beautiful – their silvers, blues, slate greys.

Ammie is crouching to look at something, the bold red of her jacket standing out against the winter ground. She is child-like in her focus, examining the intricate patterns of ice crystals. When she looks up at him, smiling, it cuts into him: the realisation that he might have lost her for good, his agony of waiting swept away by the sweetness of reconciliation – that first night.

Now, they are in a kind of hiatus. Tobias feels they're drifting on the tide of the days. Part of him treasures this time; but he also knows that he needs resolution. To stay, or return? They both need to address the question. Filling their days with pleasure, they've been deferring the decision. He's been deferring other things too: asking questions about the lodger whose clothes are scattered around the place, whose razor has a place on the bathroom shelf. Tobias doesn't want to think about what other claims he has on the place.

Ammie is beside him now, reaching for him. He moves to embrace her. Every time he touches her, he has a sense of homecoming. All the other doubts are forgotten.

'The waiting's over,' he says, more to himself than to her. His lips are close to the crown of her head, his words muffled. 'I waited so long for this.' He holds her tighter, slips his hand under the layers of clothes until he finds warm flesh at her waist, her hip, her sacrum. 'All the time you were away, I didn't stop thinking about you.'

'You missed me?' She pulls away and he sees her face, coy and teasing.

'You know I did.'

'Then catch me.'

She breaks free with one clean movement and heads further into the woods. Tobias follows, chest aching from the effort, breath sharp in his lungs. Quickly, she doubles back. She laughs as she runs, goading him. He speeds his pace and runs, snatching at her as the wind sweeps across the valley. It's strong enough to knock the breath from him. But with his arms around her, still laughing, he feels solid, complete. *If you evade suffering you also evade the chance of joy.* The words he'd read had astonished him; he'd been amazed at their rightness and how they spoke to his condition. Standing now with Ammie on the hillside, they are once again resonant and alive.

Their breathing slows. Ammie has stopped laughing. Her hand is icy as it moves under his shirt and across his back but he feels the blood pounding in his ears. They won't need to wait for the proximity of bed because how right it would be, he thinks, to consummate everything here in the open, despite the cold air; high above the city with no sound but the wind in the branches and the far-off cry of the birds.

Afterwards, Tobias watches Ammie move above him, shaking her garments free of dead leaves and twigs, dressing again in a hurry. Those small gestures – inconsequential but so filled with significance, with the absolute presence of her – are what he missed most. He rolls onto his front, puts his head between his arms and breathes in the smell of raw earth. Soon he'll need to move but for now he wants to savour this: their intimacy, this ground, high up and away from the rest of the world.

'Do you like being here, Tobias?' Ammie's words are sharp, jolting him away from his thoughts.

'It's …' He pauses, surprised by the sudden question. 'I'm finding it – disorientating.'

He rises to his feet, begins to pull on his underpants, his trousers. His temperature has dropped quickly; he needs to put his clothes back on.

'You're different here.'

'Am I?' He can't disguise the anger in his voice. He's been patient with her, not pressuring her. Now she's accusing him of something that she isn't making clear. She leans against a tree. 'I don't know you.'

'What do you mean?'

Ammie bites her lip. 'You're so fearful. The way you look at me. You take my hand every time we cross the street, like I'm a child. And with Libby – you're so … closed.'

'I'm not sure what to say. It's difficult. I feel – out of place.'

'Why? You go away from Marah all the time.'

Something in him snaps, then – anger at her inability to empathise. 'Why do you think? You've made a life here – one that doesn't include me. You don't try to help me fit in.' He's shouting. He didn't intend that. He tries lowering his voice. 'I don't have a relationship with Libby. Or with him. Finn.'

The night of Tobias's arrival. The way Finn looked at him, then at Ammie, before he left the room. It set something churning in Tobias's guts. Now, he knows, he has not been giving Ammie space to talk about him because he's been too fearful to ask.

Ammie pushes away from him, begins to pace between the trees. To the oak and back; to the rowan, back. He wants to catch her by the wrists to make her stop. He is shocked by the extent of his irritation and the thought that he might actually, at this moment, want to inflict pain.

'I need you,' she says. Her words are mangled, come out in a half sob. 'I need you to be strong.'

Tobias feels a rush of sympathy, protectiveness; he's forgotten how young she is, how heady and exciting but confusing this all must have been for her. He tries to take her hand. She moves it away but the gesture is gentle, not snatched. When she looks at him again, her face is stricken.

'I don't know what to do,' she says. Her eyes fill with tears. 'I'm pregnant, Tobias.' Her chest heaves with the effort to breathe. 'I can't believe it.'

It's so unexpected – that now, when there are so many paths in front of them – Marah or the city; staying or returning – that there should be this thing that complicates everything. Tobias feels like he's slipping down the embankment, away from her. His life, his future, sliding out of reach.

For a moment her dark eyes meet his but he can't read them. Then her gaze is fixed on the ground, and her words tumble out so rapidly he can hardly hear them.

'If it had happened before ... But here, everything's moving so fast – I've been hiding here. Pretending there was no other way.'

There is another way, he wants to say; there are so many ways. He can't imagine that it would be anything but together. But Tobias has swung between the resolve to return and the decision to stay so many times that he no longer knows what is best. There are so many factors – Rebecca, his daughters, his father, the village. And now, here, too, another layer of responsibility: this child.

She reaches for him and fastens her hands around his neck. He feels the cold touch of them on his nape, warm under so many layers. She finds him out, always, finds out his weaknesses and how he can be moved. He is shaking, he realises.

He closes his eyes. More than anything, he knows, he wants to be with her. He doesn't want to think about the future or the past. Or whose child she is carrying; the shadow of the possibility that it might not be his.

When he looks again he sees the city in the dusk, a bird moving against the skyline. It could be a miracle, he thinks, out here with all this noise, this traffic, pollution: a swallow, ageless and weightless, soaring and floating with the breeze.

Tobias looks up, imagining that he himself is riding the thermals; high above the city, in control of the wind.

It's almost dark when they come down the hillside. They approach the city from the east. Tobias is amazed by the difference between the Northern Quarter and this one; the houses are more cramped here, with narrower spaces in between. There is so much more colour in the facades of the buildings, the clothes of the inhabitants; their faces. They're animated, talk more with their hands; stand in groups in the street, talking. The shops are open, even at this time – newsagents, brightly lit grocery stores, their shelves loaded extravagantly with tins, vegetables stacked in boxes. Tobias smells, through an open doorway, something frying. Chicken, he thinks, and spices. His gut churns; he's hungry.

They find a café tucked away in a back street. The food is good and plentiful but neither of them has much appetite. When they leave, Ammie places a handful of coins and notes in a saucer. Something tugs at him, wondering what she might have done in exchange for the money.

He tries to shake the gloom that has descended on him. Now, while they're in the open and away from the others, now is when they should talk. There should be only the truth – no more secrets, no more procrastination. But Ammie closed herself off from him as soon as they finished making love.

They turn down a narrow street. Ammie takes his hand. It is tentative, a gesture of reconciliation. But now that the shock of the news has worn off, Tobias's mind dwells on the questions: how do they resolve this? Lot, or Marah? Might there be a middle ground: like Aroer, not the city but less remote than they're used to? The more he thinks, the more labyrinthine it becomes. At each turn, he reaches an impasse. He has the skills and knowledge to make a living here. It would be so much less complex: he and Ammie, and the child. And yet. He can't turn his back on Rebecca and abandon the girls. He can't imagine returning home with a pregnant Ammie – whose child, it's possible, might not be his – and pretend that nothing has changed.

Ask her the question. Whose is the child?

Ammie's hand is firm in his; she leads him through a connected series of alleyways. He's astonished that she has grasped the geography of the place so quickly. He is only aware of the darkness, the smell of damp and the narrowness of the walls. He has a sudden, fleeting image of home, the open vistas of the hills from Goran's atrium, the way the sky opens up as though pulling you into the future. Something grips him, a sudden, painful sense of having lost something. Coming here, he has given up these things.

He stops dead.

'Tobias?' She pulls on his hand.

'I can't.'

'You're not in pain?'

Pain. It is pain; a sort of paralysis. But he can't describe the pressure that bears down on him, as though everything is shifting inwards.

She rips her hand from his. 'For God's sake!'

The words ring out in the alleyway. It is not the irritation in her voice that shocks him most but her use of the word she knows will hurt him.

God. It is so deliberate, so flagrant.

In the distance, there is shouting. Ammie hears it too, and freezes. The noise comes closer and they turn to see where it's coming from. Automatically, she heads towards it. He calls out to her – Ammie, no – but she's moving to the end of the alleyway and he has no choice but to follow.

The alleyway gives onto a small square with a fountain. The only light comes from a café bar, its awning extended outwards and metallic tables and chairs in front. At first Tobias is aware only of sound – a table being knocked over, the smashing of crockery and glass and a crunching as they are trampled on. There are guttural noises, grunts. It takes him a moment to realise that they accompany the blows of fists or kicks. Metal on bone. Tobias shivers. It is unbearable.

He senses the movement before he sees it, in the half light: a bundle of bodies, men rolling over each other, towards the fountain. When they come to a stop one of them staggers to his feet, uttering obscenities. There's a pause, the length of a couple of breaths; a movement, a protest, the battering of a head into stone. Then a terrible cracking that rings through the night.

Tobias wants to cover his ears. He knows he will never erase what he has witnessed. It will taint everything else that has happened today: the view of the city from a height, the graceful swooping of a swallow; Ammie's yielding body, the news that she is pregnant.

Lot, or Marah?

They stand in the shadows, he and Ammie, watching with a horrible, unreal detachment as the men walk away. The victim is still on the ground. The waiter from the bar rushes out from the doorway, incredulous, worried. Already, he's shouting inside for someone to call the emergency service.

In a moment, they should move – see if they can help, say what they witnessed.

Tobias turns to Ammie. She holds her hand over her mouth and he hears her breathing, panicky and shallow. He thinks suddenly of the child inside her, of protection, and fear, and the intense love it will engender. And of words he has read, echoing over and over, in his head. He clings to them now, to drown out the fear, to obscure the acts of violence he has just seen.

Pleasure. Suffering.
Homecoming.
Joy.

MARAH

After a winter of lying dormant, the Aroer valley was coming to life. If you stopped long enough you'd see a swallow darting between the trees, on the hunt for twigs. You would notice pale green buds on the branches, which would soon unfurl into leaves. Drizzle in the air, like the lightest chiffon scarf.

There was movement, too, along the roads below the town: a motorcycle picking its way through the lanes, heading deep into the countryside. The noise disturbed the tranquillity of the place but the driver was not immune to the beauty around him. He was captivated by the light moving through the trees above him and in front of him. Even though he was wearing a helmet he swore he could taste the rain on his tongue, like a benediction.

In Aroer, they had given him directions. He stopped from time to time, in a lay-by or at the entrance of a field, to check his map. When he reached the fork in the road he stopped. He had left behind the town a long time ago and was high on the hillside now, looking down; below him the valley spread out like a ribbon of green; the river, the woodland and – there in the distance – the settlement he was searching for: Marah. The beauty of the valley stirred something in him. He had been curious to see it for a long time. He had heard much about the people who settled here. At one time, he had known some of them well. For a moment he stood, looking down on it, swaying slightly on his heels. He wished – only for the briefest moment perhaps – that all those years ago, he had decided things differently. The man thought about the reason he had come. He took a breath, replaced his helmet, kicked the starter motor and moved off.

*

Frania was in the schoolroom, reading the morning's story to the younger ones, when she heard it. The distant sound of something motorised; a vehicle. It took her back to the city, the visceral memory of crowded streets and the smell of fumes from passing buses.

She held her breath, sure it could mean only one thing. *Julius.*

125

The children reacted instantly, twisting round to look at each other, eyes widening with curiosity – in some cases, with fear. Frania reassured them but felt a tightening pressure in her forehead, nonetheless.

Rebecca appeared from behind the partition, where she had been coaching the older children in grammar. 'Perhaps we should go and see?' she said.

It wasn't what Frania had imagined for their reunion.

On the porch, the children crowded behind them. But there wasn't anything to see. No sign of a car, of anything other than the usual view from the schoolroom: the Meeting House and Congregational Hall across the Piece, the edge of the gardens surrounding it. Around the houses, Frania saw others coming out of the houses to check on the source of the noise; the Cuthberts across the grass, Micah, standing as though far off, with his hands on the rails of the porch.

Frania tried to guess what she'd heard; she could just make out the shape of something metallic behind a tree at the far edge. It was a motorcycle. She saw a movement, someone in black walking across the Piece. One of the children saw it too, and nudged the others and there was a minor explosion of chatter and questions. At that distance it was impossible to see. Frania held back the impulse to run into the middle of the Piece to meet him. Not here she thought, not in front of the others. She wished he had chosen a better time to arrive.

Then, as the figure grew nearer, she realised. It wasn't Julius at all.

For an instant the world seemed to tilt. Frania gripped the handrail and when she refocused Rebecca was watching, a question in her eyes. Frania shook her head and the look of sympathy on Rebecca's face brought ready tears.

Closer, he came. He had a lilting gait she would recognise anywhere. It was Jude. Jude dressed in black, come to the village. He had come, no doubt, to see her.

The pain in Frania's head intensified and she saw the dark spots at the edge of her vision. Her stomach fluttered wildly. What had happened? Had something happened to Julius, that Jude was here in his place?

Jude was smiling as he walked across the grass, raising his hand to wave to the children. Some of them clapped, as though he were putting on a performance. Frania was aware of Rebecca at her side, hesitating, anxious about restoring some order and calm to the children. But it was a matter of moments before Jude was there in front of them. They looked down at him from the steps of the porch, saw the thinning hair that was pulled back into a ponytail and the patches of skull through the places where it was showing through. The black clothes he was wearing were leather. She had not seen leather worn in that way for a long time.

She almost stumbled down the steps to meet him. 'Is Julius ...?'

'He couldn't come.'

'But he's alright?'

Frania sensed a moment's hesitation, a brief flicker in Jude's eyes. He nodded. 'He is.'

Frania looked around her, not wanting to talk in full view of the children and the whole of the village, in fact. She didn't want to go to the woods – it would take too long and she wanted to know immediately why he was here. In the end she led him to the back steps of the Meeting House.

Still, her body felt charged with adrenalin. Something wasn't right. 'Then why are you here?'

Jude's smile was indolent. He stepped forward and touched her lightly on the face. It felt like an invasion. She brushed his hand away quickly. She couldn't bear his games.

'Jude? Please. Just tell me.'

He looked at her thoughtfully. 'I've got something for you. A note. It's all in there.'

The sound of the zip as he unfastened his jacket, a sound she'd forgotten. With his movement, she caught the whiff of engine oil and old leather. Jude removed something from his pocket, an envelope; it was virgin, had nothing written on it, not even her name. Instructions, she thought, his plans. After weeks of waiting she'd finally hear when he was coming. Soon.

She stared at it for a while, put it into her pocket. When she first came here, she continued to wear her city clothes but now her pregnancy was advancing, the pinafores suited her perfectly. She'd been given an old one of Leah's in dark grey.

Frania caught Jude scrutinising her stomach now. When she caught his eyes, he looked away, scanned the hills in the background. 'You know I could have been here too?'

'What?'

'I was part of the group. With Leah and Goran, and the rest of them. Did Julius not tell you?'

No. He didn't. Why didn't you?

He fumbled in his pocket and brought out a packet of cigarettes, some matches. For one delirious moment, she remembered the rush of that first inhale. Then she thought of the baby. Jude cupped his hand around his mouth, screwing up his eyes, and lit it.

'She was a child when I left,' he said.

Frania raised her eyebrows, quizzical.

'Rebecca – she's grown into a fine woman.'

'It's only a matter of time before she'll be called to be Sealed.'

'Sealed?' The tone of his voice was mocking. Even though there were things about this place, these people, about which she wasn't sure, she felt herself wanting to defend them. Again and again, she had wondered what would happen when Julius came. Could they continue as they were? Would they be allowed to live in the caravan at the edge of the village, to contribute to the work even though their spiritual beliefs were different?

It occurred to her now that when Julius arrived, things might shift. She hadn't ever thought about the prospect of sharing him with another wife.

Jude leaned against the Meeting House wall.

'How do you manage here?' He took a draw on the cigarette, screwed up his face and picked at something, a stray piece of tobacco. 'It's so isolated.'

She felt a sharp jab from her baby, a heel or an elbow high up in her womb. 'It's a shock,' she said, 'you coming here. I'd forgotten how noisy it can be – all those engines. Here, if we go anywhere, we take the horses.'

'You miss it?'

The breeze caught Frania's face. She brushed it back, looking around, inhaling the freshness of it, the smell of the recent rain and the background scent of hyacinths.

'Actually, I don't.'

'You're welcome to it,' he said.

When he'd gone Frania sat on the hillside, holding the letter in her hand. She had read it so many times. If she let go, it would have been whipped away by the spring breeze and Julius's words would be gone as though she'd never received them – blowing around amidst the trees, perhaps, or coming to rest in a river or a stream. The ink would dissolve as though the words had never existed.

Such words. She never thought she would receive them. *Proximity to anyone suffocates me. You can't imagine. It's difficult to describe. I thought with you it was different but now with time to reflect ...*

Julius wasn't coming. Oh, he'd meant to, he said. He really had. But now he couldn't.

And there she was, with their child on the way. His words would never dissolve. Now they were swimming and blurred in front of her eyes but now that she had read them, they would never go away. They would mark her life forever: Julius wasn't coming. He didn't love her, not enough.

Frania looked over the valley. From here she could see the road snaking through the bottom of it, where Jude was already on his way back to the city, to the life he had always known. She wondered what words he would take back to Julius to describe her: ripe, beautiful, close to her time. Whether, closing his eyes, he would be able to see her in his mind's eye; and whether he would regret his decision.

She could never persuade him out of it. Because now she saw that it would always have been like this, that she had been deluded thinking she could ever snare him. That he could live here, so far from the stimulus of the city. His talk had been empty; now her life would be empty of him.

Frania's gaze moved to the gardens. She couldn't make out who it was moving between the rows of vegetables, hoeing or clearing the ground for more planting. Frania thought of how things always continue: seed is sown, it is helped to nurture, it produces fruit. The dying back, in readiness to repeat the cycle. She lowered her head into her arms, and wept.

When Tobias and Ammie reach Marah, there's no welcoming party. They haul themselves over the final field into the village, along the footpaths of the gardens, backs and necks aching from the weight of their baggage. Standing on the Piece they are suddenly overwhelmed to be here; that they have made it on foot from Aroer in such wintry weather. The landscape is white and clean, and it as though all their memories of the place are buried underneath.

No one knew of their homecoming, just as no one in the city knew of their departure. It was best that way. They had left hurriedly, crossing Lot before dawn. The night before they left, they slept fitfully. Tobias fell repeatedly into a dream of being attacked by alley walls. As they bore down on him, they sprouted knives that slashed at his skin, baring muscle and bone. He woke sweating, and sobbing, and Ammie held him. Only when he slept again did she allow herself to weep, thinking of all she was leaving behind – Libby, Finn, a home in the city, a life of freedom.

For Tobias there was no choice. He couldn't live with what the fear would force him to become.

Amarantha's decision had been determined by a photograph. She found it the day after the fight, tucked into the inside pocket of Tobias's jacket, a long ago image of herself in the woods, a girlish and sentimental smile on her face. What she saw was not a picture cracked from so much folding, but the future, lovingly held and often caressed, that her husband kept next to his heart.

*

Sitting at her kitchen table, Rebecca works through a list. The children have long since gone to bed, and she must spend tonight planning: December's lessons as well as the communal meetings, the chores, the meals, the Christmas duties. She works methodically, checking off each task, scheduling it, making a note here and there in her journal. There's a pull of pain in the middle of her forehead. Too much frowning, she thinks, as she catches sight of her reflection in the uncurtained window, far off and desolate.

She has spent too much time alone these past weeks. In Tobias's absence, what else was there to do? Leah stepped in with practical help. Her mother, too. But it was Rebecca who guided the family, deftly and single-handedly, through the days. It was only in the darkness that Rebecca woke with a clenching sensation in her stomach. His absence. Her aloneness. She would curl into a ball in the wide bed and try not to let memories assault her: Tobias's face as he left her but also, from childhood, the strength of her father's hand in hers, his pained expression when he was arrested. So many years ago.

Rebecca has been strong. Now she wonders if it has been a mask, merely to disguise her weakness.

And now that they're back: is she strong or is she weak?

Rebecca pushes back the chair, and stands up. She must check the bread. It should have thirty more minutes to bake, which means she has to stay and finish the notes and lists. She wants the solace of bed. The ache in her calves has become almost unbearable. The fact that Tobias is back, but she still has to share him is also unbearable. Her mind runs over those moments of his return: Naomi coming to fetch her, shouting that Papa was home.

Running towards the Piece, her heart soaring with the realisation of love for him. The relief rising in her throat telling her she will appreciate him more now, that time has done so much to knit them together – she and Tobias – through the years and the children they share.

Seeking out his face, from those crowding around him – his parents, brother, Per and Lucia, all embracing him in welcome. Seeking out his face and seeing the expression on it, the joy bubbling up in his eyes and feeling the surety of his arms again.

Opening her eyes and seeing Ammie. A sinking sensation, like the weight of a stone being thrown into the river. Ammie here, Ammie returned.

She wonders now if it's Ammie who gave him the book. Was she the one who had scored under the sentences Rebecca read and re-read for them to make sense? Rebecca found it a few days after his return, stuffed into the arm of the chair in his study, as though Tobias had not intended her to see it. With all its fine words, its talk of pleasure and joy and being complete, she wanted to tear it, piece by piece, and throw it onto the fire.

She wanted to make a pyre of its pages.

The bread. Rebecca opens the door of the oven. She eases the loaves out of their tins and knocks at the hollow centre. There is no need, she thinks, to consign Tobias's book to the flames. Its words sear through her already, as though she has been branded. She burns enough already, with desire for what she doesn't have, and never will: knowledge, freedom. The whole of Tobias's heart.

*

At Advent supper, Tobias surveys his family around the table, grateful for his return, grateful for this occasion. It pleases him, all of it: the rich smell of cooking that fills the house, and warms it; the way the table is set, the earth tones of the napkins contrasting with the white linen, vases of flowers in burnt orange and yellow, branches of greenery with smatterings of berries. Ammie's work, he thinks, surely. She has such an eye for colour.

What pleases him most is the sight of so many of them round the table – the girls, Goran and Leah, his wives – and the thought of Rebecca and Ammie working together once again. Rebecca would have been busy with the chopping, rolling, baking; the pastry and pie making. He thinks of Ammie decorating the table, moving one way then the other around it, standing back and squinting as though to gauge the pairings of colours and textures. When he thinks of that, he knows he is home.

Tobias smiles around the table at them, at Martha's flushed cheeks, Esther's bubbling enthusiasm; the earnest expression in Naomi's gaze. 'Shall we light the candle?'

Esther's words tumble out, unchecked. 'Can I, Papa – please?'

Tobias picks up the taper. He strikes a match, lights it and holds it in front of him for a moment. Then he looks at Ammie. 'Amarantha? Would you like to?'

He notices Rebecca's hand move from the table to rest on her lap. She bites her lip, and turns towards him with an accusatory look on her face. He knows he should have consulted her first; the lighting of the Advent candle is a family tradition, after all. But to see this raw jealousy, this bitterness distances Rebecca from him. It is ugly.

It is what it does, he thinks: possessiveness makes us ugly.

The other man's face hovers for a moment, in his memory. Finn: with the easy smile, the beautiful eyes, the charm. It makes him go cold. He knows. He knows how it feels. How much it eats away at the soul.

Ammie is reaching out to light the candle, closing her eyes, saying something under her breath. Though the words are inaudible, Tobias knows it will be something that expresses gratitude for the meal, for the family; for love, for understanding, for peace in their home. Then she speaks aloud.

'Before we begin,' she says, 'I have something to say.'

She lifts her head and looks around the table, at the children, at his parents, at Rebecca and, lastly, at him. 'Something marvellous.' She pauses. 'I'm – I'm bringing another soul into the world.'

Tobias senses an edginess around the table. Leah looks quickly at Goran. Naomi looks from him to her mother, and the other girls look confused.

Esther touches Rebecca on the arm. 'What does it mean, Mama?'

Ammie smiles at Esther as she answers. 'It means I'm having a baby.'

Naomi looks with disbelief at Ammie but when gradually her understanding grows, her face melts into a beatific smile. Esther is up from the table, dancing, and is ordered to sit down again by Rebecca. Her face is rigid, white. Her gaze flicks across his face: disbelief, betrayal. Tobias sees her mouth open and from the movement of her chest, sees that her breathing is quick and jagged.

'So this,' she says, 'this is why you came back?'

Tobias feels his hands go hot. He can't comprehend it, her judgemental coldness and lack of joy. The extent of his anger catches him off guard.

There is a long silence. Then Ammie speaks. 'You aren't pleased, Rebecca? I was sure you would be. Another child. A sign of God's blessing.'

Leah moves forward in her seat, interrupting. 'Rebecca? The food. Should I … ?'

Rebecca looks towards the stove, at the food that is waiting to be eaten. She looks at her daughters, then at Leah. 'Perhaps,' she says, 'you could take the girls off to play? Just until dinner.'

A look of relief crosses Leah's face. She gathers up the children, who have sensed their mother's displeasure; they look at one another, confused and deflated, Martha clinging onto Leah's hand. After a moment, Goran also rises to his feet. He doesn't speak but Tobias sees he is uncomfortable. Tobias is aware, too, the painful silence that has descended on the room.

Now, it is just the three of them.

'How many months?' Rebecca snaps out the words.

'Not many, I think. Weeks, not months.' Tears roll down Ammie's cheeks. She wipes them away swiftly with her sleeve.

After a long silence, Rebecca speaks. 'Forgive me, there's no way to say this without being blunt. But – we don't know where this child comes from.'

Ammie's face drains of colour. 'What do you mean?'

'Who is the father?'

Tobias feels a burning sensation in his gullet, like bile rising. 'Rebecca!'

Rebecca turns to him, quickly. 'Do you know, Tobias?' Her eyes are hard with anger, but there's something else there, a kind of request or pleading. Does she want the child to be his, or not his? Tobias is struck by a wave of nausea. If it is not his child, how can he love it, care for it, support it in the way he does his daughters? Another man's child.

Ammie's voice breaks the silence, her voice thin and cracked. 'Whoever the father is – this child. It's mine. Isn't that enough?'

Rebecca begins to move the cutlery around in front of her, lining up the knives and forks, shifting the position of the water glasses.

'You're asking a lot. If this child doesn't belong to Tobias.'

Ammie looks for a moment at Rebecca. She stands, slowly and the chair scrapes back as she moves. The noise is curdling, excruciating. Rebecca winces.

'As you have asked of me.' The words are quiet with contained anger. 'What did I do while you were in the schoolroom and Tobias was

135

blowing glass?' She points at Rebecca and Tobias sees that her hand is shaking. Her voice rises in volume. 'I had no choice than to look after your children – children that aren't my own. And I've come to love them. And now you say you won't accept this.'

'I didn't say that.' Rebecca's retort is swift.

'Then you're saying what? That I can only stay if the child is Tobias's?'

Rebecca takes a breath. 'If the child is someone else's then – no doubt he will want to be with you.'

'But there's no way to know.'

Ammie looks for a long time between the two of them – her husband and sisterwife. Then Tobias stands. He stares at Rebecca for a long time. Without a word, he turns and leaves the room.

*

In the orchard, Ammie feels empty. Underneath her feet, the earth is hard; the new year's frost and the crisp snap of the leftover leaves that have frozen to the ground. The light has a watery intensity. The trees stripped of leaves, rows of dark bark. Ammie wraps her shawl more tightly around her. She is so much more aware of the cold this winter of her pregnancy; of all physical sensation, in fact, as though her body is growing more alert. Preparing her for the birth, she supposes, readying her for danger.

Despite the cold, Ammie had an impulse to come to the garden this morning. A sudden need, once Tobias had risen from her bed, to look at the place that – in time and with work – will be her home.

It stands at the end of the garden, a low stone building that Tobias and the others will convert into a house: the shell of an old Bothy, a shepherd's refuge. It might have been there centuries. The roof has lost most of its tiles and the wooden beams show through like rotten teeth but Ammie doesn't care. She hasn't told anyone about her pride at having the shell of an original building for her home, something different from those of the others, something solid and more substantial.

It will root her here, provide her with an anchor.

They agreed. All three of them. What they needed was space, a separateness that meant they could live together without tension. It was Rebecca who suggested it and went to speak to the Elders. She didn't tell anyone what passed between them but on her return her face was tight and red from crying. It took the Elders only a day to agree. And then they had to field the shock and resentment – some unspoken, some overt – from others in the village.

Wasn't the difficulty of plural marriage a kind of test? Wasn't it a way of isolating and overcoming the limits of the self and individual desire and to make them all stronger through sacrifice? Why had the Elders agreed it? Endless questions, taking up time and space in prayers and discussions, in the Meeting House and in the Congregational Hall.

No one spoke of the real reason: everyone's fear that if nothing was done Ammie would leave again. And that this time, Tobias would go for good.

Ammie reaches the end of the garden. She steps close to the wall of the Bothy, touching her nose to the stone, running her hands over it. The mortar is beginning to crumble and she finds a place to push her finger in. The grey stuff comes out in small chunks. She thinks how fragile it is, this building, all buildings, without upkeep and proper care, how quickly they disintegrate. She remembers Tobias embracing the excitement of it, the originality of it: two houses, two wives. The swiftness of his hand over the paper, designing it. *A simple structure. Two rooms for living in. A kitchen large enough for all of us.* She remembers Rebecca nodding and trying to keep the relief from her eyes. Tobias was lost in detail about the size of the range Gervaise would source and blacken, the colours of the distemper for the walls, the oak beams he would run along the length of each room.

In Ammie, it provokes expansion, an opening up.

Here, she can breathe; she can escape Rebecca's scrutinising gaze.

At night, Tobias will come to her through the darkness and the silence. She can light a candle and put it in the window for him.

She ducks under the broken lintel of the doorway. Inside, the stone floor has broken up completely; there are patches of weeds and nettles where once there would have been a stone hearth, or an animal's manger. It is like being inside a skeleton, the shell of the building all exposed, the empty spaces in between. Ammie looks up and sees through the spaces in the roof, the blue of the sky, without even a cloud just yet. The baby turns inside her, the briefest of flutters and she holds a hand across her stomach as though to capture it, the freedom and the grace. Up through the rafters, the clouds are gunmetal, skimming across the paler grey of the sky. Ammie feels dizzy looking up at them, thinking of the future. That she will have a child, who she will love and be responsible for. She leans against the wall for support, feeling the stone damp and cold against her palms.

The light around her seems to swell for a moment as a cloud lifts and the sun breaks through. Ammie's eye catches on something in the corner, by a clump of bindweed. She crosses to it, crouches beside it. It's metal, old and tarnished but the shape is unmistakable. A horseshoe, shot through with a couple of rusty nails. The rust is crumbling and she flakes off a patch of it with a fingernail. She holds it in front of her, feeling like a child who has stumbled on some lost treasure, something definite that can pin her to the world and help her define her place in it. She has something she can put in a box and bring out when she needs comfort.

Through wisdom a house is built. She remembers the words, sees them as her fingers speed across the sepia paper in scripture class. She hears Rebecca's voice as she reads it: *rooms filled with knowledge, filled with precious and pleasant riches.*

Knowledge; riches. Ammie came so close. Since returning to Marah, she has tried not to think of the freedoms of Lot, the ones she touched and tasted with her tongue. She tries not to miss Libby, her easy laughter and her kindness. She pushes away all thought of Finn. To make a success of things here, she knows she must focus on the simplicity of life: the nourishing of her child, the building of a house. Restoring things. She tries to do all this through her actions. But no one prepared her for how difficult it would be.

Ammie stands again, imagining where the door will go. A wide door, open and welcoming. She can request paint at the provisions meeting, a bright colour that will make the baby laugh when it sees home. She imagines windows: the ones in the roof that will open up to the sky and the ones Tobias will set all along the back wall. They will have a view of the field that slopes behind the Bothy, the river just visible in the distance. She won't, from here, be able to see the hills that bound the village. She won't be able to see the roads that wind up the hillside to Aroer, and beyond that, to Lot.

IV

As she's wrenched from the fug of sleep, Rebecca's first thought is of Ammie.

She's been waiting for the knock – even poised to hear it in her sleep, with Ammie so close to her time. Now Ammie is here, an indistinguishable shape in the darkness but a presence next to her bed. Rebecca hears the grasp of breath, then a low moan, and Ammie uttering her name.

As Rebecca fumbles for the matches, a taper, the lamp, she is aware of the tension of the days of waiting. As the light of the candle catches, Ammie's shape emerges. Her face is frozen with fear. A ball of tension begins to gather in Rebecca's stomach: if she stays that way, the labour will be so difficult. She needs to be calm.

'Ammie.' Rebecca places a hand on her sisterwife's arm.

Rebecca watches Ammie's face, sees the lashes lowering as she closes them. The action is slowed right down as if time has suddenly outgrown that single moment, has become bigger than both of them here in the room. Ammie's next words are quiet.

'The Bothy. Please. Just you, Rebecca. Nobody else yet.'

Ammie needs her. She knows what will come once Leah is informed, then Sarah; it will set in motion a whole chain of movement and bustle and events. What Ammie wants is respite, the comfort of intimacy.

Rebecca smoothes the hair back from Ammie's forehead. The skin is clammy, more transparent even than usual. She feels the heat emitting from her body, even though her arms are pricked with goosepimples. Rebecca thinks of Naomi's birth, of the long hours alone with only her mother before Leah was allowed in the house. Those hours were a gift.

'Rebecca?' Tobias stands in the bedroom doorway, silhouetted in the light of the hall. He's been sleeping in the tiny box room at the end of the hall. Until the arrival of the baby, it seemed to be the best thing. He looks out of place here, in Rebecca's room, in the middle of the night. He rumples his hair, trying to rouse himself awake. 'Is it …?' When he sees Ammie, he moves quickly, tries to take her into his arms. Ammie takes a step backwards, the look on her face fraught and panicky, as though he were a stranger.

'We're moving to the Bothy.'

'Of course,' he says. He begins to look around him, readying himself.

'No. You must stay.'

A look of confusion crosses his face. Is it irritation, too, perhaps? 'The girls.'

'We can't call Sarah to be here for them?'

Rebecca shakes her head. A firm no. She will not argue with him here, now. Birth is a female thing – something to which they have always adhered. She's not about to allow it to change on Tobias's whim. She won't have him there for Ammie when he couldn't be there for his daughters. The irony of it strikes her now: after all the doubt about the paternity of this child, it will be she, not Tobias, who will be there to see the matted head emerging, to witness the initial gasping breath, the slippery marvellous first embrace.

Tobias is disenfranchised. His arms hang loose and awkward by his sides.

Rebecca doesn't have time to think about that now. She swings her legs out of bed, reaches for her wrap. After the heat of the bed she is shivering, despite the summer night. The change in temperature galvanises her into action. Braiding her hair quickly, methodically, she decides on the order of things. She will dress. She and Tobias will help Ammie downstairs. They will leave Tobias at the kitchen door and she will issue instructions as to what to do next. Rebecca herself will support Ammie's weight across the lawn and down the path to the old stable, where the child will be born.

The room is filled with jasmine. Rebecca remembers the dense smell of the oil from her own labours. When she was having Naomi it overpowered the room, but Leah insisted, she remembers, and after a while she hadn't noticed. Even now, when she passes the jasmine bush in the garden, Rebecca recalls the darkness of shuttered rooms, the heady pain and the closed door of her bedroom with Tobias on the other side.

Naomi's birth: long and puzzling.

Esther's, startling and sudden.

Martha's, swift and intensely painful.

The memory of each is overlaid onto the other: the beginnings of three small lives; three remarkable days out of her own.

Rebecca crosses to the window in the corner, where there is a lamp. She lights it, dims it, pulls the curtains across to shut out the blackness of the garden, shutting the two of them into the room. They work wordlessly, in the lull between Ammie's contractions, to prepare the room. Rebecca rips open the packaging on the plastic sheeting and hands the end of it to Ammie. The action is familiar, like folding the weekly wash. They pull each end taut at the corners – eliminating ridges, uncomfortable folds – until it crackles between them. They lay it flat.

Rebecca finds a taper and instructs Ammie to light the candles. There is a slow reverence about the way she leaves a trail of flames behind her, as she moves along the mantelpiece and around the room. Her earlier agitation has gone.

Rebecca busies herself with cushions. Big ones for the floor, square ones, bolsters. Cushions to lean on; to be tucked under the abdomen, beneath the knees. She has a flash of an image of Leah and her mother at Naomi's birth. The way the two of them handed things to each other – plastic gloves, a towel, a thermometer – without the need for words, just by catching each other's eyes. Even in her rawest state Rebecca had seen it, had been jealous of that connection, isolated as she was by her own pain, as if stranded on a rock above a dangerous sea.

They wait. Rebecca supports Ammie through the next contraction, enclosing Ammie's hand in her own.

She supports her through the next one.

The hands of the clock on the mantelpiece appear hardly to move. She wonders whether it is time to call Leah but she doesn't want to leave Ammie alone: the contractions are clearly deepening.

She remembers Leah's weathered hands on her abdomen. She doesn't remember which daughter, but she remembers the thick, strong-smelling oil. It did nothing to ease the pain tearing up her insides but freed up her mind to focus anywhere other than the relentless clenching, her body working to expel the baby inside her. The pressure of Leah's hands was surprisingly gentle.

Rebecca thinks of the basket. Leah would have brought it here in advance and now Rebecca knows what to do. She needs that oil.

The basket is next to Ammie's bed. She finds what she is looking for: a blue glass bottle with a greasy label. Rebecca can't remember what type it is; the words on the label have been smudged out. She runs her fingers over it briefly, wondering when it was last used. For Martha, probably.

In the sitting room, Rebecca leads Ammie to the cushions. She has already found the old bale of towels and she spreads them over the top. Rebecca sits, legs splayed wide, and directs Ammie in between them, telling her to lean back against her. She unscrews the lid from the jar and holds it to her nose. It is woody, bitter even. She rubs her hands to warm them, as she remembers Leah doing. She tugs gently at the hem of Ammie's nightdress, pulling it from underneath to lift it high around her breasts. Then she pours the oil into her palms that are tingling with heat.

Rebecca has never seen Ammie's abdomen this close up before; the pregnancy has brought out faint white lines, like silverfish, under the surface. Rebecca begins slowly, rubbing in small concentric circles, watching the sheen as it appears on Ammie's skin.

She is aware of the raggedness of her own breathing. She must slow down. She exhales, a long, conscious sigh. Move the hands with the breath, Leah had said, and try to synchronise it with your own.

Rebecca tries to focus on her hands. They move rhythmically over the mound of Ammie's belly. She keeps the action symmetrical, so that whatever shape she traces on the right, she repeats on the left. The simple action empties her mind. She pushes away the memories of Ammie's childhood body, lissom and straight, how much it has changed. Pushes away, too, images of Ammie with Tobias. The roundness of her breasts caressed by his hands and tongue; his hand soft on her right hip, following the curve of it down.

Her fingers brush against Ammie's belly button; it thrusts upwards, hard and prominent. She allows the fingers to stop there for a moment, circling its small folds of skin. Then away, to trace the shadowy brown line that runs the full length of her abdomen. Her hands move back up again before she reaches the hair – black, springy, brittle. She is surprised by the density, and yet its expansiveness, single dark hairs thinning out, towards the hip bones and over the top of the thighs.

Breathing. Hands moving – deeper now, more vigorously – with the breath. The oil soaking quickly in and Rebecca having to pour more of it into her cupped palms. Some of it escapes and drips directly onto the skin, beginning to slide down Ammie's belly. She rubs it in, then resumes the rhythmic action. It soothes her. Soothes Ammie too, perhaps, because she isn't moving, isn't speaking. Rebecca is aware only of the contact of their bodies: Ammie's back against her front; the weight of Ammie's head against her breasts.

When the last of the oil has soaked in, Rebecca slows down her hands again. She remembers what Leah has taught her: finish with a few minutes' still contact with the skin. With the flat of her hand on the belly, Rebecca realises that there has been no movement from inside; no sudden kick of the baby's foot against the wall of the womb. Just the slow motion of her own hands, Ammie's skin glistening under her fingers, the flickering of the candles illuminating the far wall, the one Ammie painted red. And the jasmine, catching the back of her throat.

'How does that feel?'

She doesn't respond. Rebecca wonders if she has fallen asleep, leaning against her like this. She remembers it happening with Naomi, in the lull between pains.

'Rebecca?'

'Yes?'

'I'm glad you're here.'

The contraction of Rebecca's throat at Ammie's vulnerability and Ammie's willingness to voice it. Rebecca feels, suddenly and acutely, the intensity of the years surfacing, all of it surfacing: sharp words spoken long ago in a classroom; the nights covering her ears with a pillow, shutting out the sounds of the next-door room. Tobias's dark face after the tensions and rows, his pleading. She feels it lodge in her gullet, the emotion hard and balled up there. She feels it release, slide like oil down her face with the salty droplets of tears.

*

145

The passing hours. Leah arriving and taking charge. Ammie, falling into occasional dozing and Rebecca herself catching her chin lowering, letting go, momentarily, of consciousness.

Then playing a card game. Rebecca amazed at Ammie's knowledge and the two of them laughing and being struck by the absurdity of it, but the necessity. Like humouring a sick child.

Then Ammie, nauseous and racked with intermittent pain. Rebecca, then Leah, supporting Ammie as she walks the length of the hallway and back.

All of them, trying to tunnel through it.

Rebecca, timing with her watch: ten minutes with Ammie on her feet, circling the room, stopping for Leah to massage her sacrum. Ten minutes down on the floor on all fours, arching her back against the worst of it.

*

Rebecca has napped for half an hour, wakes to a guttural howl. Leah is standing in front of Ammie, with her arms locked under her armpits. Ammie is naked, half slumped, half squatting against the wall. Her legs are shaking visibly. Her head is bowed and her hair falls forward. Through it, Rebecca catches a glimpse of her breasts, the aureolae huge and round, like dark ripening poppies.

There is something obscene about what the pain is doing to her body.

'Amarantha.' Leah says the name as though it were a summons, an order. 'Amarantha. Look at me. You mustn't forget to breathe.'

A groan from Ammie as she buckles and braces herself against the wall, face screwing up in anger, in disbelief. Pinned underneath Leah's slight but capable arms, unable to do anything but wait for it to pass.

'Rebecca.' Leah half turns to her. Ammie starts to moan again and Leah struggles to speak over it. 'Clear up, can you? Over there.' With her head, she indicates the corner of the room.

Rebecca is hit then by the force of it, the smell that won't be masked even by jasmine. Excrement. Rebecca imagines it: Ammie

146

squatting, having an urge to push. Pushing out not the baby, but the contents of her intestines instead. Rebecca goes through to the kitchen, her face burning at the intimacy of it, the shame that Ammie will feel later, when she remembers.

She searches the drawers for what she might need, for cloths, detergent, rubber gloves. She retrieves the bucket from a cupboard near to the sink. She turns to go back into the sitting room as another yell rips from Ammie's lips.

A shock of alarm surges through her when she returns to the sitting room and sees Leah's face.

'What is it?'

Ammie lies between them on the floor, curled in a ball, her eyes closed. She has retreated into herself. Leah's encouragement, her commands, suggestions, are being ignored. Ammie wants only to rest.

A strand of hair has escaped Rebecca's braid. She pushes it away.

'Leah?'

Leah looks up from the notebook in her hand. Her pen has been poised above the paper for the last minute without writing anything. There are smudges under her eyes, grey and brown. She's exhausted, Rebecca can see that. Ammie is exhausted. They all are.

'Have you any idea how long?'

Leah shakes her head. Glances swiftly at Ammie, then speaks in a low voice. 'She should have progressed by now. She's getting urges to push. But she's still not dilated enough.'

'But if there's the urge …'

'It would be madness, Rebecca. She'd tear.'

Rebecca chews on her lip, looks at Ammie's body. Such supple thighs and rounded hips. Rebecca had been in no doubt about the strength of the muscles of her womb, how easily they would expel the baby.

'What can we do?'

Leah joins her palms together and touches her lips with her forefingers. 'The contractions are dropping off.' She speaks evenly. 'We have two choices. We could leave her for a while, try to get her to rest and conserve her energy and hope that it won't be too much longer.'

'Or?'

147

'Or we can be more interventionist.'

'What do you mean?'

'I've exhausted all the herbal remedies, Rebecca.'

Rebecca can't grasp what Leah is saying.

'Meaning?'

'I'm worried. I think … ' she swallows, blinking slowly, 'I think this may be beyond me now.'

'Oh, Leah. No.'

Rebecca sees tears in Leah's eyes and realises how difficult this is for her. She will feel she has failed. But it is not her decision to make. She will have to refer it to the family.

'Do you need me to find Goran?'

'No. It isn't Goran's decision to make. It isn't his wife, it isn't his child.'

In the silence, Rebecca tries to glean Leah's meaning. Leah continues. 'We must ask Tobias.'

A flurry of activity: swift kisses for her girls, fetching Sarah to look after them. She is aware of an urgent pull to return to the Bothy. She needs to be there. When she and Tobias cross the lawn she looks with amazement at the bloom of colour in the sky. A night, and a whole day? Surely not.

Tobias is startled to see Ammie lying like an injured animal on the floor. His brows furrow with concern as Leah explains the situation to him, calmly as though he were still a child. The three of them, on their feet, huddled into the corner of the room, whispering so as not to alarm her.

Tobias shakes his head, trying to find some clarity. He's rendered speechless.

'What do you think is best?' Rebecca says.

Leah looks uncertainly in Ammie's direction. 'If she sleeps now, gets rest, she might be fine. The body won't be rushed. If things don't start happening soon …'

'But – the baby. Shouldn't we think of the safety of the baby?' He is desperate, she thinks, and something tugs at her heart to see Tobias in pain.

'Intervention will mean the outside. Hospital, more questions. More risk.'

'You think she should go?'

Leah shakes her head. 'I don't want her to. It would be better to wait.'

'There's no question. We must go.'

Leah sighs, exasperated. 'How? We're too far. By the time we got there, it would be too late. Besides ...' She looks round again at Ammie, who is on all fours now, swaying and groaning. '... moving her in that state. It would be unbelievably painful.'

Rebecca thinks of the long stretch of time ahead. Ammie growing more tired. The danger to her, to the child. She bites her lip. There must be a way.

'I agree. With Tobias. We can't let anything happen to the child.'

Leah turns to face her. She isn't able to hide the surprise in her eyes. Something in her slackens, as though she's defeated.

'There must be a way,' Rebecca says. 'Could someone – Ciaras, or Seth – take a buggy to Aroer? From there. Well there must be someone who would let us use the telephone. We could get them to come here. They must have something. Emergency vehicles. A plane, even.'

'You'd allow them *here*? For what? The body will respond in its own time. The child will come when ready. Amarantha is young, strong. There won't be any ...'

A scream splits the room. Amarantha, shouting obscenities, the pain ripping words from her mouth. And then all their own words, their plans are lost. The three of them run to her, prop her up. Leah places a hand on Ammie's rippling belly. She checks her watch. She looks at Tobias and Rebecca and nods, stony faced, hardening herself in readiness for the other woman's pain.

*

When Ammie opens her eyes she doesn't know if it's day outside or night. She doesn't know how long she has slept. Her breasts are tight, tingling as though being jabbed with pins and there's a sticky wetness oozing from them. The unexpectedness of it makes her want to cry.

The sound is unfamiliar in the first instant, a snuffling – as though from a tiny animal – coming from the middle of the bed. Then she realises. It is him – Lucas. She can't believe that today will make him already three days old, wrapped in a bundle of white blankets. She reaches out and feels for the head, the warm skin at the back of his neck. As her eyes adjust to the level of light, his features become clearer to her. She sees all his constituent parts, his closed eyes and the lashes resting softly on the cheeks, but somehow it's as though all of those parts don't add up, as though he might belong to someone else. He has a yellow brown tinge to his skin which makes him almost exotic. Where has he come from? He can't possibly be hers. He hits out at the air with a jerky and uncontrollable movement.

She catches hold of his fingers, stroking them until they spread out from the tiny fists he'd made. Not fingers like hers that are long and bony. More like Tobias's, she thinks, with fleshy pads on the ends of them. Ammie can't even remember what Finn's hands looked like.

The door opens, a fraction at first but then wider and when Ammie looks up, she sees Leah's face through the gap. She turns her face away, tracing the shadows that emerge through the curtains, the patterns they cast onto the floor, the simple chest of drawers, the wooden chest beside the bed. Late morning, she judges, from the quality of the light. Ammie doesn't feel ready to engage with anyone, and especially not Leah who now knows everything about her: every detail of her anatomy and all the things she utters when in extreme pain. It is too close. Everything about this place is too close.

Leah stands above her, waiting for Ammie to acknowledge her.

'How do you feel?'

'Still sore.'

Leah nods, smiles. 'But here, at least. Home. We so nearly had to move you, you know that? To hospital.'

Ammie feels the impulse to cry. She bites her lip and looks away, feels the touch of Leah's hand on hers. When Leah moves to sit on the edge of the bed, there's a waft of something strong and sharp, something

150

like tea tree. It clarifies things, Leah told her once, but here, now, it's not clear what Leah is thinking. Her face settles into a blank receptiveness. She reaches forward and adjusts the sheet around Ammie, tucking it further around her torso. It makes Ammie feel like a sick child and she can't decide whether it comforts her or makes her resentful.

'Your breasts hurt?' Leah almost smiles as she says this.

'How do you know?'

'It happens around now – two or three days later. It's a good thing, you'll see. He'll be feeding much more often now. You should expect to feel tired.'

How can she possibly feel more tired than she is already? Leah's eyes slide sideways to look at the child, and it raises a smile of affection. Then her eyes move to Ammie, thoughtful, as though searching her face for clues. Her hands fall loosely in her lap and she holds the silence for a few moments.

'Amarantha?'

Something about the question, about Leah's tone, alarms her.

'There's someone downstairs – someone to see you.'

Finn, come to carry off his son. Ammie's stomach contracts with resentment, with expectation, with relief. She tries to remember Finn's face but she can't recall anything except how he made her feel. Open and free and alive. And here she is now, confined to a bed with a tiny infant who is completely reliant on her. Her arms ache even with the thought of it.

Leah's voice interrupts her thoughts. 'It's Frania.'

The sensation is like being stung. 'Why? Why now?'

'She heard, of course. Tobias, I think. I'm not sure.' Leah hesitates. 'She'd like to see you, and the baby. Will you let her come up?'

Frania. Ammie stares at this face that is at once so strange and so familiar. There are more lines there than there used to be, some of them etched deep across the forehead; some saggier skin around the neck and chin. On each of her fingers – even her right thumb – she wears a ring. There are broad silver bands with Celtic knots, chunky ones with engravings. She is so out of place in this room, which is otherwise sparse and simple.

Her mother is holding Lucas. Ammie watches as Frania's jaw moves up and down. She isn't speaking but as though she is mouthing something, shock or disbelief as though at a miracle.

Lucas's mouth widens, he screws up his face. His fists agitate the air and Frania is suddenly surprised, looks fearful. She hands him back to Ammie who brings him quickly to her, finds the right position and tenses until his mouth has locked onto her nipple. She feels that sharp dart of pain that Leah warned her she would feel, and then a release. The only sound then is of Lucas sucking; she feels the strong motion of his jaw against the flesh of her breast.

When she looks back at Frania, there are tears in her eyes.

'He's beautiful, Ammie.'

'I don't know why you've come.'

Frania's head jerks back, as though shocked. 'Of course I was going to come.'

'That's not what I said.'

Frania looks stricken. She stands up and begins to move around the room, her heels tapping on the wooden floor. Then she moves to the window and pulls the curtain across. Her actions are swift and determined and the room is filled with the light of outside. Frania stands for a moment, looking out, then returns to sit beside Ammie on the bed.

Lucas has stopped feeding and fallen asleep but Ammie holds him to her, like a shield.

'Tobias found me. He told me – Ammie, I didn't even know you were pregnant. I'm so sorry.'

'For what?'

'That I haven't been there.'

An invisible thread. Lengthening, tautening. For a long time, Ammie had lost sight of it and couldn't feel it but now, now she feels its power. She isn't sure she wants to be connected to this woman any more. Just now, she doesn't feel connected to anyone.

Frania reaches for Ammie's hand. The skin is cold on hers. Ammie doesn't respond, and she sees Frania's hands go to her mouth to bite at the skin around the fingers.

'Why did you leave?' Ammie has wanted to ask the question for so long now that when the words are forced out they sound strangulated.

'It was ...' Frania looks at her hands. She joins them in her lap, turns them over and over as though looking for the right words. 'It was your father. He sent for me, Ammie.' A pause. Frania's face is tight, stricken. 'He was dying.'

Her father. The mysterious presence he has had in her life. Frania has never spoken of him, even at Amarantha's insistent questioning as a child which Frania always managed to deflect. Ammie got used to it being just the two of them; and now here he was, even in his absence, even in his death, coming between them.

'He ...?'

'He died two months ago. He had no one else, so I had to go to him. I hope you understand – I felt there wasn't ...'

'You could have taken me with you.'

The bedroom door opens, swiftly and with no warning. Leah stands on the threshold and Ammie wonders for a moment if she's been listening. Ammie looks at the two other women: her mother, alien, dressed in long swathes of fabric of different colours, her hair cut short. Leah, dark, drab, her silver hair pulled back into a braid.

This, she thinks, is what can happen. Two women, two choices. Their different lives. She sees then that Frania can never belong back here, even if she tries.

Leah looks briefly at Frania, then her eyes rest on Ammie holding the baby. 'I could take Lucas if you want me to. Give you some rest.'

'There's no need, Leah, really. I'm fine, thank you.'

'You're sure?' Leah hesitates in the doorway. But she waits, eyes fixed on the child as though to check whether Ammie is telling the truth. Then Leah looks at Frania. Ammie can't interpret the look that passes between them but she knows there's a history there she might never understand.

*

153

Frania was late. Late getting up, late leaving her caravan at the edge of the settlement, late to arrive at the Meeting House. The door was ajar, which meant that her workshare partner must be there already. She hadn't had time to check the list, so she didn't know who it would be. She knew, though, that the task was cleaning the Meeting House and that she would rather have done anything else – even shovelled manure in the gardens.

The air was fresh, the bluebells still out but she hadn't time to stop and look today. She hurried along the path with Amarantha strapped in the sling, her head slumped into Frania's neck. It had taken time to adjust to carrying her that way but she was grateful to Lucia for suggesting it. It made such sense, keeping her daughter close like that.

Leah. Frania felt her stomach lurch: it wasn't the partner she would have chosen. There was something about Leah that made her edgy. During her labour she had been extraordinary – efficient but kind – and Frania had much to thank her for. But still, Leah made her feel uneasy.

Leah stood in the centre of the Meeting room, looking up at the high windows. Her hair was braided in a thick rope which coiled around her right shoulder. Frania stood for a minute, observing her from behind: the waist that was thickening, the broad calves and ankles. There was something about her, Frania thought: solid, impenetrable.

Leah must have heard Frania approach and she turned, slowly. Frania couldn't tell but thought that she might have been crying; her eyes were puffy, and narrower than usual.

'Oh,' she said. 'Sister Frania.'

Sister Frania. She hated that form of address. Frania noticed they used it more with her than with each other, as though they were being ironic. Sisterly was the last thing she felt sometimes.

The women worked wordlessly for a long time. The only sounds in the room were the thwack of Leah's broom against the skirtings as she worked methodically across her section of floor. There was the sound of voices drifting across the green, where the children were playing. The sounds for a while seemed to mix – the swish of broom on the floor, the thwack of the mop and the clear high laughter.

They moved to the kitchen, wiping down the surfaces with vinegar and lemon juice. Frania's eye caught the pictures tacked to the walls – the

154

things the children had produced in the children's meeting. Stick people with heads larger than their bodies, blue stripes of sky and uniform houses with square windows and a door right in the middle of the building. It was curious, she thought, how some things were universal.

'So,' Leah said, 'do you feel settled here with us now?'

'It's my home.'

'You don't … regret anything? Being here alone.'

'I'm not alone. I've got a whole community to be part of.'

Leah paused thoughtfully, dipping her hand into the bowl of water. It was muddy brown from the greasy residue they'd cleaned away. 'It's just that – others have left. Single women, I mean. It's a difficult place to be – if you don't ...' A meaningful look crosses Leah's face, completing the sentence without need for the word.

If you don't believe.

Frania was amazed, even still, that the Elders had accepted her proposal: that she should stay here, living on the edge of the village – for now, in the tiny caravan that was hardly big enough to stand up in. No plural marriage, no Sealing. She would receive her share of produce from the garden in return for her workshare and teaching in the schoolroom. She was half in and half out and most of the time that suited her. But some nights, when Ammie had stopped feeding and Frania fell into a fitful sleep she cried with the hollowness of her life and at the rash decisions she'd made: Julius, believing him, coming here.

It was still raw, that grief. Even now, a few weeks after his letter.

'It's a brave thing for you to have done.' Leah resumed her wiping. Frania paused to look, watching the movement of the other woman's hand. The sharpness irritated her nose. She fished in her pocket but had nothing to wipe it with, so she used her sleeve, surreptitiously so that Leah couldn't see. 'It must be hard, being … left like that.' Leah turned to look at her now, the cloth hugged close to her.

Frania felt a twist of grief in her stomach. She wouldn't say – not to Leah – how much it hurt, how hard she still found it. Her eyes filled up, but she turned her attention to Amarantha, adjusting the weight of her body in the sling. She was still sleeping.

'Can I ask you something, Frania? How did you meet?'

'Julius?' Frania was knocked off guard by the directness of the question. What was it to Leah? Why did she want to know? Frania wanted to keep all that to herself, hug it to her like some special childhood treasure.

'It was in a café. I was working there and he came in.' Frania felt a sweeping feeling of warmth at the memory, the connection she had with him. She wanted Leah to know how it was; that the relationship was more than the shallow thing everyone thought it must be.

'It was ... ' Frania smiled. 'He seemed somehow – exotic. Different – you know?' Frania looked at Leah but her expression gave nothing away. 'He wanted vegetarian food and it completely threw Peg – she was the chef in the kitchen.' Frania thought of the smile he'd bestowed on her, and how she put up the closed sign in the door as he left, but that her heart, having met him, felt unbelievably open.

She didn't say any of that to Leah.

She said: 'If he'd come ...' She found herself rocking, automatically to and fro to comfort Amarantha. Even though she was still asleep.

'But he didn't,' Leah said. 'If he had – I wonder how it would be for you.'

'He abandoned me.'

Leah took a step forward. 'Abandoned is a strong word, Frania. I don't think ... well. None of us should judge anyone. We never know, do we? What's really inside someone else's mind?'

It was curious. The expression on her face was curious. It seemed like Leah was defending him.

'You don't know him,' Frania said. Sometimes in these past weeks, she had battled inside her with the black rages at what Julius had done. But she loved him too. She couldn't bear the thought of other people commenting, or judging.

'I knew him once.'

Frania couldn't take it in; the fact that she hadn't known this.

'You know he was the officer who led the raid?'

'The raid. The one that made you move?'

Frania felt a skipping sensation in her stomach. Julius had been

156

vague about his familiarity with this group, with how he knew about them; he said only that he had been dismissive at first, but when he got to know more he was taken with it. The ideas of communality, the principles of sharing and simplicity. It had made him humble, he said.

There was so much of Julius that didn't belong to her.

Leah crossed to the door to empty out the bowl. She didn't look at Frania but concentrated on the task of reaching the door without any spillages. Frania saw the straining muscles in her arms, the effort of her gripping it. Frania watched as Leah stood on the step, blinking for a moment into the spring sunshine then tipping away the dirty water away.

Ammie leans against a tree. She runs her fingers over the gnarled roots that surround her and closes her eyes to feel the thickness of silence in the place. The shade is a balm, not only from the heat but from the noise near the water, down the bank. She listens to them now: Leah and Goran, surrounded by the love and pain of three generations; Goran's sons and wives and nephews and nieces and their growing sprawl of children.

A scream from the water forces Ammie to open her eyes. She hears it echo around the hollow and realises that it isn't a scream but the sound of pure distilled happiness. It wasn't so long ago that she herself was swimming with friends in a river like this. And now. She scans the small crowd by the water, her eyes searching out Lucas. Rebecca holds him close to her, has turned him to face outwards so he can see the rest of the children.

Ammie's days of lightness and laughter feel too far in the past.

Ammie watches Naomi and her cousins at the edge of the water. They have their grandmother's string-bean limbs, clutching each other, laughing at Ciaras as he emerges from the water with his dark mass of wet hair plastered to his head. There's such pleasure, Ammie thinks, in looking at their long brown legs and the way the sun catches the edge of the pool of water. When Ciaras emerges from the water he's shorter and broader than Tobias, his chest tangled with tighter hairs. When he shakes himself dry, the droplets surround his body, suspended in the sun, before catching all those standing around him.

'Ammie.'

She hadn't heard the movement. When she looks up there's someone standing in front of her. The face is blocked out by sun, and there's a glare around the head. Rebecca. She holds something light, a bright bundle in a blanket. Her son.

'You look like a saint,' Ammie says, 'in this light.'

Rebecca comes and crouches next to Ammie, still with Lucas in her arms. She is poised so effortlessly on her haunches. She has such a fine sense of balance, her sisterwife. With her free hand Rebecca peels back the blanket from Lucas' face and Ammie thinks about the gestures her body must learn in order to care for her child. Rebecca is so practised at them.

'Time you took him back,' Rebecca says, 'I need to watch Martha. She wants to go in and I know the older ones can swim but she's still so small.'

Ammie hesitates.

'He needs the contact. You know that, don't you?'

Ammie feels Rebecca's eyes searching her face. Even though her arms still ache and she's desperate for sleep, she sees that there's no choice. She holds out her arms to take him. She caresses one of his feet with her fingers, beginning to stroke it gently. Even though he's asleep it startles him, his arms flaying outward and his foot pulling away from her hand.

Rebecca watches them. A look of exasperation crosses her face. 'You might sing to him. It's good for him to hear your voice.'

She turns and strides long and fast down the slope to the stream. She doesn't look back, but picks up pace as she nears the water, joining the girls at the edge. The light is entrancing, sparkling on the surface of the water, tiny jumping stars. It's calmer now that Ciaras has moved away from the children but their excitement still crackles. Rebecca speaks to them in a low voice, suggesting a game, gathering them around her in a huddle: her daughters, her nieces. Her girls.

*

158

Ammie lies under a cotton blanket with Lucas curled up beside her. The sun is higher now, its heat penetrating even the canopy of green. She pulls the blanket further up to Lucas's chin, feeling the skin on her own face begin to tingle.

Over by the flat rock near the edge of the stream, a thin plume of smoke rises in the air and there's a smell of burning charcoal. Ciaras has a hat on, a fish slice in his hand; he's organising the older girls into lining up the food to be cooked. Tobias, Seth and Caleb are putting up trestles. Sarah and Hannah flutter around with cloths; they hold one up between them and it floats up for a moment, billowing out, red and white checks against the blue of the sky.

Ammie sits, watching. There are days when she feels so distant, still not part of this family with their unspoken connections, their responsibilities, their knowledge of each other – even though she has given birth to its newest child. To understand it will take far longer than she imagines.

Leah stands a way off from the other women, taller than her daughters-in-law, with a head constantly swivelling, keeping track of all the grandchildren, the ones in the water swimming and the smaller ones faltering near the edge. Ammie looks at her long limbs and wonders, too, about the different bodies of her sons. Seth, tight and compact. And Tobias, loping and rangy but with a crown of thick hair and solid forearms that when she was a girl she used to love to watch as he worked.

When Ammie looks up again, Leah is approaching. Her steps are small and sure, and make no noise so it looks like she glides into the space under the tree. Ammie thinks about how she has probably spent a lifetime doing that, practising stealth and being silent. She joins Ammie on the ground and sits for a minute or so, watching Lucas asleep.

'No question whose son he is. He is so like Tobias at that age.'

Ammie feels a flare of anger, the heat creep up her neck, tingle in her cheeks. 'Did you doubt it?'

Leah's gaze is level. 'I didn't. No. I know that …' She turns briefly, looks towards her family at the water's edge, then back to look at Ammie. 'Some did. I didn't.'

'Why?'

'Because I believe that you love my son. Whoever conceived him – well, the father will always be the one you feel a commitment to. I don't doubt that.'

'But some do?'

'Forgive me for being frank. Some only see that you have been selfish and unthinking.'

Ammie bites her lip, and wills the tears not to come. Not here, not now. 'And you? You think that?'

Leah looks down the bank, to where the children are beginning to emerge from the stream. 'I know about selfishness.'

'Then what …?' Ammie hears the note of anger in what she's saying, and the pitch of her own voice rising. 'What have I done that is so selfish?'

'Leaving when things got difficult with Rebecca. Causing all that pain …'

'What do you know about it? About me and Rebecca?' Ammie knows even as she says the words that she has said the wrong thing, but she is unable to help it. Since Lucas came, she has been so confused by the conflicting emotions: needing Rebecca and being grateful for her help, the isolation and being overwhelmed at the things she can't do, at the life she holds in her arms and is unable to relate to but is unable to talk about with anyone. Above all Rebecca.

Leah says nothing. She looks away and Ammie follows the line of her gaze, watching the children crowded round on the picnic rug, waiting with their plastic plates and cups and Sarah crouching in the middle of them, pouring juice.

'I know you found it hard, but it is a challenge for all of us. Don't think the pain is exclusive, Amarantha. Otherwise it will maim you.'

The tears that prickle Ammie's eyes are involuntary. She turns her head the other way, looking deeper into the woods. She concentrates on the trunks of the trees, tracing the straightness of them, the strength. *You weren't bearing his child,* she thinks, *and you didn't know the love we had was different from everything else.*

'Let me tell you something,' says Leah. 'Duty comes first. I've told you that before, I'm sure. But I know …' Ammie watches as she

160

looks down at her hands. 'I do know how difficult that is.'

'I don't know what you mean.'

'The being faithful.'

'To God, you mean?'

Leah hesitates. Her eyes lock onto Ammie's and for a moment Ammie thinks that she might about to speak, to open her heart about the pain of being a sisterwife, of all that means. Then Leah sighs. Her eyes drift towards the rest of her family, now gathered into a group. 'We should join them,' she says.

Ammie wonders about trying to keep Leah here and trying to extract from her what she was about to say. But Leah is on her feet and the moment has passed and, above all, Ammie feels exhausted.

'You go. I don't want to wake Lucas.'

With a movement of her chin, Leah indicates where he lies on the ground. 'Look at him. He's in the deepest sleep. You won't disturb him.' Then her eyes are back on Ammie, scanning her face. 'You are part of this family now. Remember that.'

Part of the family. Tied to Rebecca, as well as Tobias. Tied to Lucas, always.

When Ammie stands her legs are numb; there's a tingling and a sensation of the blood running back into them. She leans over and adjust Lucas's blanket again, bending over more than she needs to so that Leah can't see her face. She doesn't want her to see what must be written there: confusion and fear and the raw want. Wanting Tobias, wanting to belong. But wanting more than anything for that tugging to stop, the desire for silence, to be alone, and for the numbing tiredness to end.

Ammie stands. Leah indicates for her to take her arm.

As they descend the slope, there's a shout and Ammie sees the children jump up from the rug. Esther is first, rushing ankle deep into the water without hesitation, headlong right onto the log they've been using for their game. Standing there, arms wide for balance and feet so sure she must surely have been born a gymnast. She points at Tobias in the water. And there he is, her husband, bare-chested, holding up one arm and shouting with delight.

He is holding up a fish.

It retches and jerks, tugging at the line. Dancing on the end of the sharpness as the sun hits the water and bounces off again to light the summer day. The grin on his face and the delighted shouts from the bank. We can cook it for lunch, he's shouting. Clever Uncle Tobias, someone else says, and there's clapping and he looks right at them, towards her and Leah. Just then he turns his attention to the crowd of children, hinges at the waist and, with his hair sweeping forward, bows to the audience. Arms wide, still clutching the fish that struggles on the line.

The kitchen door is open and the midsummer light filters through it. Ammie stands at the window, holding Lucas, looking out into the garden where Esther is chasing Martha round the garden and Naomi sits cross legged on the lawn, making daisy chains. Rebecca is still picking peas. Ammie catches sight of her dark skirt as she moves through the cane wigwams at the edge of the vegetable patch.

In a moment, she'll be finished. Ammie crosses to the stone larder, leaning across with Lucas still tucked into her shoulder, and picks up the jug of lemonade. It's cold and the beakers on the table are clean when the sunlight catches them. When Rebecca comes up the step and over the threshold, she has the trug over her forearm, full of the pods that are better this year, she says, than in a long time. She is flushed from the sun; it takes so little for her to burn. Just half an hour and already her skin is pink. She smiles. She smiles more, in fact, these days and Ammie wonders if it's the sun or the long break from school or the fact that she has made lemonade without Rebecca having to ask her.

Rebecca places the trug on the table. There are flowers on top, pink and purple ones; delicate stalks and wide petals. Ammie picks one out and holds it to her face. The scent of it, so distinct, brings back Frania's face. Sweet pea. The name Frania used for her sometimes.

'I thought we could put them in jars,' Rebecca says, 'to decorate the table.'

Ammie nods and turns to the sink. On the shelf underneath there are glass jars piled on top of each other. With her free hand she fills one with water, puts it on the table, then Rebecca puts the flowers in.

Frania, folding at the waist, legs perfectly straight as she bent to pluck out chickweed or bindweed from the beds.

'There,' Rebecca says, 'I'll wrap the rest in paper. Naomi can take some to Leah. And Sarah.' She moves to the sink to dampen the newspaper so that she can put the flowers into bundles to give as gifts to the wives. It isn't something Ammie would think to do, and she thinks that Rebecca is thoughtful like that. She hasn't mentioned Hannah but realises now that it's often the way with first wives – there's unspoken support for each other. Hannah never visits their house, while Sarah is there always, calling by with recipes and cakes, taking away vegetables or bunches of flowers in paper.

Lucas begins to stir, tiny mewling sounds. Ammie sits at the table to feed him, watching as Rebecca takes the sheets of sodden paper and lays them across the counter, dividing the flowers between. Today, unusually, she has her hair loose; it reaches half way down her back, always with the same sheen to it that Ammie has admired since Rebecca taught her at school.

Rebecca turns round and catches sight of Lucas feeding. Ammie sees her flinch, a sudden catch of breath, a turn away. She recovers quickly but Ammie has seen the reaction. She doesn't move but stands at the window. Ammie only sees her back and the stiff way she stares out of the window, watching her girls in the garden. Ammie looks down at Lucas, at the way his jaw moves as he sucks, rhythmic and strong. That need. Her responsibility to him.

'Rebecca?'

When she turns back to Ammie, her face mouth is hard but her eyes are filled with something else: regret and repression. Ammie wants to touch her, wants to know what she's thinking. 'Is it something I did?'

The green eyes on hers don't move. Ammie sees how they're filling with tears, she sees her sisterwife swallow.

'It's not you.'

'What then?'

'Just … seeing you with Lucas.'

Rebecca closes her eyes, as though today she's afraid to see what the world holds for her. She looks smaller, somehow, fading. Her eyes snap open but she sighs. 'This is difficult to say but I don't think I can hide it. I want …'

What will she say? That she wants Ammie to leave?

'I want another child. And so … so, seeing you …' Her voice cracks and Ammie feels a twinge in her abdomen; Lucas feeding, the flow of the milk. Rebecca's raw need, so exposed now.

'I'm sorry.'

It doesn't matter. Should she stand up, go to her? Should she try to comfort her?

'Does Tobias know?'

Rebecca nods. She looks lost in the middle of the kitchen, a small girl in an oversized school yard.

'He isn't against it. But he isn't for it, either. We don't really ...' She stops, abruptly, biting on her lip as her eyes fill. She can't divulge the most intimate of details, and Ammie can't blame her. Rebecca catches herself before she speaks. 'Lucas coming along has meant ...'

Her words trail off and Rebecca can't face her, can't look her in the eye. Ammie sees then, why things have been so much more difficult. It isn't just that Tobias might not be Lucas's father – and still, it was impossible to tell from the shape of the eyes, the turn of the nose – but that her son arriving means Tobias is less invested in another child so soon.

'But surely – isn't that why we do this? Why the community chooses it. Plural marriage?'

'Tobias is less invested in that than you realise.'

It's as though Ammie has been hit by something hard, something she didn't know; a realisation that Rebecca knows him more than she does.

'What do you mean?'

'You don't know how much he struggles? With the prayers, the rigid systems? Goran's inflexibility.'

She didn't. She didn't know. How could she have been so close to Tobias and not known? How can they have desired each other so much but she missed that detail? 'But he's an Elder.'

'Sometimes. I feel I've lost him, Ammie. And I don't know what to do.' She sobs. 'There's nothing to do,' she says, 'but continue.'

Ammie is struggling to breathe. Continue. With what? With how things are now? Continue how it was before he left? She concentrates her mind on Lucas's fingers, stroking the soft skin, there, the feeling of young life in the strong fist.

Rebecca's tears have gone but there's a high spot of colour in both her cheeks. 'Strange,' she says, 'how life doesn't work out how you think. I used to dream about being the wife of an Elder. It was expected, I guess, being Micah's daughter.' Her eyes are bright and steady, and there's a glow in them that is excitement, eager, happy brightness at a possible future. 'And when, with Tobias – well, I'd always hoped ...' She stops, looks away suddenly, as though aware that she is revealing more than she should, more than she intended.

'Hoped …?'

Ammie feels the silence like a charge in her body, the pulse of it.

'It's just – our lack of say in it all.' Rebecca's voice explodes suddenly and when Ammie looks up she sees that she is shaking. But then Rebecca bites her lip and her eyes become more hooded and she has closed off again – that anger, that disappointment. *I know,* Ammie wants to say, *I know too how that feels.*

Rebecca lowers her voice to a whisper. 'I'm sorry.' Her voice cracks then. 'I shouldn't complain. But it's hard not to, when we're not meant to have feelings one way or the other.'

'I didn't … didn't realise that was how you felt about it. How we do things. I thought, always …'

The smile on Rebecca's face is ironic. There's even something bitter about it. 'You thought I didn't have doubts?'

'You don't show it.'

'I wouldn't be human if I didn't doubt. The hard thing is to keep the faith and to carry on through it. To keep the values anyway. To pass them onto the girls.'

Ammie thinks of the family meals together, the prayer times, the Friday evenings when Rebecca has sat straight backed, in control. The strength it must have taken for her to act like that, for Tobias, for the girls, for Goran and Leah and for all the friends and family, every day, every week.

'I think …' Ammie feels the heat rising in her face. 'What I think is that you're very strong, Rebecca.'

She smiles, and Ammie thinks that they've never shared a smile like that before. There have been other moments between them over the months, moments of comfort or agreement that have raised a smile to her lips. But this time, Ammie sees from the light in her eyes that her words have made Rebecca happy.

'Shall we start on the peas?' Ammie says.

Ammie pulls the trug between them, so it's in the centre of the table. Lucas is restless and she looks at Rebecca, trying to decide if she should put him down. Rebecca's gaze is direct, something shifts in her expression and it occurs to Ammie then that they want the same thing. It might be that Lucas has changed something – not just his presence, or the joy people have at having a baby around, but the act of him coming into the world. Something changed that night. Rebecca's eyes, fastened on hers, telling her to be strong and wipe out the pain: something unique that she can't share even with Tobias.

Ammie moves to the Moses basket, pulling it under the window so he can gaze at the coloured light being refracted through the crystal that hangs from the curtain pole.

Back at the table they work together. Their hands enter the rhythm without the need for words as they free the peas from their husks: basket, bowl, bowl; basket, bowl, bowl. Ammie watches Rebecca's fingers dart to retrieve the next pod, thinking how pleasure doesn't have to be a complicated thing at all, just a purpose, a focus and a feeling of doing things in tandem – even if just for a moment – with someone else.

Ammie glances towards the window, to the blue of the sky and the branches of the apple tree next to it and in her mind, there it is, from the past. The image of the open door behind Frania's shoulder, leading out to the garden with its high wall, to the shapely curve of the hills. Beyond that, further still, the woodland opening right onto the border with the next county.

Tobias is tired of bowls. He's tired of the automatic way he has begun to churn them out, from habit or because the design is popular at the craft fairs. Each one is exactly the same to him, and in some senses he's longing to make a mistake because, even flawed, it would be different. In all the years as a glass-smith, he doesn't remember feeling this creeping sense of malaise.

At the bench, Ciaras holds the blow pipe for him, the molten end glowing with all the promise of a new piece. Wedging a hand against the marble top of the bench, Tobias begins to shape the glass into frills with the tweezers. Today, though, the glass won't do what he wants it to. It's as though something is blocked between his head and his hand: the worst possible thing in his trade. When Tobias makes a mistake with the fluting he continues, but beside him he senses Ciaras's hesitation. Tobias looks up, sees the ironic look on his friend's face and the mockery in his eyes.

'We can't sell that.'

And there's the problem, Tobias thinks. He has to travel outside the community and trade on their terms in order to justify being here at all. His profits at the fairs ensure the community can buy the goods they can't produce themselves; if he didn't sell outside and earn money, real money, none of them could live here. He sighs, wishing again that he was involved in the farming. At least there'd be a direct correlation between the food on their table and the work of the hands.

Without looking at him, Ciaras lifts the misshapen bowl with the trowel and crosses to the glory hole. In the time it takes for the glass to reheat, Tobias tries to find his focus. He runs his hand across his forehead, tries to gather himself. When Ciaras returns, Tobias is calm again. He applies his mind to what he is doing – moving aside thoughts of Goran, Amarantha, Rebecca, the craft fairs.

When he's finished moulding the edges of the bowl, Ciaras asks him the question he's been expecting: 'What is it?'

How to find the words, even with Ciaras?

Ciaras prompts him. 'Is it Goran?'

An image of his father floats into his head now: the loose folds of skin around Goran's face, his father's effort to listen. The bout of pneumonia left him weak. But he worries that Leah alone can't help him.

'Partly that. Partly …'

What he wants to say is that although his concerns about Goran's ailing health are very real, he is troubled by something else. The strength and commitment he has shown to the village and their faith are slipping away the weaker he becomes. And Tobias isn't sure if he's afraid of this, or if he welcomes it as a time for change.

Back from the furnace with the gather on the end, Tobias pauses again. He feels Ciaras's eyes on him as he rolls the glass along the marvering bench.

'What bothers me,' he says then, 'is how to broach it. That things need to change.'

'What things?'

'Our exclusion, as a village. The old ways. They feel dead to me.'

'It isn't all down to Goran.'

'Isn't it?'

'It feels like that to you because he's your father.'

Again, with the jack, he's shaping, defining. All he hears is the steady hiss of the furnace from behind. He can't even hear Ciaras breathing.

'Your trouble, Tobias, is that you can't separate parental authority from the church.'

'Church? That's not what we are!'

'Do you know who we are?'

Ciaras's voice has a challenge to it. Tobias is heavy handed with the jack and cuts too far into the glass. Another piece wasted: one more for the glory hole. Ciaras's eyes flick over his face for a moment. Again, he crosses the workshop to reheat the glass.

Tobias sinks down onto the bench. He realises how the muscles in his arms are knotted with tension. He flexes his arm at the elbow. He needs air. A glance outside shows him the intensity of light on the leaves – red, gold. He wants to be out there, breathing it in. He doesn't want to suggest a break, though. They still have so much to do.

Half an hour later they have a whole shelf of bowls in the annealing ovens and Tobias decides that enough is enough. Ciaras clears up without a word, angry, he knows, at the lack of focus he's shown this morning, at his irritability and intolerance. It isn't that Ciaras thinks their system is perfect. But from some boyhood loyalty, he always defends Goran.

Goran's hand. More bone there than Tobias remembers seeing, the outline of each tendon jutting out of the flesh. Such vulnerability. It will come to him, too.

Tobias damps down the furnace, and switches off the lights. It's rare to be finished so early in the day. He watches Ciaras's back disappear down the track, accusatory. Tobias is left with the afternoon; wonders about going home, to spend some time with Ammie and Lucas, and with Martha. But no. The lure of the woods is too great. He breathes in the peaty smell of leaf mould.

Along the edge of the river, watching the play of light on the water, careful to avoid the prominent roots of the trees. He knows where he is heading, and when he reaches it is overcome with familiarity. Despite everything, all the shifting and changing of the last months, this tree trunk, moss grown and embedded in the woods, is still here.

Tobias sits down on it, feeling the roughness of bark under his fingers that are sore from the morning's effort. He hears the call of a bird, far off, something harsh, like a rook. He thinks of when he was here with Ammie. So much has happened since then, and he remembers the image he captured that day when she smiled into a hopeful future.

Rebecca, Ammie. And something else that he can't understand. How the warring between them has stopped. He remembers Ammie's hand on Rebecca's forearm last night at dinner, offering to clear, a gesture of sympathy, a gift of service. Rebecca has been at school all day; Ammie will do this one small task. He remembers, too, the swift look of gratitude in Rebecca's eyes.

His wives befriended. He has wanted it for so long. They have come a long way, all of them. He can't tell what makes him uneasy: the leaves that float gently in the corner of his eye, but alert him, somehow, to movement, to change. The sounds of his breath, the view of it in front of him, the vapour: showing that he is here, now; alive in this moment.

*

'I've tried. He won't talk to me.'

Ammie watches Rebecca on her knees, sweeping the dusty corners of the pantry. School starts again next week, and the place needs to be clean, she says. Ammie is afraid of Rebecca's energy; the way she throws herself into things sometimes, it's as though she's afraid to be still. Now, Rebecca sits back on her heels and runs her hand across her forehead. Her face has the sheen of effort, and tendrils of hair have escaped from her braid.

'He's worried about Goran,' Rebecca says.

'It's more than that. He's so distant. Ever since ... since Lucas. Is he ... is he like that with you?'

Rebecca eases herself up from the floor – knees stiff, no doubt, from being in the same position so long. Even from here Ammie sees the frown puckering her eyebrows.
She moves to the sink for some water, and when she tips back her head her throat moves with the action of drinking. The whiteness of exposed skin. She finishes the drink and puts down the glass.

'On my nights, we're so tired we barely speak.'

Ammie thinks of them lying together in Rebecca's brass bed, their backs turned, their breathing deepening as they move towards sleep.

'It will only be worse. After next week. When you're back, I mean – at school.'

'I don't want to think about it.' There's something conclusive about Rebecca's words. She's already turned her focus back to the floor, her wrist moving with swift, insistent sweeps and the sound of the brush banging against the skirtings. In the corner of the kitchen, Lucas lies on his sheepskin, kicking his legs and punching the air. His gurgles are the only other noise in the kitchen; with the girls out the silence in the house is dust-thick and unfamiliar.

'If ...' The words she wants to say feel too full in her mouth, as though something is stuffed into it. 'If there's more I could do here,' she says. 'To give you less to worry about ...'

Rebecca turns, gets to her feet and crosses to the table, where they've stacked the jars and boxes of provisions they moved off the shelves to clean them. Rebecca doesn't look at her, and Ammie thinks she can't have heard her, but she looks up suddenly, a strange, confused look on her face.

'Thank you, Ammie.'

Ammie can't remember being thanked by Rebecca, not since she was a girl.

Rebecca loads the preserves into her arms – Sarah's blackcurrant jam, Ruth's best rhubarb conserve. The things that will see them through the winter: tomatoes and peaches they've bottled, bags of flour they milled a couple of months ago. She notices how Rebecca stacks things in the same place they came from. Jars the same size, labels outwards, at the back and nearer the front the things for immediate use, the butter and milk. Picking up the chutney, Ammie joins Rebecca in the pantry; and for a while there's just the sound of the bottles being placed on shelves, a harmonious satisfying noise. When Ammie turns to her sisterwife, she sees the clean parting in the centre of Rebecca's hair, the delicate line of scalp.

A strand of it has come away from her braid, hangs by her cheek. Ammie wants to stroke it back, tuck it behind her ear. When Rebecca reaches for another jar, the strand of hair swings further in front of her face and Ammie's hand is moving towards it, placing it between her fingers and stroking it behind her ear.

Rebecca flinches. For a moment Ammie thinks she's gone too far. They are close now and Ammie smells the orange aroma from the cleaning fluid, but also the floral scent of the lotion Rebecca uses on her hair.

Rebecca, wearing only a slip, leaning over the basin to wash it, rinsing it with Martha's plastic cup.

The room lurches, but everything seems somehow slowed down. Then Rebecca lifts her hand, and echoes the movement, tucking the strand of hair behind her ear. Her hand hovers for a moment, then it closes on Ammie's. The skin is warm but rough and she is entering a new world; no longer just Rebecca and Tobias with Ammie, but a world that can contain all three of them, all wanting the same thing: to be loved.

There's a wail from the corner: Lucas, reminding them of his presence. Ammie feels a pull of loyalties. Her child needs her, but she doesn't want to move from this place next to Rebecca with her hand on

172

hers, with the closeness between them they haven't known before. Part of her is relieved though. She doesn't trust the words that might come out, too soon, too raw.

In the kitchen, there's light and more space; her head clears and she is conscious of the breaths she takes. Lucas's face is dark, purple and wrinkled, fists angrily thumping air. When he sees Ammie's face he stops and she has a rushing sensation of guilt, somehow, at her disconnection. Her body responds to his distress, but his presence doesn't penetrate her being in the way she knows, from Rebecca, that it should . Ammie pulls Lucas towards her, pacing the length of the kitchen to soothe him. When she reaches the window she stops for a moment to look out onto the square of garden, the start of the path that links the house to the Bothy. Already, there are signs of the summer ending: the fruit beginning to show on the blackberry bushes and apples falling onto the path through the orchard, browning and bruised, pecked by birds.

Behind her, she hears a scrabbling sound. It's unnerving, the rattle of something hard. When Ammie looks round, Rebecca is leaning over something, her hands in a plastic tub. She lifts up the tub and shakes it, frowning. Ammie sees then what it is: the magnetic letters they have in the kitchen for the girls to amuse themselves with, sometimes. They're often arranged on the table in random words, consonant, vowel, consonant – simple, concrete words: cat, mitt, bat. Rebecca shakes the box, looks at Ammie and smiles. Then her face clouds as though a thought has occurred to her.

'We should wait,' she says, 'until the girls get home.'

'Esther ought to be learning some new words by now.'

Rebecca laughs. 'If Naomi will let her.'

Her smile fades to a frown as she reaches into the box and picks one up. Red. Letter A. 'Do you remember we had these in class?'

She had forgotten, until that moment. Now in her memory she feels the edges of the shapes and how bright they were, standing out amongst a classroom where everything else seemed to be made of wood. They fascinated her, those bright plastic shapes that surely were from somewhere else. Her adult self knows now that they were from another world: they could only have come with Micah and Ruth from the city, found one day by Rebecca and appropriated for the school room. Ammie remembers the white board in the corner they could stick things to. The day Emilia trod on a blue B so that the magnet fell out and it stopped sticking. Ammie nods. But she doesn't move. She's aware of holding her breath, of squeezing Lucas tighter towards her.

Rebecca is holding up the A.

She reaches forward and puts it on the floor in front of them. Hitching Lucas up in her arms, Ammie moves next to her, looking at the mêlée of colours, all bold, all primary. Rebecca reaches into the box again and brings out two 'M's – green and blue. When she places them alongside the A, Ammie spots a yellow E. She reaches to pick it up, and hands it to Rebecca. Rebecca places that one too, leaving a space where the letter should be.

'Just one letter left,' she says.

The letter 'I'. The I of her.

They crouch there, the two of them, Ammie with her infant son in her arms, trying to spot the missing one, guessing the colour even as they look. Rebecca finds it first. Her hand darts in and retrieves it, the colour bright in her face and Ammie thinks how simple life is sometimes, how pleasure doesn't have to be a complicated thing at all, just a purpose, a focus and that feeling of doing things in tandem – even if just for a moment – with somebody else.

'There!' Rebecca comes to kneeling, sits back on her heels. So simple to see it like that, reduced to letters, to colours, to code. But the letters are unmistakable: Ammie's name.

A smile plays around Rebecca's mouth, as though something in her is lifting. It suits her, Ammie thinks. She could be a girl again.

'Look,' Rebecca says, 'we could rearrange it.'

Her head is angled to one side, her tongue curling towards her top lip as though trying to solve a puzzle. Ammie looks at the pattern made by the letters – the red, yellow, red again, then green. It's her name. And yet, laid out like that on the wooden floor, it is rendered strange by margins of the space around it.

Rebecca's fingers reach the 'I' and slide it upwards, so it hovers above the line of the other letters. She removes one 'M' and takes the other between two fingers, moves it across. Slides the 'I' down into the space left by the 'M'. It is no longer Ammie's name but something else entirely.

'Do you remember?' Rebecca says. Her voice hardly reaches above a whisper. 'Do you remember I told you what it meant? That word?'

Rebecca's eyes are fixed on the word on the floor. Even so, Ammie hears the smile in her voice as she speaks, and her throat is so tight she can't move her head, or neck. She feels as though she's swaying, holding onto Lucas to keep her afloat. In her head there's an echo of the way Rebecca says her name. It was she – all those years ago – who first gave her the name, the shortened version: Ammie. The vowels aren't short and crisp like everyone else says it but roll long in her mouth with a final expansive E.

'I remember.' Ammie curls her chin into Lucas's head. Rebecca leans forward to straighten the letters and Ammie looks down again onto the crown of Rebecca's head, to that line of white, the exposed scalp. Then Ammie isn't sure if she actually says the words that crash in her ears, or if she just imagines it. In any case, she remembers. The word is right on her tongue.

The word comes from her name, an invented name from years ago that has sweetened over the years as Rebecca has rolled it over her tongue.

Amie. In French, it means friend. And something else. It also means love.

*

Tobias traces his way across the field, the thin beam of the torch illuminating frozen tufts of grass and thistles, a random rabbit hole. There is only the sound of his boots on the frozen ground, the regularity of his breathing; the vapour that comes out of his mouth in clouds. He plays with it a little; breathing out hard and watching the volume increase. After the heat of the furnace, the cold makes his cheeks sting. He thinks of their sitting room, the fire; the evening ahead with Rebecca and Ammie, and how quickly it's come round again, the Advent meal. He thinks he'll encourage a period of silence before bedtime. They should make it a daily habit, he thinks, a few moments of still connection instead of spoken prayers; he'll suggest it tonight and see if they agree, contemplation for a year of being reunited.

The kitchen is in darkness. Tobias sees signs of earlier activity, the shadow of implements left on the drying rack: a mixing bowl, a pan. He sniffs the air – an unmistakable smell of cake dough. He crosses to the range and feels its heat near his thighs, but when he reaches for the kettle, it is cold. They must be next door, a spontaneous invitation to supper, perhaps. Tobias's stomach tightens: eating with Goran is not what he wants to do tonight. When it happens, he needs to steel himself. He scrabbles in the drawer for matches to light the lamp then warms his hands against the range, breathing consciously and trying to prepare himself to don a smile and greet his father.

He notices the hallway door is open. He crosses to shut it, to keep in the heat. There is a sound from down the hall, a dull thud. It isn't loud; but it is loud enough for him to pause, still holding the door handle, feeling the metal cold against his palm. He listens. Outside the world is stilled, calm. Perhaps he imagined it. He returns to the range, picks up the empty kettle. With the rush of cold water comes a sense – nothing rational, nothing definite – that something is wrong. He places the kettle on the counter and crosses to the hall.

The cold is what he notices first; he shivers, but his senses are focused down the hallway. He fights two contradictory impulses: the voice in his head that tells him not to worry; the need to proceed and be sure. Since witnessing the fight in the city he's carried the fear inside him constantly, the fear of what the outside can do. But who could reach them here? Who would want to trespass?

He inches down the hall in darkness, avoiding the obstacles in his way: the settle, the bureau in the corner with the tidy piles of family and church administration. The sitting room door is ajar. From this angle he sees the fire in the grate. No fireguard. He experiences a moment of irritation that Rebecca should leave the house without remembering the guard. And as if to prove him right, at that moment a log falls from its place at the top and there is a hiss, the glowing spit of sparks.

Inside the room, there's a movement. It's out of his line of

176

vision, something he senses rather than sees, like a soundless vibration of molecules he experiences in his body. He hardly dares breathe. He calculates how long it would take for others to come and help but there might be no way of raising the alarm against this person: this intruder, outsider. Thief.

Tobias is aware of the pressure on his finger pads as he pushes open the door.

A woman is standing before the fire, undressed. It takes him a moment to register it is Ammie.

His breath stops; he feels a charge in his body that is all at once a question and an instantaneous rush of desire. She is trance-like, eyes focused on the middle distance, and the smile on her face is one of invitation. And there's something about the emotion it radiates, something distilled: pleasure.

It makes her mesmerizingly beautiful.

Tobias's eyes take in the gracious sweep of her hips and waist, the pointed breasts, the neat triangle of pubic hair. Skin lit by the fire and yet still extraordinarily white. She could be a sculpture in a gallery; he remembers going as a boy and wanting to run his fingers over the blue threads, like capillaries through the translucent stone. There's the urgent twitch of his penis, and Tobias wants to touch her, floor her, consume her; there is only this, the pinpoint concentration of need, this tumbling, rawness of wanting.

Tobias steps forward and his line of vision opens up. He sees where Ammie's gaze has been fixed.

Rebecca.

Rebecca naked, with her arm in the air and a rapture on her face that transforms her. He recognises its beauty but he is repelled by it, because it is something unrecognisable, something from outside him, outside any realm of their experience together. Rebecca's hands move, stroking the air in front of her, tracing the shape of her sisterwife's body even from across the room. Caressing Ammie through the space; defining her, loving her, creating her.

It is too much. Tobias is falling, closes his eyes to regain balance and catches the glint of the fire on Ammie's fingers, the light reflected in

177

that thin gold band. His eyelids seek respite, blackness, but pressed into relief is that image of the two of them, a doubleness that sickens him, stokes something immense in him: larger and more animal than he could possibly have imagined. They face each other; an exact reflection, even though there's the difference in their bodies – bodies he has cherished, slept beside – Rebecca's slender shoulders, Ammie's rounded biceps. The convex curve of Rebecca's stomach and Ammie's flattened abdomen.

Rebecca, Ammie.

Ammie, Rebecca.

The sound that comes from his mouth is deformed. He gags, wanting to vomit up excess emotion, shock, disbelief, rage. He sees their heads turn in a slowed-down synchrony, sees Ammie's eyes shoot across the room; sees the stricken expression on her face, the panic. And then Rebecca's haughty gaze and fear on both their faces, looking for the intruder who has disturbed them, who has found them out.

Then he is running. Thinks only to find help because his wives must have been drugged. He must alert the others. As his feet strike the ground, mucus rattles in his lungs as though protesting at the way he snatches the air. For the first time he registers the cold of the outside, stumbling towards. Towards ...

He lurches to a stop.

Tobias has no idea where he is going. He has run past Goran's house and his ears are pounding with effort, with the sound of blood pumping through his body. His body is trembling. He thinks of Ciaras. Ciaras can help him figure this out, what has happened, will help him restore order and calm to his family, his wives.

Then he sees his wives' faces again, their slow gesture of turning together to face him. He remembers their recent laughter in the kitchen; the way at mealtimes they moved around each other in their elaborate dance, with no need for words. The tenderness of Rebecca's fingers reaching for Ammie; the two of them locking each other into their glance. No room for another.

He is standing by the old stable on the rise, breath coming in heaves. He didn't even notice the incline. Now he feels a surge of energy, of blind anger and his fists hit the wall. It is already crumbling, and he dislodges another brick, brings his fist to his mouth, finds the wound with his tongue. His skin is grazed and in the next instant there is the pain, the sharp sting of it, the ache of the bone where it has struck something hard and the welling of emptiness in him.

He has his head in his hands. Wonders how he has been so deluded, and for how long. And he knows then that he can't go to Ciaras, that he needs to crawl into a space, somewhere dark and familiar, that will hold him and protect him. His sobs are a heaving push of effort, expelling the memory of Rebecca, Ammie, Ammie, Rebecca, the whiteness of their skin, the brazenness of their bodies in the firelight. Something swims up, too, from the depths of childhood; a face. It is undefined in features but the threat of its presence is clear. The face is bound up with a memory of crying at shards of glass and wanting to sink the edges of them into the man's pocked face.

Glass. At once vulnerable and strong. Pliable when hot, but quick to shatter. His father's fear, he remembers; the pulling sensation in his six-year-old bowels that night watching his father being led away and the sound of his mother's shrieking and his awareness of fallibility, human fallibility, that things are not always safe. That his father will not always be there.

Tobias is here, now, where he needs to be. He slides open the door to the workshop. The weight of it, the sensation, is something familiar, at least, and the old oilcloth he spreads on the floor has the smell of years on it. The blanket he pulls around him is too thin but Tobias does not care. He lies on the stone floor, shivering, sucked into a raging emptiness.

V

LOT

'He asked to see me.'

To Frania, the defensiveness in her voice was obvious. But the nun wasn't interested, merely glanced sideways and continued in her tasks: tidying, refilling the water glass, opening the curtains so there was enough light to see by. It was more like a prison cell than a hospice room, with a sink in the corner, a flimsy chest of drawers, a wooden-armed chair by the bed. Its sparseness amplified everything: her fear and grief. And relief.

Julius had sent for her. He wanted to see her. Proof – after all these years, that she still occupied space in his heart.

He was asleep, the white sheets pulled tight across the bed, a blue blanket folded over his feet at the end. The nun left the room without a word, closing the door decisively. Frania moved towards him, hardly daring to look.

He was so diminished. This man; once her lover. Tears pricked at her eyes, hot and unexpected. His face was lined, drained of colour. It was nothing like the face of his younger self. His arms were shrunken. She thought how responsive she'd once been to him, the places on her body that his tongue had found and made his: the patch of skin behind her ear; the cleft between her collarbones. There was nothing in this man of the Julius-ness she had desired and – sometimes – even hated.

She reached for his hand, expecting a papery dryness but finding it extraordinarily soft. Someone must be caring for him, coming each day with creams and lotions, gently applying them to Julius's skin and making comforting circles with her fingertips. She couldn't imagine it was the nun who'd shown her in. Whoever it was, the thought of it was more moving than the sight of Julius himself: the thought of all that quiet love.

Frania traced a finger along the protruding veins on his hand, following its journey up his wrist. Julius opened his eyes, the same dark hazel eyes she remembered and Frania was thrown, suddenly, into the past. She was startled by the juxtaposition of his dying body and his eyes so ageless and alive.

Julius stared. Her heart thudded in her chest. He didn't know her.

He'd send her away. Then she saw the flicker of recognition, realisation. He sighed her name, like relief.

'I didn't think you'd come.' His voice was so thin.

'I came when I heard,' she said. 'I'm glad I …' She paused, not knowing how to say that she was glad she wasn't too late. She remembered the challenge on Jude's face as he leaned against his motorcycle in Marah – still the same one, the one he drove out all those years ago to find her. *He needs you. Will you come?* Then a swift decision. The pain in her gut, the voice in her head she must follow.

It was too much. Seeing him was overwhelming. Frania covered her face at the thought of his grief and pain, all the lost years. Her reaction had been instinctive: Julius needs you. Come. But now she felt – across the distance, across the space – a powerful sense of her daughter's need. What had she done? The realisation hit her hard, like a blow to the gut, and she could hardly see Julius through the tears. To be here, to be with him, she'd left Ammie behind.

Oh, her dear girl.

Julius lifted his head. It was slow and painful; an agony of time before he spoke.

'Bloody cells.'

'Julius …'

'Multiplying too fast. That's what they said.' His lips curled into a smile. She heard a throaty chuckle. 'Body never did know when to stop.' The laugh turned to a wheeze, a pronounced cough that caused her body to tense, poised for the nun to return.

She put her hand on his arm. 'What do you want me to do?'

His eyes softened, clouded over for just a second. She heard random footsteps along the corridor outside and the regular tick of the clock at his bedside. She thought: if we could put it in a vacuum, this life. If we could only do that.

'Thank you. For coming. I don't deserve it.'

'Sssh …' She reached for him. Reassurance. Her eyes kept being drawn to his face. It was gaunt and yet pockets of skin – around his eyes, near his earlobes – sagged, with folds of skin hanging loose where flesh should have been.

'Tell me what you need,' she said.

'Water.'

Frania crossed to the sink in the corner. She filled the glass, set it beside him, rearranged the sheets around his shoulders. There was a faint waft of something deodorised. Underlying it, something stale and rotting. She helped Julius to sit, lifted the water to his lips. It's how it would have been, she thought, growing old together. Days spent caring for him. Perhaps it was not so late, yet, for that.

The door opened briskly. The nun. She threw a look at Frania. 'What are you doing?'

'Helping him.'

'Helping? You're only a visitor. Please remember that.' In her hand she held something – pills, painkillers. She held out four of them, white and oval and shiny on her palm.

'There's no point,' Julius said.

'Please take them.' The nun snapped out the words.

With a shaking hand, Julius picked one from her palm and held it up to his lips.

When the nun left, he lowered his head to the pillow, fixed his eyes on hers. 'There are things,' he said, 'that I need to …'

'No.'

Tears obscured everything; the room, his face. All the years of pain, the rejection; the anger. It wasn't that they didn't matter. It was just that, now, they seemed so small.

'I should have come,' he whispered. 'Before she was born. I left you alone.'

Alone. It was Frania's guilt, now, that had her by the throat. Not anger at Julius's absence any more, but regret. She'd managed to push it away – the memory of Ammie's face as she stood on the doorstep. *Leaving?* Something in her hands, still, a book maybe. Staring at Frania in disbelief.

Frania had made her choice. There was no return.

He was speaking again. 'When I met them, I didn't know.'

She closed her eyes. She'd been waiting for this, the incoherence and confusion. But she'd glimpsed it, at least, for a few moments – the real Julius. And she'd be back, tomorrow. She'd be with him again.

'All that stuff they spouted,' he said. 'About inner spirit.' He was sweating, eyes fixed on the ceiling, as though the answers were all there. Frania reached for a handkerchief, wiped his forehead. 'It was only – after – it was when I got to know what they believed.'

'Hush.'

His body stiffened. He reached for her arm; she leaned towards him and he was whispering. 'I've left it too late – for the truth. To find it.' His breath in her ear, rasping. In and out, painful. Then: 'Would you read to me?'

'Of course.'

Frania crossed to the window and snapped the curtains back. She wanted to let in the sunshine so it might heal him, so Julius could breathe in the hyacinths from the garden. Spring. Surely a torturous time to die.

He turned to indicate the book by his bedside. She caught sight of it – dark red, leather bound. She walked around the bed to retrieve it, fingers brushing the lettering. She stopped. It couldn't be.

'Julius. It's a bible.'

He closed his eyes, a gesture of agreement. Or, at least, acceptance.

'I've marked the page,' he said.

She opened the book but the tears swam into her eyes, the words blurring. When they cleared she tried to concentrate, to make sense of them. She would never have guessed that Julius believed in this, took comfort in it. And yet the words were familiar; words she hadn't heard or seen for many years, words from her childhood that echoed in her head and brought back the texture of the bench under her buttocks, the intoning voice of the pastor. She hadn't heard them in Marah, even, for all their talk of God. Though they might benefit from them, she thought, because in themselves they were beautiful: *blessed are the meek, blessed are the peacemakers.*

For they shall be called Children of God.

He was asleep. Frania felt the chair arms digging into her flesh. She felt the heat rising in her body, around her neck and up her face. Another phrase began to surface; it was like diving to the bottom of a lake, retrieving things – all the objects brought up from the darkness. Words reinventing themselves in this room, where Julius was struggling towards the end of life. Suffer the little children.

She thought of Ammie. She and her – they'd suffered because of Frania's love of Julius. But his thoughts and dreams, his love, had coloured her life. She couldn't let go. Fragments of memories were there, still, tucked at the back of her consciousness: making love in the forest, the hush, and pine needles working into her back.

She needed air, and light. She placed the book on the floor, began to get up.

His eyes snapped open. 'The children?' His hand hovered in the air, searched for hers.

She whispered then: 'Which children?'

'Mine.'

'Amarantha?' *Think of me, and I'll feel it, that pull.* The tug in Frania's abdomen, sudden and quick. She swallowed. 'Don't worry. They'll take care of her.'

'And the other?'

'Other?' There was the rasping sound of his breath.

'The other girl.'

'Which girl?'

Julius turned to face her. His face was so earnest, like a child in a schoolroom.

'We had to – she couldn't have stayed …'

This was the tragedy of life, she thought: that the mind invents a narrative to aid the body in its efforts, to help with the pain. She couldn't reach him; this place he was in – of the imagination – it was so far removed.

He sighed, closed his eyes again. She was left to watch the steady rise and fall of his chest as he slept. She couldn't stay. She needed to be outside, needed to think.

She crept out of the room with Julius's words resounding in her head. *She couldn't have stayed.* Frania didn't understand. Was he saying Ammie had to leave?

The main door slid back automatically, she caught sight of the brass plaque outside the door. Above the name of the hospice – St Anthony's, engraved in squat lettering – was the image of a man with a halo around his head. There was a glimmer of a memory, her grandmother on her knees with beads around her hands, praying for lost things.

St Anthony. The patron saint of lost things. Lost causes.

She thought of Julius, lost himself. And how she herself had been lost for a time too. Was it duty that brought her here or was she, like some compass guided ever northwards, drawn by her fascination for him? It was more than that, now. There was something she needed to know; she could divine it.

She couldn't have stayed. Who? And why?

Outside, a gardener was hoeing the beds, whistling as he pulled the handle to and fro. Frania pulled her scarf closer around her, shivered in spite of the sunshine. She followed the meandering path round the side of the building. She took a breath and pulled back her shoulders, resolute. The stone arch of the gateway was in view now, pulling her towards it, as though for something else, vivid and real. Frania knew what it was she was heading for. She was heading into the truth.

MARAH

Frania was the one Tobias looked for. Even before first light, he was hammering on her door and she opened it, dishevelled and bewildered. She'll understand, he thought, because she lives on the fringes of things. He knows he'll feel safe with her, out of view of the rest of the community, tucked away in her caravan overlooking the woods and gardens; far from the Piece. And so it is that – as the sun rises and colours the sky like an artist's backwash – he finds himself at the table that is crammed between Frania's kitchen and her tiny living space.

They've said everything that needs to be said. Tobias explained what happened; Frania listened. Then she said some things of her own: past truths, information that's left him reeling. It changes everything, and nothing.

He's still lost. Lost to the self he left behind, the one who lay last night on the workshop floor. Tobias would give anything to be back there now, in the darkness with nothing but the soothing hiss of the furnace and the gleam of light on the finished glassware. He's so close he hears Frania's breathing; feels the pressure of her hand between his shoulder blades as she massages in circling movements. Her fingers move across his back, still gentle. They have a vocabulary of their own, unlocking what he has kept buried since last night.

And so he finds he can weep, finally. For his pain, for his shame and for the overwhelming sense of being excluded. The not knowing is the worst; that he should discover the truth in such a way.

'Tobias?'

He can't respond, just yet. But Frania doesn't push and he's grateful for her patience. Gradually, his crying subsides. He pulls himself upright and turns to face her. Concern flickers across her face and the watery light of afternoon illuminates the grey in her hair. She's intent, though, poised; as if her whole body is engaged in listening. Her shoulders pulled back, hands folded in her lap. He feels himself growing calmer.

She puts a hand out to touch his arm. 'Don't be hard on anyone,' she says, 'yourself, most of all.'

Hard on himself? How can he not be? How can he let go of all he's heard? He wants to punch something hard and unforgiving. It is how he feels, in that flare of white light in front of his eyes. To punish, not to forgive.

'How can you say that? After what I saw. And what you've told me …' Layers of lies have sedimented over the years, he realises. There's a rushing in his ears, time moving too fast. He'd always stood on solid ground. That's what he used to think. Now he sees life as it can be: unwieldy and malleable, unable to be controlled, like glass refusing to gather on the blowpipe.

Without glass, how can he work?

He lifts his head; shakes it quickly, as though to rid himself of the thought.

'It explains so much,' he says. 'I keep seeing flashes of things that happened. Memories. Strange things I couldn't explain – like coming home and her not being there. The house dark …'

Frania stands up and moves to the tiny stove. She fills a kettle from a large container of water and puts it down on the stove, lights it. She begins to spoon tea into the pot, then pauses. 'Don't judge too harshly, Tobias.'

'How can I not judge?'

From here, he can reach out and touch the window. He puts his hand flat against the glass and feels its coldness as a comfort. He thinks what a complex substance it is, that he works with. It can create distances. It can harm, it can separate. It can create illusions and make people believe things that have never been there.

Outside, the world continues as usual. Far off, at the edges of the garden people are beginning to move about in the glass house, scurrying to their activities. Already, even this early in the day, the routine is beginning. Care of the garden, the list of tasks for the day.

The kettle rises to a boil. Frania looks round for a glove or a towel to protect her hands then eases it off the heat.

'You're a man. It's hard for you to imagine being a sisterwife.'

'But you never were.'

She shakes her head, philosophical. 'That's true. But I've seen what it does. Those Friday meetings, being excluded. The lack of freedom

…' She crosses the caravan, sits beside him, hands him a cup. It is too hot, burns him, and he puts it down quickly. 'On the face of it, it's easy. Other wives to share the burden, the work and the children. A big happy community that you feel so grateful to be part of. But it's so lonely – so excluding …'

'I do know. I've seen it – I saw it with my mother and Deborah.'

Frania's lips set into a line. 'But you can't relate that to your own wives?'

'I did. I mean, I do. I know how hard it must be to share. I found it – the thought of it – hard myself. With Ammie.'

He has a sensation like something falling away from him, but of things making sense, suddenly, truth revealed. His own blind spot, revealed. All these years, he thought the richness of the wives was in sharing. He's been blind, he sees, to how they feel, these women. Everything their way of life asks of them. It's not that he didn't know. He was too afraid to think about it.

Frania continues: 'And there's no place for it, that other thing. It's suppressed. No one talks about it.'

She's speaking in riddles now. 'What thing?'

'Desire.'

'Desire?' He laughs, hard and bitter.

Frania looks at him, bites her lip. He feels her eyes on his, the intention of her gaze. Then she turns to look out of the window, looking at the same view he sees now: the edges of the woods and the track down to the garden. Frania sits, completely still.

At last she says: 'I want to show you something.' She stands abruptly, crosses to the cupboard in the corner and crouches to look inside. Tobias hears her grunt with the effort of looking as she rifles through the contents. Will it provide the answer for the secrets and transgressions? Will it tell him what he did wrong, as a husband; as a son?

Frania thrusts something in front of him. A photograph. A full-length shot of a woman, smiling at the camera. The first thing he notices is her posture, relaxed, loose limbed. He takes in the surroundings: a street in the sunshine, tall buildings behind. The city.

He picks it up, examines the face. It's only then he sees who it is.

His mother.

'Leah?'

Frania nods.

'In the city. It was a few months before they left, I think.'

'Why? Why show me it?'

Leah: younger, thinner. Something liberated about her.

Frania sits still, considering her reply. Slowly, a smile plays around her lips and she edges forward in her seat. She touches the corner of the photograph with the edge of her finger. 'She's beautiful, don't you think? Happy. Look at her face, her body. She's in love.'

'I don't see …'

'It's proof.' Frania exhales suddenly, deeply, turns her eyes to the sky. 'How repressive this all is. This.' She points at the photograph. 'This is your mother in love. Before all this – the repression; the duty.'

'It doesn't prove anything.'

Then from nowhere a question comes to him. He stops to consider it, then it hits him with full force. 'Did she love my father, do you think?' He hisses the words through clenched teeth. Even as he asks it, he's not sure he wants to know the answer.

Love. Desire.

So much he doesn't know.

Frania leans forward and gently takes the photograph from him. She fingers its edges, looking at it. 'I can't answer that. I've said too much already. You need to ask Goran.'

'I don't want to speak to Goran.'

Tobias leans forward, massages both his temples with his fingers. His head throbs, with the lack of sleep, the crying; and all he's learned this morning. He remembers the call to the Meeting House, the Elders' direction to be Sealed to Ammie and his stomach fizzes with anger at the subterfuge. He doesn't want to speak to Goran. But he must.

'I still don't understand,' he whispers, 'why you're saying all this.'

'So you could salvage something good – from all this. It's too late for me. I've lost my daughter, I think. But you – you can rebuild things. I was hoping – it might heal a breach.' Her face begins to crumple. 'I love Ammie. I know you do, too. I want what's best for her. Love her, Tobias.

But love your father too.'

'You want to heal things,' he says. He hears his voice, flat and lifeless. 'Or destroy them?'

Frania leans forward. She places her hand on his head, as though he were still a child. He sobs at the gesture, and he hears from her broken voice that she's crying too.

'What you do with what all this – it's your choice. This information – it's a kind of power. But if you use it wisely, it can heal things. It's a chance, Tobias. A new beginning, maybe.' She pauses. 'It could be what you were waiting for.'

His hand, flat on the window pane.

In the hands of a craftsman glass is transformed from grains of a substance of the earth, to contain air. It transmutes into something beautiful and is made into objects that not only give pleasure but which sustain, are timeless. Around him, the sounds of now: a shout, one of the villagers greeting another at the other end of the garden; above him, the feet of a bird scuttling against the thin roof of the caravan. Beside him, the rise and fall of Frania's expectant breath.

'What will you do?' Frania says.

Tobias makes no sound. He jams the heel of his hands into his eye sockets. He wants to feel something physical, something that will stop the pain on the inside, but most of all, he wants to be able to see. And to find his way through the labyrinth of lies.

*

The days that follow are strange and tumbling. Ammie goes walking, strides out along the track towards the town with Lucas strapped to her back. Each time she wonders about continuing but when he wakes, cold and hungry, she turns back. She avoids seeing anyone, lives off root vegetable soup from her stockpile of swede and beetroot, wrinkled from being stored too long in sawdust. Even when Frania taps at the window, Ammie hides behind the door, willing Lucas not to make a sound.

Rebecca walks around her house like a ghost. She claims illness, keeps the girls at home, drinking chocolate with them by the fire and fending off offers of help. They bake cookies and eat pancakes. When Martha asks a question, she forces a smile and finds an answer, tries to keep things light. She tries to avoid Naomi's puzzled gaze.

Tobias sleeps on the floor of the workshop, refusing Ciaras's offer of a bed. His friend doesn't probe but he tells Tobias he can't stay there in midwinter; he'll catch his death. Tobias only shrugs, tells him that the furnace lights the space enough to see by, that the blankets keep him warm and that he prefers the solitude. In the mornings, when Ciaras arrives for work, he finds his friend staring into the furnace, ineffectual, moving the blowpipe along the surface of the glass.

*

He finds solace in the glasshouse. At least, working in the garden, he's nowhere near the house; he can do something with his hands. There's a lot to do before they start planting, a season's worth of tidying and sorting to be done; the glasshouse panes to clean, algae to scrape away methodically, with vinegar and a scourer. It leaves behind smears of green on his clothes and hands. Inside, the pain won't stop resounding – in his stomach and his chest; part of him feels missing. He is anchorless, weightless. He'd give anything to see his daughters; Lucas. He isn't up to seeing his wives. Or his mother.

When he's done with the cleaning, Tobias readies the seed trays for planting, lining them up on the bench. He tips compost into each tiny container, into which they'll sow winter lettuce. He tries not to think about anything but the loam between his fingers; the fertile smell of it. It's comforting, elemental.

'You forgot these.'

The voice comes from behind him. When he turns, it's Goran, holding out gloves like an unwanted gift. Tobias nods wordlessly and steps forward to retrieve them, trying not to meet Goran's gaze. He knows his father will wonder why he's here. For a moment, he considers telling him. But what would he say?

Goran leans against the doorframe, watching Tobias, blowing into his hands. The vapour escapes from the sides. He looks small and fragile and there's an unspoken question hovering in the air. *Why? Why are you here?*

'Ciaras tells me you've been sleeping in the workshop.' A pause. 'Tobias? What's wrong?'

The compost though his fingers, moist and crumbling. Like everything else, he thinks, disintegrating; coming apart.

'I know what happened,' Tobias says. The words echo, bounce off the glasshouse walls. Tobias sees Goran squint against the low sun but it's the pain not the light that does it: the pain of truth finally revealed. There's no need for Tobias to qualify it; he sees that Goran understands. And his face is stricken. He looks so much older, his spine beginning to bend with age as though beneath an invisible weight. What should Tobias say? He can't possibly tell him. And yet, he thinks now, Goran might be the most likely to understand.

'You misled us,' Tobias says.

'What do you mean?'

'You lied to us. About why we came here, all that time ago. You lied about …'

'It wasn't like that.'

'Then how was it?' Tobias snaps. He's claustrophobic, suddenly; the air inside the glasshouse is too hot. He's overwhelmed by the smell of earth.

'We decided together. All of us. It wasn't just me.'

'You were angry.'

Something in Goran gives way then. His knees buckle and he looks wildly around him, arm outstretched, looking for support. Tobias rushes to find a chair – an old wooden one with no back – and helps Goran into it. Tobias squats beside him; Goran holds out his hand. The pain on his father's face is obvious now. It makes Tobias dizzy. He's weak with lack of food and sleep, and now, with this: the knowledge that to confront the truth, he must remind his father of his past pain.

'Father …' The impulse is instinctive. Tobias moves towards him, seeking his embrace. The anger is fading now and Tobias is dimly aware of sounds from the garden: the cry of a rook, someone's voice, far off, calling: peaceful sounds of the everyday. But inside, he's fighting with the emotion: the pain, confusion and fear.

He grips onto Goran. 'I found them,' Tobias says. And there they are. They're out, the words before he can check them. His only need now is to share. 'They were together – Ammie and Rebecca. Together.'

Goran tenses and pulls away. Tobias sees the sheen on Goran's pale skin that makes it look waxy; he sees the threads of red, the veins in his eyes. His lips move but Tobias can't hear the words and he doesn't recognise them, words from his old language. It's as though he's praying.

He whispers: 'Oh my boy.'

Tobias is pulled in to Goran's chest, held there. His father breathes with him until Tobias feels it pass, the urge to cry.

*

By the time they've exhausted their stories, the afternoon light is fading. Tobias moves away from the bench, leans against the glass wall. He leans his forehead against it, feeling the cool as a balm to his forehead. It's a barrier – keeping the outside out, the inside in – an invisible force field. All his life, he realises he has been surrounded by something similar, something that holds things in.

'What will happen, do you think?'

Out in the garden, Tobias spies people moving between the beds; an adult and two children, bundled up in layers against the cold afternoon. She stands up, the woman, pulls her shawl around her and the gesture is so familiar it makes his throat constrict. Rebecca. Rebecca in the garden with the girls, issuing instructions. They're hoeing, turning over the ground in the far corner. A gust of wind sweeps the hair across Naomi's face and she pulls it quickly back. He watches Esther's unsteady movements as she handles the tools; Rebecca's patient explanation and demonstration. It ignites something inside him: sadness, regret, admiration at this simple act of love.

He sees Goran watching him.

'If it comes out,' he says, ' – everything that's happened. It's got to change. Do you see that?'

'It can't stay hidden. It's too late for that. The best we can do …'

'This is about faith,' Tobias says. He's surprised by his passion. He looks onto the garden again, sees Rebecca ushering the girls away. They're picking up their things, moving towards the east gate of the garden. 'It's all we have.'

'I don't know,' Goran says. He leans forward, elbows on his knees, head in his hands. 'I don't know what to do.'

'I don't know either. They won't understand. I don't myself.'

The silence is unbearable. When he thinks of Goran going to the Elders, he wants to run. More than anything, he wants to leave, to not have to face anyone; to start again. But he has no choice. His home; his children. They're here. He has to make peace with Rebecca, with Ammie.

As for his parents: they must make peace between themselves.

He needs to move, to do something. Crosses to the bench, looks out onto the grey of the garden, the dramatic gunmetal colour of sky. He pulls the seed trays towards him, filled with nourishing earth and he makes a depression in each pod, a finger's width. He takes a seed and jams it into the compost. Without a word, Goran stands up to join him, picking up the dibber and beginning to jab holes in each of the pots. Tobias fills them with seeds. They work together silently until the seed tray is complete.

Tobias gathers up what they've planted and lifts the trays onto the top shelf. He thinks of them resting in the earth through the winter; how, with the first sign of sunshine, they'll sprout, spindly but full of intention; seeking the light.

Dawn rising. It is low, still, the winter sun; the light has a watery golden quality. The woods echo with that silence that comes after a deep snowfall. The fields are empty; the garden is empty. In the workshops, tools lay on benches where they were set down yesterday. In Tobias's studio, the furnace remains at the same slow burn it maintains overnight. All it needs is an injection of air, some more wood, to resume its intensity.

The Meeting House bell rings through the valley.

The clanging is insistent, somehow more mournful than when it last rang – to gather people for Amarantha's Sealing to Tobias Christensen. It's a signal; a sign of something not right. It brings the villagers out onto their porches. Hephzi Carter pulls her shawl tighter round her and frowns at the sky. Despite the snow, Alpha the dog runs barking in frenzied circles, and the Miller children spill onto the Piece to chase him. Slowly, the community emerges: the Carters and Cuthberts; Fitzgeralds, O'Gradys. They trudge across the Piece, closing their eyes against the sting of sleet on their cheeks, vapour issuing from their mouths. They crane their necks to watch the bell as it swings. The expressions on their faces: curiosity, fear. Some are more open, trusting that the reason is important enough to pull them from breakfast, from their first tasks of the day. They can be patient; they will know the reason for the ringing soon enough.

*

Goran has told them. This is what Tobias thinks as he finds his seat in the inner circle of the Meeting House. There are two possible reasons to have called the meeting: either Goran wants to tell his own truth; or they're here because of what happened with his wives.

Tobias counts around the circle: the Elders are all here.

He feels the pressure of fingernails digging into his palm. He tries to remember how he described it to Goran, the words he used about that moment of finding them together, naked flesh, pale skin. The invisible charge between them, reverberating through his own body. He couldn't tell his father – or anyone else – what it aroused in him: desire to touch them, both of them together, and an opposing need to run. How would anyone here make sense of that? He can barely make sense of it himself.

196

He feels his lungs constricting – from the wood smoke, perhaps, of the stove; or with the anxiety at waiting. But these things are somehow out of his control now; beyond them all. He'll lose everything: wives, children, his status as an Elder.

Tobias watches as they enter: Eliza and Jed Cuthbert, Malachy, Hephzi, Mariah Miller, stamping their boots on the mat in the porch, removing scarves and mittens. He puts each hand under an armpit, glad of his fleece-lined jacket. He registers Ciaras's face, but his friend's smile is distant and gives nothing away. Frania sits down hard on the chair, clearly agitated. Her grey eyes flit around the room, darting to Goran and Leah, sliding sideways at Ammie, then off around the room again. When, finally, she looks at him, she smiles, a look of encouragement. He thinks of what she told him: *be strong*.

Lucia gets to her feet. Something has occurred, which needs their attention, perhaps a decision. Tobias can't control his breath. The words are muffled by his heart thudding, the pulse of it amplified in his ears. What will he say if he's called to witness? He flushes hot with sudden anger – at Rebecca, and Ammie; at Frania, and at his father.

Rebecca is told to stand.

He knows, then. Goran has told them everything, the Elders will have discussed it and it will be replayed, all of it, in this room. The whole community will see everything he has lost: his wives, himself.

Rebecca looks smaller, somehow, shrunken. Tobias can't control the swift flutter in his gut at the sight of her. Her eyes are swollen. Her face, usually so pale, is covered in a rash.

'Can you tell us what happened? The other evening?'

There is the brief, bubbling sound of laughter from the next door room. The voices of the children. They're with Hannah and Patience, and the eldest Miller girl; they're singing, a folk song he recognises from his own childhood, about change and the turning of the seasons. *A time to rend, a time to sew.*

Rebecca chews her lip. She stares at Lucia. At the back of the room, Tobias sees Mona Fitzgerald, shifting in her seat and straining to hear.

'Tell us how Tobias found you. With Amarantha.'

In the corner, a log in the woodstove catches flame and spits, hisses into life.

The energy in the room tightens. Tobias watches as people visibly straighten in their chairs. They are caught now; they are listening.

He watches his wife, the distress on her face. He watches as her fingers creep under the sleeve of her blouse. She scratches, frowning, and he knows what the skin will look like there – dry and flaking, fiery with heat. It is nothing to the pain he has felt, the pain she has caused him. He's caught between wanting to accuse her, to rip the answers out of her, and wanting to defend her from all this – this public inquisition, people's judgements.

'We – we were …' A breath. She bows her head, hiding her face from the rest of the Meeting.

'Tobias found you – together. Is that right?' Lucia pauses. 'You were naked.'

The gasp echoes around the room, the sound of people moving, shifting; their horrified faces turned to each other. Someone in the outer circle – Niamh or Emilia – calls out: *No.* Tobias watches the charge of shock on Sarah's face. She reaches for Seth's hand, closes her eyes; shakes her head.

'We were undressed, we …'

'You were making love?' Lucia's voice is accusatory.

'No!' Rebecca's eyes are wide with alarm. 'It wasn't like that, it was …' She swallows. 'I can't explain. It wasn't about – sex. It was about … it was ...'

'Sorry.' Lucia raises a weak smile, intolerant now. 'I'm not clear what you mean.'

'It was … our way of … being connected. It wasn't sex,' she flushes. He knows how difficult Rebecca will find it to say the word. 'It was ...' She takes a breath, starts again. 'We were – are – close.' Rebecca looks at Ammie for the first time. Ammie doesn't smile, doesn't acknowledge her; she stares blankly ahead.

The baby in her arms stirs, moves his head, jerks his arms suddenly. Lucas. Tobias had forgotten that his son was even here. His face turns purple, he screws up his eyes. His cry punctures the silence. All eyes swing to look at him, at Ammie, who frowns, lifts him over her shoulder, rubs his back. Lucas still fidgets, and the volume of his wailing rises. Ammie shoots a defiant look around the room and begins to unbutton her blouse, exposing her white breast to the room. She guides Lucas's head towards her.

Everything stops. They watch this infant – his baby son – suckling. There's shock in the silence. It radiates through the room. Then, from the next door room is the sound of the children's high, sweet voices, singing: *a time to keep silence, a time to speak.*

Tobias watches Rebecca sway on her heels, looking at her sisterwife. Her jaw is clenched against crying. As though she's battling with herself: what to say, or not say. Finally, she forces out the words. 'Ammie is my sisterwife. All I did was love her, as I was called to do.'

'You weren't called to sin,' Lucia says, 'or deceive your husband.'

'Don't we believe in ...' Rebecca falters. 'What we do – it's about sharing, and supporting, and love.' Rebecca's voice is loud now, the anger evident in her pale face. 'It wasn't sin.' She takes a breath, exhales, a sob catching in her throat. 'It was ... it was something pure.'

Pure. Tobias has glimpsed that: the essence of both these women, Rebecca, Amarantha, and how their selves are distilled in lovemaking. Amarantha, whimpering with pleasure at the point of release. Rebecca's green eyes fixed on his, a quick shock of a frown, as though she's in pain.

But together. No.

Something Seth said, not so long ago, when they were laughing together in the kitchen, his wives: *little witches.* When Tobias heard the words, it disturbed him. Now, though, he wonders if his brother wasn't so far from the truth. In another time, another life, they would have been strung up and set alight; burned together, their flesh and muscle fused by the flames.

*

Rebecca is shaking. Sweating; despite the cold air in the room. It has sucked everything out of her, standing in front of these people she's known all her life. She sinks into her seat, longing suddenly for her children. She wants to lose her lips in their hair, smell their sweet girl smell; speak their uncomplicated language.

Now it's Ammie who's speaking. She's dressed perfectly for the occasion – laundered blouse, properly buttoned; her best skirt; her boots, even polished for the day. On the surface she conforms; beneath, because she knows her so well, perhaps, by now, Rebecca realises that she is galvanising herself. She has learned so much from Ammie: courage being the greatest.

'Tell us how it started, Amarantha.' Eliza has taken over the questioning. She is finding it difficult, Rebecca notices, to hide her disapproval. Her head moves stiffly, her body closed.

'How what started?'

'Your relationship with Rebecca.'

'She was my teacher.' Ammie pauses. A defiant look crosses her face. But the irony is a mistake, Rebecca thinks. It's too insolent. It mocks everything, this room, these people; their belief system. In spite of everything – her own shaking limbs, the way she's loved Ammie – she feels shame at her sisterwife's lack of respect for the proceedings.

Eliza bristles. 'We know what she was to you. We want to know when it began.'

'I don't know what you mean.'

'At what point did you seduce her?'

Nothing on Ammie's face betrays her emotion. Rebecca's eyes dart to Tobias. She sees the pain flash across his face. She has a sudden sensation of falling, as though from a height; the inevitability that this is what they will assume: that she and Ammie were lovers.

But perhaps they were: she loved her, after all; she loves her still.

There is a sudden scraping in the centre of the circle, chair legs on the wooden floor. It reminds Rebecca of catching her nails on the board at school. It sends something ringing inside her.

Frania. Frania is on her feet, face tight with anger. 'This is wrong. It isn't a court room.'

Micah gets to his feet, tentative, pulling himself up on his stick. 'With respect. This must be difficult for you. It is difficult for us all …' He breaks off and looks at Rebecca. She feels her stomach plummet. The pain she is causing them. Ruth will not even look at her.

'You've made up your minds already.' She is shouting now. Rebecca can't remember anyone shouting in the Meeting House before. Micah holds up a hand, trying to restore calm. 'You'll believe what you want to – that my daughter is guilty.' She pauses, sucks in her breath, eyes wildly looking around the room, 'That she led astray the dutiful Rebecca.'

Dutiful. The word is a jab to the stomach. Is this how Frania sees her? How they all see her? Rebecca always thought duty was noble but in Frania's mouth it becomes a bitter, shrivelled thing.

'We have to go through this process,' Micah says, 'to discern …'

'Don't spout such utter crap.'

Micah stares at her, stunned. His face crumples, his hand goes to his forehead. He looks wildly around him, at his wife, at Goran and Leah. There is a shocked buzz. Frenzied whispering, someone calling out that she should have more respect.

'You.' Frania is pointing now; pointing at each of the Elders in turn. At Micah, who is back in his seat again, at Lucia, at Eliza – still standing – and finally Goran. 'You talk so much about discernment, and truth. But you cover up the lies.'

Rebecca sees Ciaras reach for Frania's hand, try to stop her or calm her. He whispers something, but she doesn't hear him. Her focus is still on the gathering in the Meeting House. She's intent on finishing what she's started to say.

Ammie. Ammie holds Lucas to her, but the expression on her face is absent. There's something so remote about her, as though she is in a bubble, a capsule of existence. How bewildered she must be, Rebecca thinks. Her mother leaving, then returning. Abandoning her, now defending her. Everything is shifting, so uncertain.

When Rebecca was a tiny girl, she went on a fairground ride with a swing that turned her almost the whole way upside down. Since Ammie came, this is how she feels: that the world she knew is constantly tilting. She is disorientated. She feels a hardness gathering in her; anger. At Frania, at this whole thing: the village meeting to pick over the bones of what has happened, to pass judgement. How do they know? she thinks. And how, after this, can things remain the same? How can Rebecca stay?

201

Where else does she have to go?

*

Ammie's anger bubbles through her like molten glass. Anger that Frania should leave and not explain why; anger at being ordered to be Sealed; towards Rebecca, that she should have made things so difficult and then so easy. She's angry with Lucas for tying her down; with Libby for not persuading her to stay, with Finn for showing her how sweet life could be on the outside. That longing is embedded in her, so deep. It won't ever go away.

She's angry at herself for not having had the courage to stay.

Frania's voice is too loud and too angry and it makes Ammie want to curl up somewhere, sleep for hundreds of years and pretend that none of this is real; her unconscious, maybe, playing out its images and thoughts, alive and malleable, like Tobias's glass.

She wants Frania to sit down, but she won't; she's looking at Leah. 'It's time for the truth,' she says.

Ammie actually hears the silence in the room. It's like a buzzing in her head. Ammie realises the limitations of her knowledge, that what's happening is bigger than she can imagine. She takes Lucas's hand and strokes the smooth skin, feeling that his softness, his vulnerability, might somehow protect her.

'I don't know what you mean.' Leah's face drains white. She clutches the edges of her chair. She looks only at Frania. Leah remains in her seat but she looks deflated. Defeated.

Goran stands up. Ammie can't interpret his expression as he looks at his wife; but it's something like sorrow or regret. All Ammie can think is that he's looking down on her, not beside her, helping her, but looking down on her.

'It is too late, now,' Goran says, 'to keep things hidden.'

Ammie watches as their eyes meet and their gazes lock. There are tears in Goran's eyes and when he reaches forward and touches her face, it's as though they're the only ones in the room. Ammie feels her eyes prickle; he looks so vulnerable, carrying pain that has been there for a long time. He's loyal, Ammie thinks; a good man. Tobias has inherited those traits from him.

'It is time to tell the truth, Leah,' he says. 'Remember? *Trohet.*' His voice cracks. His face crumples. Leah covers her face with her hands.

LOT

The fever made Goran unhinged, that day. He was sent home early, couldn't get a grip on what he was seeing or doing. The ground swayed under his feet. Everything was exaggerated.

The tenement steps; the grooves in the centre of them. The traffic of centuries' worth of feet.

The border of red paint on the wall all the way up the building. Chipped on the third level, right next to the Gonzalez apartment.

A sense of walking into light as you ascended, coming closer to the window in the roof. He needed his bed, only; the sanctuary of sheets and blankets and darkness.

The key in the lock of his own door. The way you had to rattle it to open.

Goran stood in the hallway. There was something wrong. He paused to listen but heard nothing, except that he knew he was not the only one home. It was strange, so, at this time of the day when he thought he'd come back to the solace of empty rooms.

As he moved to the open doorway, the warmth hit him. The fire was lit. The curtains drawn. Someone must be ill – one of the boys, perhaps – and Leah had stoked up the fire so he would not get a chill.

Goran stepped into the room, looking for a son lying prone on the sofa. He saw someone else: a man.

Naked.

He stood by the fireplace. He was looking away from the door, his gaze intent on something further inside the room. His arm was draped across the ledge of the fireplace, his face was in profile. All Goran could take in was the length of his thighs, the elongated chest. Narrow hips. The penis, half erect.

Goran's stomach lurched. He tasted bile, suddenly, in his mouth.

As though he'd sensed someone there, the man turned to look. Then everything was slowed down. His face. A jarring sensation of recognition: the pocked skin, the cheekbones, the lengthy nose. This man. Months ago Goran had sat across from him at a table. He'd been asked all manner of questions about his beliefs, his actions. His marriage.

Goran stepped into the room, turned.

Leah.

She was naked too, from the waist up, her breasts exposed; nipples like petals, exquisite. His, his for the taking, and no one else's.

He wanted to slam his fist into the man's jaw. But there was something not right. When he'd entered the room, Leah's arm was raised. She had one eye closed, squinting. Measuring him in the air, from across the room; a paintbrush in her other hand.

Goran could not help the gasp that escaped his mouth. Painting, drawing: all these things, the Disclaimers had spurned to concentrate on the simplicity of living. Yet here she was, Leah, painting him. There was something in it, so sexual, so raw. Goran could almost smell it in the air; the reek of sweat and bodily fluids. He began to shake uncontrollably.

Looking around the room, he saw cushions on the floor, a rumpled throw. Then, as he stepped towards Leah, he saw the easel, half hidden by the door. His first thought was how she had hidden it, where she had hidden it, in their cramped apartment.

The frozen look of fear on Leah's face. She stepped forward and there was a sound, an exclamation – a protracted 'oh' – but it was lost in the room. Lost on him. He couldn't take his eyes from her breasts – the smooth roundness of them, the way the nipples protracted with the exposure to the air. Fixed there, he could not move. This other man – the stranger – was looking at him, still.

Leah had been drawing him. Almost, that was worse than the sexual act. It was a way of owning him. Of owning herself.

The reality hit him with such force that he could not even see Leah in front of him. He felt the touch of her hand, first on his forearm.

'Goran …'

'No.' He pulled his arm away from her, not wanting to be touched by her. Her stricken face, the panic there. Her eyes were wild.

Across the room the man began to move, crossing to the chair in the corner and pulling on his clothes. Dark items, heavy fabrics. He struggled to put on socks, had to sit down. Goran was so fixed on him, on the man, that he didn't notice Leah putting on her own clothes.

'Goran – I – there's nothing I can say.' He hears the break in her voice, the contrition.

'I don't want to hear it.'

Julius. His name. He was pulling on his shirt, fastening buttons. Casting around him, a final glance at the cramped room. Then he was gone, the door slamming behind him. In his wake there was the scent of something – something floral – that made Goran want to retch.

'It isn't what it seems.'

'Then what is it?'

'Goran. Please. Let me …'

'Which is best for you, Leah? You tell me. The sex? Or the art?'

There was a noise from the corridor, the sound of a child calling for Leah. Goran watched as she froze. He turned, hastily, automatically stepping towards the door. But too late, Tobias entered just as Leah was pulling on her blouse. He looked at her, his wife at the firm line of her lips and the way she tried to tuck back a strand of hair to tidy it. So help him, he was filled with disgust.

Leah was buttoning up her blouse.

'Mama?' Tobias was wary; Goran saw his son's gaze swerve to take in the easel, Leah's flushed and defiant face.

'Why is Papa home?'

'I am sick, son. I'm home because I need to be in bed.'

'Is Mama sick too?'

Goran looked at Leah, saw the plea in her eyes. *Play along, for my sake. Please.*

He realises how weak he feels, how he's trembling. He takes a breath, tries to control himself. 'A little. Go now. Go to the kitchen.'

'Is that why she's undressing?'

Goran looked at Leah. It would be for her to explain, to find justification; to have the guilt of lying to her own son.

Leah intervened then. 'Tobias. Please do what your father says. There is bread in the kitchen, and pickles. I'll be there in a minute. Go.'

Goran turned from the room. He wiped his forehead, slick with sweat. The heat of the room was making him nauseous, but his stomach was hollow.

In the hallway, he leaned into the wall, resting his head against it. Closing his eyes, he saw Julius's naked body. The sheets and cushions, the moment he had disturbed. Saw again the intensity of Leah's gaze. Looking at the man. Painting him.

In all the years of their marriage, even in the early days, Leah had never wanted to paint him.

How could he live here, now, with this knowledge?

How could he live at all when he felt so hollow?

From inside the *familjrum* there was the snap of curtains being opened again, sounds of his wife moving around the room. Fatigue washed over him. He held out his hand. Still trembling. Goran walked the length of the hallway, seeking his bed, wanting only to stay there for the rest of the day, and the days beyond that, alone.

MARAH

The eyes of the whole village are on Leah. She's exhausted all she has to say but still she stands there and Ammie is relieved it isn't her now; that soon she'll be able to escape this room, this place. She can't stand the feeling of hiding things and keeping them in. But although she knows now that their beliefs are a sham – something fabricated, something desperate – she feels not angry but foolish. It's as though she were the victim of an elaborate joke.

But Frania knew all along. How could she know something like that, and play along with it, and not tell her? How could she keep such a secret about Leah and Julius – Frania's lover, her own father?

Lucas stirs in his sleep. He lies flat on her lap and he throws his arms out suddenly, a gesture that has always amused her and entranced her. Soon he might wake and she should be gone by then – before he starts to cry – but she's desperate to hear the rest of Leah's story, wants to know why. All these years Ammie thought – everyone thought – she was an exemplary wife, and now it seems she's flawed and human. Like the rest of them.

Leah has run out of words. She looks around the circle, proud in her confession and not at all ashamed. Some quietness has come over her, relief probably. Imagine having all that hanging over you, Ammie thinks, and having to keep it secret. She's looking into the faces of each of her friends, though; imploring them to understand. When her eyes light on Ammie's, she smiles at her, an understanding, as though to say: I'm an outsider now; like you.

Niamh is the first to speak. 'What made you do it?'

'Remember what we believed in then? We talked about spirit. There being no sin. It didn't feel like sin.'

'But – Goran – your sons. How could you do it?'

'The thing is, that our perception of sin has changed. Who we are has changed. I think we lost something when we moved here.' Leah turns to Goran, then shifts her gaze to Micah, speaking to him too. 'We've become too insular. Too blind to the truth of things.'

And Ammie sees something amazing: Goran wipes a tear from his eyes, and nods.

Leah turns back to the circle. 'After that raid, we hated those who did it to us – those men. And yet ...'

She glances across the room at Tobias and watches his beautiful face darken as though at a memory of something; something that touches him deeply.

Leah takes a breath. She twists her hands together in front of her, lowering her eyes to the floor. 'Those men – they were human. Like us. They were doing what they had to. What they believed was right. Just as we were.'

There's an outbreak of murmuring, questioning, surprise. Ammie hears the volume rise until at last Micah implores them all to let Leah finish.

'And so – when he came, Julius, asking for forgiveness, what could I do? He wanted to know more of our ways. And so – I began to tell him. We would ...' Her face catches at a memory and she bows her head, eyes fixed to the floor. 'We'd drink tea at the kitchen table, with the boys playing on the floor. He was so – unthreatening. And because ... because I was afraid and things were changing ... ' She lifts her head. 'I began to love him.'

Ammie looks around the circle, taking in the faces. The anger and shock from most people. On Emilia's face there is pleasure mingled with disgust, and she exchanges a look of triumph with her mother. On Per's there is fierce concentration as he listens; she can almost see him trying to understand.

She finds the silence agonising. For herself, she becomes aware of the weight of her sleeping son in her arms and the need to put him down somewhere to rest them. When she looks up again, Leah is crying, her hands covering her face, shoulders heaving from the effort of trying to keep the sound in.

Seth stands up, crosses to his mother and opens his arms for an embrace, some comfort. His eyes are tight with tears and he swallows as he looks around the room. 'Don't say any more. We don't need to know any more.'

Ammie watches Tobias at the other side of it, holding tightly to his knees, staring at the floor; like he's remembering.

Micah gets up again. 'I think it would be right if … if we paused for a while …'

Leah half pushes Seth away from her and shakes her head; she is resolute. 'I'd like to continue, now that I've started.' Leah indicates to Seth to sit down.

'There's something else, too. Another secret. With this man – I – we … we had a daughter.'

Leah stands completely still and in the next moment Ammie sees something in her collapse. Her face crumples and she begins to weep. It's appalling, Ammie thinks, to be watching this confession. There's something brutal about this public show of shame and pain.

Through the silence, Leah begins to weep. 'And because it was so hurtful for Goran …' she glances away, 'I went away to give birth. I left her with her father.'

'Does she have a name, this girl of yours?' This is Malachy speaking quietly, with a frown on his face.

Leah takes her sleeve, wipes it across her face which is blotchy now, and red with the crying. She shakes her head, lets the tears come. They fall onto the floor in front of her. Ammie has a sudden urge to move forward, give her a handkerchief, stop the weeping.

'She's not a girl any more – she's a woman.'

Ammie thinks of her out there, a child who grew into an adult, wondering if she inherited anything of Leah – her broad face, the shape of her hips, and solid ankles.

'Her name is Liberty.' Ammie's heart begins to pound. It can't be. She thinks of the name she saw on an identification card.

'Libby.'

Ammie hears a crashing in her ears; the rushing in of knowledge and truth. Libby. Leah's daughter. Now Julius's daughter, too. Libby, out there, playing cards with Finn or laughing at leaves in the park; curled up on the sofa, quietly talking perhaps to some other girl but her. Somewhere out there: her sister.

*

And so, the truth; the silence.

If you were to look at the room from above, you'd witness a whole array of expressions and gestures amongst the congregation gathered there. Many of the faces are hard and critical; some – the women mostly – are weeping. There's the sense of something profound in the air; an awareness of truths exposed and hypocrisies revealed. Everything has changed and slowly this fact is sinking in for these people. Sitting beside Leah, Lucia Olsen sniffs. But she reaches out and touches her friend's hand and Leah turns to her gratefully, and smiles.

Ammie stands, walks unsteadily to the door, clutching Lucas to her chest. If you look carefully, you'll see Tobias's head turn; there's an uncertainty on his face, a moment's hesitation, as though questioning whether or not to follow her. The room resounds as the door slams shut. Rebecca looks at Tobias, but it's impossible to tell what's running through his head at that moment. He looks unhinged, disengaged from his body somehow. His gaze flits from face to face and it's clear he's undecided, thinking about what to do.

He remains in his seat. His eyes stray to the closed door of the Meeting House. He frowns, takes a breath, turns his gaze back into the room. He takes a breath in and his chest expands; a look of decisiveness passes over his face.

*

Lucas is sprawled like a starfish across the bed, deep in sleep. Ammie runs her fingers over his arms and hands, the dimpled fingers. She strokes the flushed curve of his cheek. His eyes flutter open, staring into the room. She places her hand on his head quickly as though, feeling the weight of it, he might stay where he is. She doesn't want him to wake. She wants to fix him in her mind, a mental photograph. His eyes close again, little by little, as though he's been part of a world he doesn't want to leave.

She sits for a long time, looking around the room, Rebecca's room. She thought she would never see it again. After what happened, after Tobias's discovery of them they hurtled apart, repelled like magnets. Rebecca in the house; Ammie back to the Bothy. Tobias, strangely, staying in Frania's caravan. That puzzled and perplexed her; but she has stopped trying to pretend to understand this world and the relationships in it. She only knows that she welcomed Rebecca's tentative visit, her invitation to dinner.

Ammie is sure Rebecca hasn't seen the bag in the bedroom, packed and ready.

But now, she is in Rebecca's bedroom. She's always been fascinated by it, by the ghost of Rebecca's scent; by the way the brushes and combs are lined up on the dresser and the muted light filters through the curtains.

One last look. The long mirror.

Her Sealing day; Rebecca standing behind her. The two of them framed in the glass. If she had known, would she have stayed? Or would she have set out then, for Aroer, then the city, walking away from her childhood as fast as she could?

From downstairs, Ammie hears the jagged notes of a piano. It's Naomi, practising her scales. Usually it makes her wince, each note brash and discordant, but today they help her fix everything into place. Ammie pictures Naomi on the stool, with her straight back and fierce concentration. Her sisters will be sitting at her feet, pushing some toy around the floor. And Rebecca. In the kitchen, she'll pause in some task to check on them, smiling in on her girls as she wipes dishes and measures out flour.

Ammie stands in front of the long mirror. She sees a girl with unruly hair in shapeless clothes; and she thinks of Libby and the way that she transformed her with the cut of different clothes, with scarves, and with colour.

A sound. The door opening. And when Ammie looks round it's Esther in the doorway. She's reaching up, holding onto the door handle, watchful eyes searching the room, and then Ammie's reflection in the mirror.

'Why are you looking in the mirror?'

Ammie's eyes dart to the reflection of the door and Esther standing in it, wondering what to say to her and whether she's guessed.

'Just checking how I look.'

'Mama says it's a sin to think about how you look.'

She wants to say: there's so much about your mother you don't know; so much she's only just found out herself, in fact. Ammie thinks of the things she never knew about Rebecca: her softness, her kindness, her vulnerability. She wants to say to Esther: be good to her, she's not as cold or strict as she seems to be. Cherish her, she wants to say to the girl, help her.

Leaving Rebecca will be the hardest thing.

The thought rocks her; that, of everything, she should miss that most. She'll miss the rhythm they've created here – the shared care of their children, the working together, the small tasks which, taken together, make up the fabric of each day.

Ammie says: 'I'm not thinking about how I look. I'm just remembering.'

'Remembering?' Esther's eyebrows lift in an enquiry. Ammie realises that the child has picked up on something; some intuition is warning her of change.

Esther lifts her chin and asks another question. 'Are you going somewhere, Aunt Ammie? Because if you are, I'd like to come with you and Lucas.'

Ammie glances at the mantel and at what she placed there earlier. Lined up, side by side, are three notes. For Frania; for Tobias; and the last, for Rebecca. All Ammie's life is contained in those notes, and yet each one holds a different story. She hadn't known she had so many selves.

Ammie crosses to the mantel and picks up the letter with Rebecca's name on it. She lifts it to her face, inhaling for a moment the scent of it. Lavender; heather. She took the writing paper from her sisterwife's drawer. She didn't expect it to smell of her.

'I want you to do something for me, Esther. Would you?'

She sees Esther's eager nod, her swift smile and it pulls at her for a moment, that thought of losing her.

'Could you give this to Mama?' She holds out the letter and Esther reaches for it, but Ammie holds it out of reach. 'Listen to me, though. This is important. I want you to give it to her after supper. Do you understand? After. Not before.'

Esther's face is ecstatic. She steps towards Ammie and wraps her

213

arms around her waist, pulling tighter onto her. Ammie tries not to think about all she'll miss in Esther's life: the loss of her front teeth, all her accomplishments over the years; the way she'll develop into a woman. It makes her empty. She has to detach herself from it, or she'll never leave.

Ammie places a hand on the top of Esther's head, trying to control the emotions. She can't let Esther know that the gesture is final.

When Esther has gone, Ammie crosses again to the bed. She remembers carrying him, the pressure of him inside her, his slow, tunnelling birth. The sweet pain of feeding him.   Her hands burn. She realises then she's been running her hands back and forth along the rough surface of the coverlet. She drinks him in, her boy, trying to imprint the image onto her eyelids.

By the time Rebecca comes, she will have gone already. Rebecca will be left holding a note, and the note will say – in Ammie's scrawling hand – that she is leaving behind a gift, a gift she'll find in her own bed. *I'm leaving you Lucas. Cherish him as a gift; care for him. Some day he'll understand why I've done this.*

She must focus on why she's doing this. Lucas will have so much: Tobias's strength to help him grow; his sisters' devotion and Rebecca's care. Alone, she can't give him what he needs. He'll draw strength from a community that will nurture him and steer him in the direction he needs to go. And then the choice will be his: whether to stay or go.

Ammie tries to ignore the voice in her head, the one that tells her she'll feel more pain than she can imagine.

She has no choice.

They'll talk to him about her. He'll grow up as though he knows her. He won't be afraid of anything, and between them there'll be a thread of connection that no one can break. It joins her to him, her present life to her past. She takes something from her pocket, something square and glossy – a photograph, taken on a warm day in a happy time. She tucks it under his arm. For now, it's all she can give him.

All this is for his future.

The light filtering through the curtains bathes the room in pink. It's how she will leave him: sleeping, as though held, still, in the womb.

Is this how Frania felt? She was leaving an adult child but the rupture, the guilt, the inevitability must have been the same. But she never came back; it was never the same. Once he died, Julius, it was too late. The thread was broken. But she knows now, making this decision, why Frania never told her the truth about the Elders, about Leah and what happened in the city: because she was going along with what would protect them, give them the best life they might have.

And now Ammie is doing the same and her throat is tight with grief and fear held in. The walk to the door takes her too long. One look back from the threshold of the room. Lucas is so still. Ammie's holdall is by the door. Not too much: books, a few changes of clothes, some bootees belonging to Lucas, butterfly pins, a brooch. So many things she has left behind: a glass goblet, marbled and inlaid with blue.

Ammie picks up the bag, testing the weight of it. She'll manage.

Her footsteps on the stairs are silent. She'll put on her boots outside the door. As she descends, she smells onions frying in the kitchen, something spicy. There's the sound of Rebecca moving around, opening cupboards and drawers. Usually as she's cooking she sings to herself or hums, but there's nothing like that today. The girls must be out in the garden because she hears distant shouting and laughter. She imagines their breath freezing on the air and wonders about taking a last look. The note. Will Esther remember the note? Ammie glances down at the chest in the hallway. Esther has left it there. Rebecca will find it, eventually. And if she doesn't, it will be Lucas himself who alerts her when he wakes.

Ammie can't say goodbye. Her arms tingle with the desire to hold them to her once more. All of them: the girls, Tobias, Rebecca.

Her arms tingle already at the absence of her son. She can't wake him because she can't bear to see the expression in his eyes; she won't let him see her actual moment of leaving.

Soon, Rebecca will come in from the kitchen to set the table for the meal.

It must be now.

Ammie moves to the door and opens it silently, running her fingertips over the metal struts in the window stained blue and green. She remembers Tobias in his workshop, a lock of hair falling forward as he leans over the firing oven, then dipping the glass into the oxide to create colours that capture the hillside, the sky and the woods they walked in. Imprinted on her memory, like the picture he took of her that day. It captured a moment, something singular and beautiful; impossible and fleeting.

Ammie looks back at the kitchen. No movement or sound now and she thinks that Rebecca will have gone outside to check on the girls, gum boots pulled on over thick socks, holding her hand up to her eyes to shield them from the low winter light and calling them in to wash hands for dinner.

Ammie opens the door. The click of the lock is quiet but firm. The garden path is in shadow, cold, but she makes for the gate and moves into the light, feeling the sunshine play briefly on exposed skin: her wrists, her neck, her face

She seizes the handle of the bag and hoists it onto her shoulder. Wrapping her scarf tight around her face, she begins to walk.

*

The path is barbed with thicket, and Tobias wishes he had brought a scythe. As he works his way up the slope, beating back the undergrowth with a stick, he remembers a phrase from his childhood. *When you walk your steps will not be hindered. I have led you in right paths.* He recalls hearing it as he sat in front of the stove, bitter woodsmoke mixed with the sweetness of bedtime milk. A biblical verse Goran recited to them at night.

What else? Something about wisdom and instruction. Tobias can't remember the source; Psalms, it might be, though it is a long time since he picked up the scriptures. These days, they don't need them. They are discovering their own way, at last, a way without words and without scripture. They have put silence at the heart of everything and Tobias turns his face to the sun, and smiles at the thought; it is enabling them to connect more than they ever have.

He hears Goran's laboured breathing behind him now. It's a long time since anyone climbed this path, and they want to be sure it is clear before tomorrow, when the whole village will gather for the ceremony in

the clearing on top of the hill. But it is hard going. The two men pause
for breath, for a swig of water. It is early in the year – not May yet – but
the sun is hot today. They stand for a while, feeling its warmth, listening
to the homely call of woodpigeons, looking over the valley. Even from
here – only half way to the top – the view of Marah is unhindered. Down
in the foot of the valley lies the circle of buildings that circumscribes their
days; their eating and sleeping, their working, their worship. Their lives.
At the sight of the smoke curling upwards from each chimney, tears spring
to Tobias's eyes. He is moved by a sense of rightness, a sense of home.

He swallows, gulps the clean air of spring.

Goran says. 'When I stood here the first time – with Micah – we
imagined it just like this. And here it is.' He smiles, and Tobias thinks how
old he looks, these days; older, but softer, perhaps, more yielding. He is
glad of the chance to be reacquainted with his father, spend time with him
in laughter rather than fear. They have learned from each other. *I have
taught you in the way of wisdom.*

A question passes over Goran's face. 'It pleases you? How things
have changed?' Tobias feels his father's eyes on his face, searching it for
truth.

Tobias's fingers stray to his pocket, and catch the hard edges of
something. He knows without looking what it looks like, the fold running
in the centre that has made the shiny paper begin to crack. He thinks of
the day the image was taken, a day of pure happiness. Amarantha's smile;
the smile of a girl with a gap in her teeth, looking into the future.

Ammie left it behind.

'I would understand,' Goran says, 'if you were angry … with me.
With the Elders. If they didn't know, then Amarantha ... she might still be
here.'

'Why would I be angry?' The anger is long gone, Tobias thinks.
At first he blamed Goran; but now, now he sees it is inevitable. 'She
would have gone anyway, I think. In the end.'

'But – even now. Seven months. You still feel pain, yes?'

Tobias looks down at the wooded valley, at the village at the
bottom. It is not the future he imagined, or expected. At times, Ammie's
face flashes before him, a memory of a look or gesture that leaves an ache,

a hollow place in his stomach.

'Yes.' He looks down at his hands. 'It still hurts.' Then he turns to survey the landscape, looking down the valley. 'I miss her.'

'We have paid the price,' Goran says, 'you and I, both.'

A lover and a wife; the child he once befriended. A friend and protector to his children: all these things he has lost. Then again, Goran has lost Seth, Seth's wives, his grandchildren, who left because there was no place for them to fit, in the end. Leah's secret led to a new kind of openness, but also a splintering and breaking away. And sadness, for all the excitement at the future.

Goran speaks again: 'For me there is a cost. Not just Seth, though I miss him here, it is true.' He sighs. 'I never said it before, but the cost to me was losing my pride. What happened to you made me – humble.'

'Humble?'

'You were betrayed, it gave you pain. But you were stronger than I – in understanding that pain and making sense of it. Since then ... I find I have learned to let go of what my ego dictates. To see things from the other angle.'

They stand side by side for a while, the two men, looking out onto the hillside. 'You are ready ...' Goran says at last, 'for tomorrow?'

'Yes.' He smiles at Goran. 'I'm ready.'

'I was thinking just now of the verse we read – when you were a boy. You remember?'

Tobias smiles at the coincidence; and he finds the words on his tongue, reciting them now for his father: *'Hear my son, and receive my sayings, and the years of your life will be many. I have taught you in the way of wisdom. I have led you in right paths.'*

Goran's eyes shine with tears. He reaches out and takes Tobias's forearm, squeezes it. Tobias moves forward to enfold his father into an embrace; Goran's body is smaller than he remembers, lighter, somehow more insubstantial than it used to be.

He closes his eyes as the men hold each other. The father continues to speak. The words span the years, so that the son might be a boy, still, sitting at his feet: *'Do not forsake her,'* the father quotes. *'Love her, and she will keep you.'*

When Tobias opens his eyes, there is a windhover in the distance. Something about the beauty and grace of that lone bird makes him rejoice, reminds him of the smallness of his existence; and of how far he has come. *Do not forsake her.* He knows he couldn't; not after everything. Not now.

*

On the morning of the next day – fresh and fragrant as a sheet pegged on the line – the villagers walk the path that Tobias cleared. The youngest and the oldest amongst them find the climb difficult. But the hedgerows are a riot of new leaves and blossom and they have allowed plenty of time. Together, as a community, they make it to the top, resting and gathering their breath. They look over the valley, to the white spots moving on the hillside – the sheep with their new lambs; to the crops that will soon fill the fields with luxuriant shades of gold and yellow. To their village; the children exclaim at how small it all appears from here. Some have never seen the village from above.

Finally, they form their circle – smaller and looser, these days, than it used to be. In parts, it is out of alignment; the children straggle, or climb between their parents' legs or wander off to investigate fallen tree trunks. It is not like being in the Meeting House. There are no chairs, here; no wooden floors, no windows; just a grassy clearing, the sound of birdsong, the open air. No Eliza Cuthbert, no Niamh and Gervaise. No Frania. These and many of the others left, after Leah's confession and the changes it brought about. Those in plural marriages have found it difficult to stay and there is talk of a new community on the other side of the valley, where Seth has built a homestead with his wives.

Looking around the circle now, you see them all, dressed in their best and smiling into the sunshine: Per and Lucia; Micah and Ruth; Gideon; Emilia, next to him, with a young child in her arms, Micah's grandchild, Rebecca's niece. Ciaras stands beside Kitty Miller, Mariah's eldest girl, young still but warmed into maturity by her pregnancy and by Ciaras's careful attention. He catches her eye, places an arm around her shoulder, and smiles.

There are newcomers too, people from Aroer who've heard of the community's openness and co-operation and requested to come, attracted by its values. More, they say, will follow, attracted by the idea of working on the land; attracted by the idea of a faith that stands for freedom and not restriction.

*

Rebecca faces Tobias in the circle. She wears a simple dress, a silk shift of watery green that was made by the seamstress in town. Rebecca has never owned anything like it before and she is amazed by how happy it has made her. Happy not just in the thing itself, but what it symbolises: a new beginning, and the beginning of something beautiful. Life here; her commitment to Tobias. Their hands are joined, and she searches his face. There is a long period of waiting, in which they absorb each other, give themselves to each other, make promises. And their friends, standing around them, in support. But no words are spoken.

The silence lasts a long time. Then Micah steps forward to minister. He smiles. 'It is a blessed day,' he says, 'to see my daughter affirming her commitment to her husband. Their promises are forged in a new context, one of love.'

Rebecca looks at the man who has been her husband and thinks that, today, she will properly, finally, become his wife. She turns her head; a strand of hair falls loose and she tucks it behind her ear. When she looks up, she catches him smiling at the gesture; knowing. I know you; I love you.

Her eyes move behind him, behind the friends that surround them and she looks at the hills. She can't help giving a thought to Ammie, out there somewhere. She thinks of the difficult and painful things that have happened here since she came. The Sealing, the destructive gnawing jealousy that plagued her. Lucas's birth; Ammie's face.

Ammie. She's been gone months now and Rebecca is heavy, still, with the lack of her. Her fingers ache at not having been able to touch her before she left. She would have reached out to touch Ammie's cheek, feeling the softness of skin on her face, the contact of flesh, the warmth between them, like a blessing. It's strange, Rebecca thinks, that she should feel it today, of all days, when it is about two people, not three, being joined together.

Rebecca and Tobias. Tobias and Rebecca. Like a mathematical equation.

She can't help but carry Ammie with her – always – her strong restless spirit, her remarkable eyes. Rebecca always thought that Marah would protect them from everything, from pain and fear as well as intruders. Now, she sees that the worst danger, the worst pain, comes from the inside.

She looks at her children. They're on the ground, sitting together, close in and leaning against each other. Martha's coppery hair has grown long now; Esther's face has rounded out. And presiding over both of them, Naomi: now a tall girl of eight, with her hair put up for the occasion. Rebecca did it herself using the pins from the purple satin box, heads of pearls and butterflies.

Lucas is with them. Their brother, now.

He sits on Naomi's lap, entertaining himself by pulling at the flowers of Naomi's garland. She laughs at him, not minding, lighter and looser limbed these days. The tight-buttoned child seems a memory now. Lucas begins to crawl into the circle and Naomi shoots a questioning look at her mother, who nods, smiles, opens her arms to the little boy.

Rebecca walks to meet him, bends to lift him, takes him into her arms. His eyes have turned brown now, like Ammie's; but he is so much like Tobias too – around the nose and the chin – that there can be no doubt of his parentage. She has come to love him, this boy, who has inherited Ammie's spirit of adventure. Rebecca longs, still, for another child of her own, touches her hand to her belly, now briefly, in a gesture that is swift, almost automatic. Tobias sees her, and smiles. Tonight, she thinks, every night, she will lie beside him and wake up next to him. In days of happiness, and hard work; in days of illness and grief.

Leah steps forward to retrieve the boy and it is clear that they have a bond, these two. Lucas laughs, tugs her hair, and Leah herself giggles like a child.

Someone in the circle ministers about children and the riches they bring. Rebecca can't see who speaks, the words come from behind her and are lost in the spring breeze. Afterwards, she will ask who spoke, ask them to repeat the words, and write them down.

And then there are no more words. Another long stint of silence; the breeze; the birds. The footsteps of the children, pattering in and out of the circle. In that silence, they are joined together in life: Tobias and Rebecca Christensen. They are joined to their own family, as well as to each other; joined to the community and the land.

Goran moves into the centre of the circle and puts a hand on the shoulders of each of them. Close up, Rebecca sees his grey eyes, weary with age but today filled with light and hope; and happiness.

'Time for the rings.'

Tobias's eyes are full of emotion as he fishes in his pocket and brings out Rebecca's ring. It is worn, after all these years of being Sealed, covered with minute scratches. When he hands it to her, there is something different about it. He had taken it to Jonas, the jeweller in Aroer who Tobias works with now, sometimes, making jewellery and vases for tourists. The shine on the gold tells her that the ring must have been cleaned. But there is something else. When Rebecca turns it between her fingers, she sees it has been inscribed in tiny writing, looping along the inside of the ring: *To Rebecca, for the completeness of being.*

Rebecca signals to Naomi, and her daughter enters the circle, carrying a small purse made of voile and tied with ribbon. She fumbles with the fastening but then reaches inside and retrieves something. She hands her mother a ring – a new one, this time – and Rebecca pushes it onto Tobias's fourth finger. It is new and shining next to the knuckle, strange to see.

The other evening, they lay in bed together and Tobias read aloud from a book, the one he found in the city. It told of separated lovers, he said, and when he came across it first, he saw it as a sign to bring Amarantha home. Now, he knows that it is something different. Now he knows what home really is. She recalls his smooth intonation as he read, the expression breathed into the words that night. She hears them now in her head. They speak of distance, journeys and fulfilment; the need to travel to know where we are from; the need to be afraid to realise that we are safe.

If you evade suffering you also evade the chance of joy.

Rebecca looks around her. There is warmth reflected everywhere: in the unfurling leaves, the blue sky, the reflection of the sun. And on faces, too. She watches her father, her mother, her husband, her children. She looks around the circle of people gathered high above Marah to see her rejoined to Tobias. Then her eyes scan the landscape: the clearing, the wooded embankment that leads to the edge. Behind it, all the clear space and air surrounding them, the paths leading through thickets and along the river, flanked with tree roots and boulders. Rebecca thinks of Ammie, scrambling over them. She wills her on, wishes her well.

She thinks of leading the children along the same path, of slowing to help Lucas climb over a rock. She thinks of his thin hand, weightless, and how it will grow in size to match her own with the passing years. Rebecca turns her attention back to the circle, to Tobias's rapt smile and the murmurings of her daughters. Silently, she feels her own hand, curling into a gentle fist, fingers meeting palm, the pressure of nails against skin.